ROXANE
GAY
BO□KS

HOT SPRINGS DRIVE

Also by Lindsay Hunter

Daddy's

Don't Kiss Me

Ugly Girls

Eat Only When You're Hungry

HOT SPRINGS DRIVE

A NOVEL

LINDSAY HUNTER

ROXANE
GAY
BOOKS

New York

FIC
Hunter

FIRST EDITION

Published simultaneously in Canada
Printed in the United States of America

This book was typeset in 11.5-pt ITC Legacy Serif by Alpha Design & Composition of Pittsfield, NH.

First Grove Atlantic hardcover edition: November 2023

Library of Congress Cataloging-in-Publication data is available for this title.

ISBN 978-0-8021-6145-1
eISBN 978-0-8021-6146-8

Roxane Gay Books
an imprint of Grove Atlantic
154 West 14th Street
New York, NY 10011

Distributed by Publishers Group West

groveatlantic.com

23 24 25 26   10 9 8 7 6 5 4 3 2 1

For everyone who's still here

PART I

A House on
Hot Springs Drive

The house didn't ask for what happened, for what it had to hold, for the echoes it muffled, the wetness it dried. It was just a house, a collection of rooms. A divided space.

One of them hadn't pushed the couch all the way into the corner, so it was a spot used for the little one to hide things or hide herself or cry when she got a little older and the house wasn't so big anymore. There was a coin there still, dusty and forgotten, but at one time it had been her special thing, her beloved. The house knew how some things could feel gifted, how they suddenly appeared or were suddenly seen, how it could stop one of them in their tracks with wonder. A beam of sunlight angled through the sliding glass doors over and over and over and over and over and over, day after day after day after day after day after day, and the child played in it, the big ones stood in it with their hands on their hips, looking around, or they rushed through it, exploding the dust motes into chaos until they settled, calmed, into the beam, twirling and falling, and sometimes there was no one at all in the room, just the house and the light, and then one day the girl noticed it, saw the sunbeam, how it looked triangular, or like a blade, how it sliced into the room and was yellow but even more colors once she looked closer, and the house could do nothing but offer it. The house had no hands to wring, no shoulders to straighten, no eyes to see, no lips to lick. The house was just a house, imbued with its people and their strangeness, the loneliness they only showed to the house, the way the mother stared at herself in the mirror and pulled at her face or stood to the side and tried to make herself into a new thing, something taller and less slouched, something that smiled, something that could look at itself without trying to make itself into a new thing. Something that could endure the mirror, and the mirror in the next room, and the one in the bathroom, and the one by the door, and the one in the visor in the car, and the one in the reflection of a window, and the one inside her that showed something ruined, misshapen, discarded. The house wanted her to see the sunlight sword her daughter stood in daily now as though it filled her with something. The mother watched the daughter sometimes and in those moments the mother was beautiful, calmed, intact. The house saw how you could thrash alone to the loud music absorbed in the walls and you could throw all the pillows from your bed and you could throw something special into the trash and take it to the curb, where it was no longer of the house, and how there was power in that. In a banishment. The mother stood. Every day she stood, the way a house does, and she made her own light, the way a house does, and the house was just a house for a time. A loveliness, when a thing can just be a thing.

Does a house feel itself being noticed? Does it know its yellow windows, glimpsed from the outside, are irresistible? Is it the house's fault for offering itself up so easily, so helplessly? Anyone can open a door; that's not up to a house. Anyone can peer in, snoop around. Anyone can lie in wait. The child in her corner, the boy in the garage, always the house's shame. Its smell, its stains, its darkness. The boy, when did he get in?

Had he always been there? Was he like the furnace kicking on, day after day, over and over, a rheumy inhale and then an endless, roaring exhale? Was he the mice scurrying inside the walls; was he the blown fuse, easily thrown; was he the stuck window, the loose floorboard? Was he part of the house? Did the house do that to the mother? Did the house make a mess it couldn't clean up? The house doesn't know. The house can only offer what it has: screams, and stains, and blood, and the mother, slowly sinking toward the floor. She had a name. The house used to know it.

Theresa

In the Lindens' garage there were plastic bins containing Christmas decorations, stockings and garland and the delicate papier-mâché angels and bells Cece Linden made in school that Theresa Linden wrapped in newspaper and sealed in bags, only to see that they'd flattened and crumpled as she unwrapped them every December. There were lawn tools, bicycles, old paint cans. High on the three inner walls were bare planks bracketed eighteen inches apart, shelves Adam Linden made himself shortly after the family moved in. They were too high up and the upper shelf remained empty. Lined up on the lower shelf were large plastic soda cups Adam used to store nails in every size, screws, washers, and bolts—things he'd bought in bulk over the years so he'd have something to put on the shelves. When the winter sun began to set, light streamed in through the wide, squat windows at the side of the garage that faced the Stinsons' and showed spiderwebs as thick in the corners as the whorls of hair Theresa pulled from her daughter's brush. Cece had never liked the garage. Later it would seem like a sign, something she should have paid attention to.

In the summer the air inside the garage turned thick, scented heavily with the smell of the Lindens' cars and the wood walls and dust and faintly with the evergreen-scented candles Theresa used in her Christmas Eve centerpiece. On the bare concrete floor there was an oil stain in the shape of a hand, its fingers splayed wide. It was a late summer morning the day Theresa Linden's body was found there, her face in the hand, her body curled as if it were in sleep, her hair blooming petals of blood and bone.

Theresa is seven years old, watching her sister use a rope to swing way out over the lake. Carissa lets go, falls, the water exploding around her, but it's Theresa who gasps just before Carissa goes in. Like she can hold Carissa's breath for her. Carissa surfaces, coughing, raking her hand down her face and over her hair. "Come on," she calls to Theresa. But the rope is too far away to reach, dangling into the mucky water. "I think the hot dogs are ready," she yells back. It seems like a sure way to distract her sister, but Carissa doesn't go for it. "Oh my God, Rese," she laughs. "You're just afraid you'll break your vagina." This is how Theresa comes to be seen, in the way that family lore clings to stories that are illustrative but unfair, as someone who is afraid to take risks. "Forget it," her sister will say any time she refuses to try a cartwheel, or a cigarette is offered, or someone holds a car door open, offering to whisk her away from school. "She's afraid she'll break her vag."

Theresa is eighteen, and Carissa is twenty and pregnant, and the sisters are walking through Sears pointing at clothes and toys and soft, fluffy blankets the baby will need. They've named him Roy, a joke name Theresa came up with to cheer Carissa up, but now the name has stuck, the baby is Roy. Roy will have ears that stick out and scrawny legs like Carissa. "Thank God I don't have to buy any of this crap," Carissa says, looking away. Theresa knows she's trying not to cry. Roy is being adopted by a couple they're not allowed to meet. The day he's born, Theresa's mother has to ask the doctor to sedate Carissa so they can take the baby from her. "Don't let them take him," she says to Theresa. Her hair is sweaty on her forehead, her face pale. She's whispering, but everyone can hear her. They all nod, of course, of course, no one will take him. Finally, she falls asleep, and Theresa watches Roy as they change his diaper, swaddle him in a new blanket, and wheel him out of the room in his bassinet. When Carissa wakes, it's only Theresa in the room. Carissa sits up, looks around, knows. "I knew you'd be useless," she says, and puts her hands over her face. They watch Ricki Lake on mute. At the commercial breaks, Theresa hands Carissa a new Kleenex.

Theresa is twenty-two, lying on the futon in her apartment, its broken spring knuckling her shoulder. She's just had an abortion. She holds the remote but the TV is dark. She turns and vomits into the trash can she'd placed there just in case. She traded shifts so she could have this and the next day off. Her boyfriend thinks she's cramming for a final. She's told no one, only written a few lines of it in her diary. She longs to call Carissa, but imagining what her sister will say is enough to stop her. Carissa has two children now, goes to church every Sunday, works as the supervisor at a landscaping company, celebrates Roy's birthday every year. *Ungrateful* is maybe something she would say to Theresa. *Evil. Careless.* None of it is louder than the relief Theresa feels.

Theresa is twenty-six, working in customer relations at the corporate offices of a national bank. She hasn't had sex in three years. She has a brief, intense friendship with Samantha, a coworker. They take long walks at lunch and feed each other from paper sacks and spend every evening at Theresa's, legs over each other's laps, watching talk shows. Samantha is gone

one day, fired, and it turns out she's been forging Theresa's signature on withdrawal papers.

Theresa is twenty-nine on a date with a man who says he plays semi-professional rugby. One of his eyes is swollen shut and he angles that side of his face away from her. Out of tenderness for his injury, she goes to bed with him but they can't kiss because her brow might bump into his wound. He has stiff sheets and a lamp on the floor and a bare window she looks out of after they're finished. "It's hard to tell how high up we are," she says. "The window is just a square of sky." He pats her shoulder. After some silence, he says, "I actually have a girlfriend." When Theresa gets home, she sees there is some blood on the shoulder of her favorite blouse, and she drops it into the trash can. "It's time to grow up," Carissa tells her. Carissa is pregnant again, and has to go, bath time is the worst. "Just pick someone and stick with them." She hasn't said the thing about Theresa's vag in years, but it's there in the subtext. *Stop being so choosy, so scared. Start your life already.*

Theresa is thirty-one when she meets Adam. She's at a bar with her manager, a new low, and he's just excused himself to go to the bathroom. All night, he's found ways to rub himself against her, standing at the bar waiting for drinks or holding her chair out for her, and it's clear he'd like her to come to the bathroom with him. But she's already seen Adam. He's with someone, a very pretty woman with a girlish headband in her hair. It's that headband that clears the way for Theresa, that lets her walk up to the bar and pretend to ask for a drink, elbowing Adam as she does. Up close, he's familiar. He has kind brown eyes, broad shoulders that curve slightly inward. He smiles at her; she sees that one of his front teeth crowds the other. "I think I know you," she says. "Don't I?" His date looks back and forth between them, the straw from her drink clamped tight in her mouth. "Remind me," he says. She wants to collapse into his arms. Finally, she thinks. Carissa was right.

Theresa is thirty-two at the wedding. She wears an off-the-rack dress that is two hundred dollars more than she wants to spend and too tight across the chest. Carissa, her matron of honor, weeps loudly through the ceremony. "My sister always seemed like the lonely type," she'll say in her speech later that evening, using the back of her wrist to dab at her eyes. She'll raise her glass and Theresa will see how happy Carissa is for her. She'll hug Carissa, thank her for seeing what Theresa couldn't see, but Theresa is uncomfortable that her family sees her that way, a lonely woman, nearly a lost cause. She's lonely then and there, with everyone toasting her and Adam, with him bending to kiss her neck and whisper that her boobs in her dress are making him hard.

Theresa gets pregnant. It's exactly like in the commercials, with the test that shows two pink lines and the husband who comes home and sees it and doesn't know what it means, then grabs her and hugs her tight. The calls to family, Carissa shrieking and dropping the phone, the standing in what will be the baby's room and imagining the stuffed giraffe, the comfy rocker, the diapers stored neatly on shelves. "This baby is so lucky," Adam will say, resting his hand on her still-flat stomach. "You are going to be an amazing mom." She drives by the abortion clinic only once. That she doesn't get out of the car, doesn't want to get out of the car, is enough for Theresa. Soon enough, the baby kicks, turns its whole body. "Do you ever think about Roy?" she asks Carissa on the phone. It's been years since they've said his name, Carissa the mom of four now. All those years ago, just twenty years old, Carissa had felt those same jabs, flops, kicks. "Roy?" Carissa says. "Oh,

Roy." They are silent, listening to each other breathe, and then Theresa changes the subject to diaper pails.

Theresa is thirty-three when she gives birth to Cece. She won't let them take her, won't let them wheel the baby out to be weighed or bathed. The baby stays with her, in that room. "You're being silly," Carissa says. "The baby still has afterbirth in her hair. Let them take the poor thing." Theresa struggles out of bed, wets a soft blue washcloth, and washes Cece's head as best she can. Her scalp feels like velvet and Theresa is positive she sees the baby smile.

And here, the day Theresa meets Jackie Stinson, is where the story—the one neighbors and acquaintances and reporters and true crime enthusiasts love to tell and retell—here is where that story begins.

There's something familiar in Jackie, too. She's brash like Carissa, and funny like her too. But unlike Carissa, Jackie seems to find something she needs in Theresa. A stasis, a peace, some quiet. It's easy to look back, after everything that will happen, and assume that there was some deeper meaning behind their friendship. More likely, it was a simple transaction—each woman needed a friend. New moms struggle to make friends, everyone knows that. Best to find someone equally in the thrall of infanthood, equally unable to talk about anything outside of diaper rash and feeding schedules and exhaustion, someone who can laugh about the disgusting state of their nipples and sit patiently during a bout of weeping.

The story ends this way: Several years from that day in the maternity ward, Theresa will find out Adam and Jackie are fucking. She'll walk in on her husband with his head between Jackie's legs, crouching the same way he does when they've lost something under the couch, his legs tucked under his ass and his weight in his hands, fingers splayed. He'll be moving his head rapidly and Theresa will want to laugh. He never was good at finding anything.

The next day, Theresa will be murdered in her own garage. They'll find her murderer with blood in his hair, on his face, in his nail beds, even some inside his socks. He'll still be holding the crowbar. "I wasn't sure where to put it," he'll tell the officer.

Jackie

There are some things, looking back, that I now believe I deserved.

I met her the day Jayson was born. Nick and I arrived at the new hospital built on the red clay of the old fairgrounds, Douglas riding Nick's shoulders and amniotic fluid trickling into my socks. They said I nearly had Jayson in the hallway outside the delivery room. "Shh now," the nurse kept saying, pushing my hair back on my head with the hot, wet palm of her hand. The rubber soles of her shoes shrieked on the brand-new floor. "You shush," I finally said. I couldn't see Nick or Douglas but I heard Nick tell the room I was a firecracker. I knew Douglas shouldn't be in there, that he could probably see all my bells and whistles and that he felt afraid. I leaned up to tell Nick to take Douglas out, go get him some crackers from the vending machine, and out the baby slid. "Jesus," the doctor yelled. The baby was scrawny and red, and didn't want to eat, even when the nurses dripped sugar water on my nipple. He bopped his face against my breast and gave up, opening his mouth as if to bellow, though all that came out were angry little squeaks. "Aw," one of the nurses said. "It's like he can't find you." They took him to the nursery for bottles and he thrived. Away from me, he thrived.

Having a baby at the new hospital was something we'd looked forward to. Douglas was born in a squat concrete building that had three beds to a recovery room and dusty Christmas holly in the corners, though it was midsummer. The new hospital had generous windows along the back of the building facing the clay and the patches of wild switchgrass and, beyond that, a new subdivision of identical brick duplexes going up. The front of the hospital faced a sprawling parking lot and a four-lane road, and I guess there were fewer windows because of it. My room was at the front of the building, no window. "It's a nice television," Nick said, aiming the remote, Jayson over his shoulder like a dish towel and a spray of spit-up trickling down his back. "You can tell they splurged."

"Mommy wants a window," Douglas said, tucked in next to me, his head lolling on my aching breast. I couldn't remember saying so out loud, but he looked at me the way he did a lot back then, proud to know something about me his daddy didn't.

"That's true, chubs," I said, combing my fingers through his hair.

"They have ESPN!" Nick said.

Walking to visit Jayson in the nursery, I'd pass her room. Theresa's. Her bed was by the window, which framed a piece of landscape that looked like a poster you might buy at Walmart for your guest bedroom. Sky, waving grasses, red clay. The TV off. Sun on her face. The baby in a pink swaddle always in her arms. Once, her husband brought balloons; another day, a box of chocolates. I watched him kiss her forehead, hold the baby like a bouquet, hand it back. Warmth spread through me and down my legs. I remembered when Nick didn't know how to hold a baby.

Finally, one day, I went in, drawn to the light in the window and the quiet woman before it.

"You seem a lot better at this than I am," I said. I was supposed to show up at the nursery at feeding times, and I did, but a few nurses had commented that most mothers showed up more. "Don't you want to hold your baby?" they asked. Theresa, she wanted to hold her baby.

"Better at what?" she said. Her voice was deeper than I thought it would be. "Having hemorrhoids? Ignoring my stringy hair?"

I moved closer and I could see now that her face was oily and her gown was stained and her ankles were swollen, massive.

She had a window, and I didn't, and it bothered me, but it drew me to her as well. Motherhood is an eternity of noticing, a prison of noticing. And once you notice, you have to decide whether or not you're going to do something about it. We're out of milk. The toilet won't stop running. Your husband comes home late and then even later. You got a crappy room in the maternity ward. Does it matter whose fault it is? What are you going to do about it?

I don't know if she'd agree with me. I never asked her. She was a good mother, and I was a bad one. Am.

All those years ago, I sat at the foot of her bed. "I'm Jackie," I said.

"Theresa," she said, and told me her baby was Cecilia, Cece for short. A banner plane flew low, crossing left to right in the frame of the window, the switchgrass bending with it. SHOP CHEAP AT SACKS, it read. Why do I remember that? Sometimes I think I keep these things for Cece. Maybe I'll see Cece one day, and maybe she'll ask me about her mom, and I'll have something to give her. *If only*, I find myself thinking, *she'd want something from me.*

"Remember when this was the fairgrounds?" Theresa asked.

I nodded. We looked out her window, trying to place what ride was where. "I let the boy who ran the funhouse follow me in once," I said. "I let him touch me under my shirt." I'd never told anyone, not even Nick. While it was happening it had seemed exciting, the boy following me closely, his breath warming my neck, his fingers cold and bony. But there was a bright bulb over the exit door, and in the light I could see he wasn't a boy but a man, perhaps nearly as old as my father, his mouth open and panting slightly, and I'd felt a rush of power and shame that made the whole thing feel unspeakable. Theresa laughed a little because I'd told it laughingly. She looked down at her baby nursing. "Honestly, I hope no one ever touches my boobs again." I loved her immediately. Isn't that how all the great hatreds begin?

I ended up having four babies, but she only ever had the one. I think about that a lot. Why give a mother like me all those kids, and a mother like her just one? It feels like I won something, some prize I don't even want.

It turns out that feeling never goes away. The wondering why. There once was a woman named Jackie, and sometimes she let life happen to her, and sometimes she didn't. At the end she stood around and thought, *What have I done? What have I done? What have I done?*

The Realtor

The house next to the Lindens belonged to an older couple who had moved south and put it up for sale. Theresa told Jackie all about it, even offered to call the realtor for her. "It's . . . brown," she told Jackie, so she wouldn't say, *It's ugly*. "But you'll have so much more space!"

It *was* brown—light-brown stucco, dark brown on the trim and nicked front door, the color scheme of owners who were playing it safe, perhaps relying on landscaping to add some color. There were boxwoods and zinnias and a jacaranda the realtor said was guaranteed to offer pink blossoms the whole month of April. There were enough bedrooms and bathrooms for everyone—the boys would pair off two to a room—and a backyard with a tree perfect for a tire swing and a kitchen in which more than one person could stand. Still, Nick Stinson was a car salesman with a nose so fine-tuned to bullshit that now he smelled it everywhere.

"You know, I once heard of this drug ring that buys houses where they can cook their filthy substances or store kidnap victims or"—he leaned in to inspect a smudge on the wall—"you know, murder someone in this bedroom, count their money in that bedroom . . ." He looked to the realtor, a woman with the determination of someone on her third career—intense eye contact, smile as rigid and welcoming as a brick wall, moist eyes—waiting for her to confirm or deny.

"Is that so?" she asked. "I hadn't heard." She looked at the mother, at the two little ones hugging her calves. She felt for the woman. She herself was just out of her second marriage, and it was occurring to her more and more that she just didn't like the sound of a man's voice. Did they have to comment on everything? Her ex, Dan, used to stand outside the bathroom door and ask her when she'd be done. Like she was on the clock, slacking off on her job. And it *was* a kind of labor. Marriage was, she'd finally decided, just another shitty job.

"Seems to me it's your job to be up on those kinds of stories," Mr. Stinson said. And that was the other thing. Men liked to smell blood in the water. They liked to circle in, readying for the kill. Not *kill you*, but everything was win-lose and losing to them meant they'd killed you. She could put on a slideshow of the times they—her exes—had held something up in triumph. Mark with a cereal box, proving the one she'd bought wasn't the same as the one he liked. Dan with her new bra, shouting about the price. Mark with a sex magazine, to prove what he wanted wasn't so offensive. Did men just walk around all day wondering why everyone was in their way?

"You'll have to send me the article," the realtor said, knowing there wasn't any such thing. She knelt down, her skirt pulling taut across her ass and making a worrisome stretching sound. She smiled harder and pointed. "I bet you boys can't wait to play out in that yard." They turned to look out the sliding glass doors, still clutching their mother in their fists, at the small patio beyond, the green patchy grass. In the far corner was a blue ball.

"The people who lived here before had a whole mess of grandkids," the realtor said. She didn't actually know that to be true. In all likelihood it'd been kicked over the fence long ago, the kicker now in high school. But she knew folks liked to hear how a home was a happy place, how the people who lived there hated to leave it. She thought of how she'd burned a mandarin-scented candle until just before the Stinsons showed up, to cover a smell not unlike the one in her own elderly parents' home. Band-Aids and ointment and rubber-soled shoes, oatmeal and the clicker and a single fried egg, a single browned toast point. Sore joints and blurry vision and difficult shits.

"I bet that's their ball, left here special, just for you." She stood up. "Why don't I take the children outside, so you two can talk?" She looked at Mrs. Stinson when she said this. The woman was there but she wasn't. The same had happened to the realtor's sister, after having kids. The realtor wanted Mrs. Stinson to make this decision. It was the right one. She needed a yard she could see from a variety of angles, out the kitchen window and out the family room window, so she could have some peace and quiet without losing sight of the kids. She imagined Mr. Stinson lifting weights in the garage, striding down his driveway to get the newspaper, hosting barbecues on that tidy patio. Children took so much from you. They took and took. They'd been in a two-bedroom across town; they'd said as much when they'd met. Mrs. Stinson had called one of the boys by the wrong name. "I'm Jayson," the boy had said. "Not Nathan." They needed more space. Mrs. Stinson walked as though she were wearing someone else's body. Mrs. Stinson needed to unpack, to fill the rooms, to feather her nest. Why did the realtor have these kinds of thoughts? What the hell did she know? She knew enough. She knew the house needed a family. Needed a fresh coat of paint on the walls, needed rugs and bright curtains and little objects that caught Mrs. Stinson's eye for some reason or another. There was a little girl who lived next door. The realtor wondered if she'd be outside, singing to herself, as she had been another time when the realtor showed the house. The girl's mother hummed along from the covered back patio. Mrs. Stinson needed that. Whatever that was, that easiness, that casual love. Mrs. Stinson needed to witness it.

The little girl wasn't out back; the windows next door seemed dark, no sign of anyone moving behind them. The boys fought over the ball, kicking each other in the shins to try to gain control. The realtor's feet hurt, as did the space in between her shoulder blades. One of the boys began to cry, though he clearly didn't want to. "I'm not crying!" he insisted. "I'm not!" The realtor didn't intervene; it wasn't her place. Instead, she watched the Stinsons through the glass doors, Mr. Stinson pacing in a slow circle and Mrs. Stinson half turned toward the yard, the picture of a worried mother. Suddenly, she turned to her husband and made a sharp motion with her hand. The realtor recognized the way he gave in, throwing up his hands, trudging toward the door.

"Now, see?" the realtor trilled. "When was the last time you were able to have a conversation without one of the kids breaking in?" She gestured at the yard. "That's worth its weight in gold, am I right?" Nick Stinson bent to run his hand over the grass. The boys ran to their mother, shoving to be the one who got to her first.

"You're smart to get in right now," the realtor added, looking at Mr. Stinson.

He stood. "I want the mower I saw in the garage added in," he said.

She nodded. "I think that can be arranged." The mower was hers, but no bother. He could have it. She watched Mrs. Stinson's shoulders settle, some color coming into her face. The boys saw it too and began tumbling over each other, pulling each other into the grass and laughing. Well worth it, in the realtor's expert opinion, to go along pretending some things were the husband's idea.

The Boys

Out back they'd begun to dig a hole. Nathan and Sammy were barely any help, just jabbing the rusty trowels they'd found in the garage at the dirt and flinging it backward, but Jayson and Douglas were making real progress. It felt good to ram the shovel through thick roots, to watch the pile of dirt get bigger as the hole got deeper.

In the apartment, the Christmas tree had looked enormous, crowding the front window and requiring their parents to move the dining set further into the TV room, which was really all one big room. Their parents talked a lot about being cramped, too cramped, they didn't like being cramped. Now, in the new house, the tree seemed scrawny and short, and their father promised to bring a new one home from the tree lot next to the dealership. The hole was a grave for the old tree. Douglas's idea.

"People cry at funerals," Nathan said.

"So?" Douglas said.

"I don't feel like crying," Nathan said.

Inside, their mother was making dinner. Something with onions and ground beef. A good smell, though Sammy would throw a fit about it, and refuse to eat it unless it was doused in ketchup. The boys hoped there was ketchup.

"I think it's deep enough," Jayson said. He raised his shovel eye level with Douglas. "Now it's just this gross wet stuff."

"It's called clay," Douglas said. The new house was still a mystery, not yet home. There was red clay all over town, and people still took dirt roads as a back way in, but Jayson had yet to see clay as sticky and wet as this.

"Think we can make something with it?" he asked. He was thinking of a Christmas present, a smooth bowl he'd make with his hands, something his mother could put her earrings in.

"Obviously," Douglas said. Sometimes their parents talked to each other this way. Sharp, disgusted, hasty. Only Douglas tried it on, used that tone on his brothers. In front of their mother he was always the one who ran to her, threw his arms around her, kept close. Jayson saw that Douglas didn't know how he sounded, didn't even know what the word *obviously* meant, but Nathan and Sammy treated Douglas like a general. Someone to obey, to approach with caution.

"Hey," Cece called. She peered over the fence at them from the top of her slide, pushing her hair out of her face. She'd gotten the metal playset the previous Christmas, and each boy burned with envy, even now. Her hair fell back in her face. "Your dad isn't going to yell at you about tearing up his yard?"

"We're going to put it all back the way it was," Douglas said, going back to the shoveling.

"Yeah," Jayson said. But in truth it depended on what kind of mood his dad was in when he came home. If it was dark enough, maybe he wouldn't even notice. Sometimes he worked late, coming home after the boys were asleep. "Mom just had to have a house," he said, goosing their mother on her rear, "so Dad's got to work some overtime."

Jayson looked at the mound of dirt, the clumps of grass. There was no way they'd be putting it all back the way it was. He stopped digging, gathered clay into his hands. It was slimy but firm and quickly coated his palms. He fashioned a small bowl, its sides quickly folding in on themselves. If he had money, he could just buy his mother something pretty, but he didn't. He knelt to gather more clay.

"Sammy shit his pants," Nathan said, also trying on something he'd heard their father say. "Sammy, did you shit your pants?"

At nearly four, Sammy was still in diapers. They'd heard their mother say Sammy was stubborn, that he wanted to cling to his babyhood, but they knew she was worn out, that her attempts to potty train him were half-hearted and rapidly abandoned, and they'd taken it upon themselves to bully Sammy into underwear. "I pooped," Sammy said.

"That's gross, Sammy," Jayson said. "You know it's gross, right?"

"You shouldn't say *shit*," Cece said. "You're just teaching him to say it."

Nathan pretended to pick at the rust on his trowel. Sammy stuck two dirty fingers into his mouth. One of them would have to bring him inside, tell their mother he needed changing, and she hated being interrupted while she cooked.

The clay wanted to stay in a lump. Jayson wondered if he could make something useful but lump-shaped for his mother. *It's art*, he could tell her. *I made you some art.*

"You think Dad's going to remember to bring home a new tree?" Douglas asked.

"Yeah," Jayson said. "He will. He loves Christmas." But it wasn't the answer Douglas wanted.

"Still," he said. "We shouldn't bury the old one. Just in case."

"You were going to bury a Christmas tree?" Cece said. She was on her knees now, leaning farther over. "That's a grave?" Jayson knew she was hoping to be asked to come over and help dig. *She's an only child*, their mother often said, pity in her voice. Cece didn't seem lonely, just bored. Jayson was never lonely and always bored. He liked when Cece came over. She was always up for the games Douglas no longer wanted to play: hide-and-seek, tag, would-you-rather. *Would you rather kiss me or Douglas?* he imagined asking her.

"Now it's just a hole," Douglas said. He dropped his shovel and went inside.

"Maybe he's telling Mom about Sammy," Nathan said. Briefly, Jayson considered stripping Sammy naked and cleaning him with the hose their father kept coiled on the side of the house.

Their mother knocked on the kitchen window. *Ask Cece if she wants to eat with us*, she mouthed.

"What's your mother saying?" Cece asked.

"Nothing," Jayson said. "She's telling us to clean up our mess."

Nick

Fridays at the dealership, there were donuts and pastries and the "good" coffee, all set up by Monica on the table by the offices. The thought was that Friday brought serious buyers, usually men on their lunch breaks, and they'd be drawn to the goodies right where Nick Stinson and the other salesmen could see them, fish in a barrel. Sales*persons*, what with Belinda. All of this was Jerome, the sales manager's idea, Jerome who shrouded his hopefulness in abject fear and, sometimes, rage. They could hear him in there sometimes, clacking away at his laptop in the darkest, farthest office. *Aw, fuck! Oh, Jesus!* Trudging out for the morning huddle wiping his mouth like he'd been told there was a war and it had been lost. But then he'd come up with the donut thing, or the raffle last month, or the summer cookout the year prior. He never gave up, and somehow they eked out their numbers, all of them getting grayer and fatter.

See anything you like?

What are you gonna drive off the lot this fine morning?

Don't let my boss see me telling you this . . .

My brother, I'm sorry, but your wife is just too fine to drive off in a car like this. What you need is . . .

Great for the kiddos, too!

You got three kids? I don't believe it. I was going to ask you what you were majoring in!

Hello, Miss! Is this your sister? Your mother? *Hang on, you're pulling my leg . . .*

They all had their schtick. They divided their customers before heading for the floor. Belinda liked the geezers. Aaron went for the students coming in with their parents. Nick liked the moms. Jerome, it went without saying, got the big spenders, identified immediately by the watches they wore. Nothing else mattered—not shoes, clothes, the cars they drove in with. Only the watch was the true tell. Nick liked to saunter up, appear by the side of a mother, identified by the size of her purse, which was usually a diaper bag, or diaper bag–sized, and crack wise.

This morning the sales floor was quiet. It was still early, hours from the lunch rush. The enormous windows that framed the floor had just been washed and the light felt focused, calm. Nick loved mornings like that, mornings when he could ease in. Leaving the house sometimes felt like he'd survived something, escaped, the boys hollering and Jackie yelling back and the TV so loud he felt flayed by it.

Belinda cackled, leaning in close to Aaron over by the coffee. Nick watched a woman with a messy ponytail and a backpack answer three calls in quick succession, staring at her own reflection in the driver's-side window of a minivan the color of mucus—*eggshell*, the sticker said. She said neither hello nor goodbye, just answered questions with increasing frustration, then hung up when she was finished.

"It's right there on the counter," she hissed as Nick walked up. "I left it in the most obvious spot I could think of." He knew she was busting her husband's balls, knew they had to take turns coming in to look at the car because the babysitter canceled or there wasn't any family nearby or whatever. He knew they both hated each other for it, these small difficulties that added up to a shitty day, day after day, knew they just wanted someone to come in and handle it for them, knew they had to realize over and over that that person was them, there was no one else. He knew when they imagined the end of this sort of stress, she probably pictured herself holding a large drink, a margarita maybe, and he pictured himself getting head from an anonymous brunette in a corner office. Nick knew people. It was his job to know people.

He also knew if he could get the wife all in on this van, which had been sitting on the floor for too long—no one likes eggshell in a minivan, turns out—and was thus now the source of an informal competition to see who could move it off first, then the husband would come in and sign whatever, pay whatever. Happy wife, happy life.

"Husbands," he said when he was right next to her. "Can't kill 'em, am I right?" He elbowed her playfully. He saw that she'd be pretty without the glasses, if she did something with her hair and the bags under her eyes. She kind of looked like that actress, the one in the movie about that heist. Girl-next-door kind of thing. She looked at him with the leftover rage at her husband and a burgeoning embarrassment at being overheard. Nick stuck out his hand and she shifted her coat so she could take it. Her hand was warm and soft and it collapsed in his meaty paw.

"I'm here to help," he said. He pointed at his name tag. "We'll get you in exactly what you need, on my father's grave." His father, a ladies' man who treated Nick like a cousin he once knew, died years ago. He was feeling her out, seeing which version of Nick she'd prefer. *On my father's grave* was boyish Nick, wise guy Nick.

"Claire," she said, glancing at her phone, then shifting it to the other hand. "I'm just looking. We don't know exactly what we want yet."

Ah, yes, she'd already deployed the *we*. A husband she could hold up like a wedge, even a blockade if she needed a way of explaining why she was leaving without signing anything. Child's play. Masterfully, Nick changed his posture from easy, casual (hands in pockets, belly out) to more formal, professorial (buttoning his blazer, folding his hands in front of his dick).

"No problem," he said. "First things first: we got a coat room in the back by the offices. It's very secure. Let me take your stuff back there, free up your arms a bit." She looked at him, over his shoulder toward the offices, probably picturing her purse held ransom until she agreed to buy that jizz-colored minivan. "I know my wife," he said, talking quickly, "she's always got her arms full. Breaks her back bringing in the groceries, the dry cleaning, some toy she tripped over . . ." He was getting through, but he knew what he had to add. "Plus all her work." That did the trick. Claire nodded and laughed a little. She was a working mom, he could see that now, probably had to fit meetings in between story time and bike rides and tantrums. He put the side of his hand up to his mouth, like he was about to share something just between them. "Feels damn good to just have your arms free once in a while, am I right?"

She laughed, handed over her coat and purse. Nick took them and tried not to show how heavy the purse felt. She carried that around day in and day out? No wonder she hated her husband. "I'll be right back," he said. "And I'll meet you over by the coffee."

He winked at Jerome in his office as he passed, knowing he'd been watching. Nick had to get Claire feeling loose, open, and getting the coat and bag was just one part of that. The coffee came next. He lingered by the "coat room," actually just the supply closet, where he could set her stuff on a box of paper and close the door, so she could make her coffee just the way she liked it, another luxury probably denied her every day. It was Nick who'd lobbied for the taller cups, the lids, the little refrigerator with its variety of milks and creamers, so customers could feel like they were getting coffee from one of those fancy places with the dumb drink names. He thought of Jackie—not a working mom, far from it—and how she complained of her coffee getting cold, of having to reheat it a dozen times a morning, how she worried over what she called *my creamer*, did they have enough, did they need more, if she didn't have *her creamer* what was the point of life?

Jackie's purse felt like she hauled bowling balls. And now she had a backup purse, a little thing she slung on her shoulder, the bigger one hanging across her body. Nick had the urge to open Claire's, see what was so damn heavy in there. Men just carried keys, phone, wallet, change. What the hell else was there to carry? It occurred to him he could just go through Jackie's purse later. Purses. If he was so curious. But he wasn't.

He took lunch at one of the picnic tables out back with Manuel, the service manager. He had half his hoagie from the day before, plus a cookie the size of a small plate he filched from the goodies table. He washed it down with a beer Manuel handed him, so cold it hurt to hold.

"The hell is that?" He nodded at Manuel's lunch, an enormous jar filled with what looked like lawn clippings.

"Esme," Manuel said, shrugging. "She calls it salad in a jar. Says if she's the one making my lunch, she's going to make what she'd eat, not what I'd eat."

"Oh yeah? What would you eat?"

Manuel pointed over Nick's shoulder. Across the street there was a Wendy's, a sandwich place, a Tex-Mex restaurant with a bustling outdoor patio. "Take your pick."

"Well, the ironic thing is," Nick said, "you're just as likely to get the runs from those places as you are from that produce aisle you're about to choke down." They laughed and Manuel shook the jar so vigorously the top of his hair wobbled.

"You sell anything yet today?" Manuel asked.

"I did, in fact," Nick said, thinking of Claire, how he'd been right, once her arms were free and she was cuddling that coffee in her hands, she became a totally different person. Decisive, even funny. She'd made fun of his socks, a zany pair one of the boys got him for Christmas, patterned with shrimp. She said the minivan was the color of breastmilk, which he took in stride, he was proud to say, even as he wanted to cough into his fist and shake it off, but she went for it, deciding on it within an hour.

"It's all over but the crying," Nick said to Manuel. "Husband's coming in tomorrow morning to seal the deal."

"Good for you," he said. "I'll make sure it's vacuumed and polished up."

The tables were positioned just beyond the garage doors to the service floor. The sun felt like a hot iron pressed to the back of his neck. He held the beer there for a moment, relishing the cold. The guys on the service floor moved languidly, lifting drills, bending over hoods, wiping their hands on a dirty cloth, almost like a dance he was watching. Every once in a while there was a burst of laughter. Someone turned up the music, a song with horns and guitar and what sounded like a whole chorus of men singing. He had the next half of his day to get through, and then the hot drive home. He didn't want to go there. Or, he did want to go home. But lately that house—his boys either too loud or too sullen, his wife who had become unrecognizable in every way—that wasn't his home. Home was something you looked forward to, not something you had to endure.

Manuel was a friend, someone he'd had over for barbecues, and they'd even hugged once or twice, slapping each
other's backs after some amazing football play they'd wit-
nessed. Esme, his wife, seemed like a sweet woman, always
going off with Jackie and Theresa to help, but he'd find them
laughing with their hands to their mouths, like they wanted
it to be quiet, like they were hiding whatever it was they were
laughing about. Like they were laughing about him, maybe.

"You like going home, Manuel?" Nick asked. Manuel
knuckled dressing from the corner of his mouth, squinted
at him.

"Yeah, of course," he said, though he didn't sound all that
thrilled. "Just got a brand-new flat-screen, my daughter is a
sweetheart, me and Esme still laugh, life is good, you know . . ."

"Totally, totally," Nick said, busying himself with tidying
his wadded napkin, the bits of lettuce he'd dropped.

"Why, man? You don't like going home?"

Nick laughed. The song switched to something mournful
and one of the guys quickly changed it. "I don't know. You
know how it is sometimes."

"Totally, totally," Manuel said. He picked a carrot out of
the jar and flicked it at the garbage can. "Jackie seems good,
right?"

"Yeah," Nick said. He searched Manuel's face for pity, for
something showing that he saw how big Jackie was. His own
pants strained; he felt like his belt was trying to squeeze the
life out of him. He knew the trend was to love your wife at any
size, love yourself, but he just felt grief. She'd been so young
when they married, just twenty. Hell, he'd only been twenty-
three. Back then, she looked at him like she was in awe. "You're
so smart," she was always saying. "How'd you get so smart?"
Her shoulders were so delicate he worried if he gripped her
too hard she'd break in two. He saw her at a dance in college,

one of those mixers where he'd show up with the best of inten-
tions, wearing his best sweater and sipping his drink painfully
slowly, and then he'd wake up the next morning asleep on the
floor, his vomit-stained sweater rolled into a pillow.

He'd been talking to a girl from his psych elective, a bossy
type who kept reminding him to make eye contact with her
when they were speaking. Finally, she folded her arms and
stared at him. "I have better things to do, you know," she'd said.
Elissa, that was her name. He'd had plans to get at least one
hand under her shirt, but that all faded away. They annoyed
each other, so why bother? "All right, see you around," he'd
said. Later, outside, he saw her rolling around by the hedges
with a TA. But at that point he'd found Jackie.

She was dancing, her arms up, her whole face a laugh.
Her drink sloshed into her hair and she didn't even notice.
She looked like something familiar, someone he remembered
from somewhere, but he never could place it. Years into their
marriage it was still there, that thing that made him feel like
they'd known each other for lifetimes, and he wondered if
that was what people meant when they said *love at first sight*.
Like maybe what they meant was *Oh, I know you. We're going
to be something important to each other*. He was recognizing the
mother of his children, that ancient instinctual mating thing
that gave men involuntary hard-ons.

But maybe all of that was something he understood much
later. Maybe he only understood it now, staring at Manuel as
he chewed near the front of his mouth, like he wouldn't be
able to swallow. Back then, maybe he just saw a girl he wanted
to be close to, put his hands on, usher out of that loud and
smelly place so no one else could lay claim to her. "Hey," she'd
yelled up at him. She kept dancing. "You're a terrible dancer,"
she said, and it made him laugh, because he was. They ended
the night thrusting fully clothed against each other in the

doorway of his dorm room, her hair and her lips so soft, her leg hooked around his, and his cock in rigid pain.

The wedding in her parents' backyard, kissing under the hundred-year-old hawthorn tree that looked as though it were twisting and clawing its way to the sky. New growth at its base held sharp spikes, and Jackie's father spent the day shooing children away from it, hollering that this was not a tree for climbing. "It'll scratch your eyes out!" he cried. They laughed all day, and Jackie smeared the cake across his face, and he kissed her hard, and they swiped at the frosting on their faces and then forgot about it.

She was pregnant with Douglas then, though they didn't know it. They made love every night, Jackie turning to him and tracing a finger down his shoulder, or Nick wrapping his hand in her hair and lightly pulling, and sometimes, mid-conversation, moving closer and closer toward each other in the rickety full-size bed they'd inherited from Jackie's child-hood bedroom, Nick pushing into her as they discussed what neighborhood to buy in, or how Jackie's professor looked down her nose at married students. They moved together, Jackie arching her back and meeting him with her hips, push-ing him deeper in, rolling him onto his back and moving faster and faster until she collapsed over him, her nails digging into his arms. This was what marriage was, a sweet, warm home full of pleasures, a woman who laughed generously, who looked at him like she knew the deepest childlike part of him. And when Douglas came, when Jackie spent the first month in the dark, never changing her nightgown, remembering with a start that Douglas hadn't had his diaper changed in hours, the TV on to the infomercial channel because she believed Douglas liked it, Nick waited for her to return to herself, knew that she would if he was patient. And one day he came home from school and she was there, his Jackie, wearing a tight red sweater and jeans, her face bright, her hair clean, Douglas on a blanket on the floor, kicking his legs. "I think he finally likes me," she said.

With every baby after, there was the month of darkness, then the sudden day when Jackie felt better. Nick had grown used to it, reminding Jackie that it would pass, even though it was true that she wasn't so quick to laugh anymore, that she seemed to be shrinking, the boys gobbling her up. Now they said maybe a dozen words to each other in a day, tops. *What do you want for dinner? Don't know. Did you pick up the— Yup. That your dry-cleaning pile? Mmhmm. I don't see why you can't just— I got it, Jesus.* At night they still turned to each other, still came together. Jackie had her tubes tied after Sammy was born. The nights were when they could talk, the door closed and locked, but Nick couldn't put what was happening into words. He wasn't some asshole, he knew people gained and lost weight all throughout their lives. Knew he had gotten stocky, so who was he to talk? Still. He made his little jokes, his little comments. This wasn't Jackie. She was burying herself, slipping away.

And once he couldn't throw the boys around anymore, he felt useless there, too. The hell do you do with a teenage boy? They don't want to play catch or help you in the garage. They don't want you to look at them, talk to them, acknowledge them. He saw how Douglas and Jackie were always huddled close, whispering, how they had their looks across the table. She spoiled him. He'd be ruined when he reached adulthood, have no clue how to check the oil or hammer a nail or earn his own goddamned money and not run to his momma's purse.

It was too hot. His beer was warm now, his shirt damp. His own father never said the word *love*. Nick never had that problem. He said it over and over. But what was love, the action of it? Feeding, clothing your children? Sticking around? Offering to play catch? What else was there? He knew he was missing something, that there was a void in his fathering, a distance that would make his boys resent him a little, all the way up until he died. Certain nights, it just felt like exhaustion. He was simply too tired to even ask the boys about their day. Even so, Nick couldn't think of his father without remembering how the old man had simply stopped talking to him and his sister once they got to be teenagers. He'd nod at them in the mornings, formally, nod at them again when he came home. He'd address their mother instead. "Dear, would you ask Nicholas to pass the ketchup?" What the hell? What was Nick's formal nod, his silence? Wasn't trying your hardest or, at the very least, simply *trying*, good enough? Whatever it was, it was in his blind spot. Or maybe it wasn't even there. He loved his sons, loved Jackie, sure. He should be more like Manuel, befuddled by the question. He was at risk of becoming one of those classic middle-aged sad sacks, mooning about how miserable he was, tossing back alcohol and junk food like coins into a well. Of course he liked going home, of course things were good. He had to shake it off, get back in the showroom, bowl another sucker over. He pushed the cookie across the table. "Here," he said to Manuel. "I owe you for the beer."

Jackie

It was Theresa's idea to go to Get Skinny. "Be my wingman!" she said, trying to make it seem like only she needed it, like I was just along for the support. We'd both lost control—sitting together and working our way through one, two, three boxes of Little Debbies, washed down with Coke (her) and Dr Pepper (me). It felt good to do that. I loved it. Like a trust fall where you just kept falling.

But now I didn't have any pants that fit, and I was getting winded walking around the grocery store, and Nick had started making his little jokes. Oinking when I went into the kitchen. Asking me to do the Doughboy laugh. "That's bullying," Douglas said at dinner, watching my face. "You're not supposed to bully people about how they look." Already he'd started twisting his brothers' arms, holding them down, and once I found him standing over Jayson, trying to get him to eat a spoonful of dirt. He worried about me, about the boys stressing me out, and it weighed on him. I could see that.

"You know I'm just kidding," Nick said. He fed me a bite of his chicken. I chewed and smiled at the boys. "Your mom is the most beautiful woman in the whole world."

At that point I wanted, more than anything, to become a different person.

That's what it felt like they were offering at Get Skinny. We all came through that door clutching purses to our middles, crossing our arms, sitting up straight to smooth it all out or slouching to show that we understood we'd failed. I was always thinking about food, about what I would eat later, about baking cookies and cakes with the boys, then putting the TV on and eating as many of the goodies as I could before one of them found me. I clipped coupons for Pizza Hut and Papa Johns and hid the boxes from Nick. I dipped Hostess pies from the gas station into nacho cheese; I ate powdered Nesquik straight from the canister. I told the boys their Christmas candy got sent to kids who didn't get visited by Santa Claus when in reality the chocolates and suckers sat at the bottom of my purse under my wallet and wadded tissues and I ate them, one by one, after they were off to school for the day. I lay awake at night, starving, knowing there was an easy fix. Sometimes, I got out of bed and ate half a loaf of white bread in front of the TV, breaking off bits from a cold butter stick to place on my tongue to chew along with the bread. It looked like I was out of control, but I was perfectly in control. I was simply free in one very small way. And when you're the mother of four, and your child has learned how to pick the shitty little lock on the bathroom door because you sit in there too long feeling guilty for sitting in there for so long, desperate to be the kind of mother who knows how to sit still, be in the moment, appreciate the fleeting nature of their childhoods, but unable to get up and just open the door and let your boys in, unable to just be their center, their north, feeling overwhelmed by how they need you to say if it's okay to go outside, need you to play with blocks, daub a runny nose—when that's your daily life, any kind of freedom, even a freedom that imprisons your body and becomes a desperate need itself, feels like a gift.

But now I wanted a new kind of freedom.

We took my car, the summer evening still bright, just a little pink at the horizon. We ate cowboy cookies out of a gallon-size Ziploc Theresa had in her purse. "One last hurrah," she said.

"I ate an enormous salad for dinner," I said.

"Oh," she said.

"So hurry up and open that bag!" I said.

We laughed. The cookies were tiny, bite-size, so it just felt like you were popping breath mints. I had a feeling in my throat, a triumph. I really had eaten a salad for dinner. I hadn't picked at the mashed potatoes and ribs I'd made the rest of my family. I'd even measured my dressing. My body already felt thinner.

It felt nice to be out, driving slowly, the windows down and the air sweet-smelling. We passed the new bank, an Italianate-style building that clashed with the nearby Chevron, Shell, and Mobil. I held my nose when we passed the Checkers—bustling with teenagers picking at French fries and milkshakes—so I wouldn't feel tempted and then heartbroken.

"I used to go there on the way home from the grocery store," I said. "I'd wear sunglasses and a hat in case anyone I knew drove by."

I could feel Theresa looking at me, but I didn't turn to meet her eye. "You'd wear a *disguise*?" she asked. I looked at her and we burst out laughing.

"Friggin' Sherlock Hams over here," I said, and we laughed harder.

Theresa only had ten or fifteen pounds to lose. Most of the time she looked fine, unless her shirt was a bit tight or she had her swimsuit on, revealing the dimples of cellulite on her upper thighs. Her ideal body was within reach. Mine was in a whole other room. Mine was a dozen flights up and hiding in the shadows. She had no idea how people had begun looking at me. Like, *Can't you just stop eating?*

"Nick told me he's worried about me," I said. Late at night, in bed, the only time we had to talk without being interrupted, his breath in my hair. *You're disappearing, babe,* he said, his hand heavy on my shoulder. *Where are you going?* "He said I'm disappearing," I said, laughing. "Uh, I'm pretty sure I'm doing the opposite."

"Oh my God!" Theresa laughed, which was exactly the reaction I wanted, needed. She gathered her hair and held it, twisting it over her shoulder. She was the ideal looker if, say, this were a 1970s ad campaign for shampoo. She was wispy, pale, her face a gentle landscape. I was jealous of her cheeks, full and distinct, as if she held half a small apple under the skin on either side of her nose, and I was jealous of her hands, how her fingers never got pudgy, always stayed long and thin and graceful.

"I'm just sick of hearing about it," I said. "Fine, I will fix my body so everybody can finally shut up."

"If only it were that easy . . ." Theresa said.

"What does Adam say about all of this?" I asked.

She placed another cookie on her tongue and drew it into her mouth. I was desperate for her to talk shit about her husband. I lived for it. I knew all her main complaints: When she asked him to cook, he often said, "I don't know how," and left it to her to figure out. He didn't like buying her pads or tampons at the store. He had to be touching her when they slept, even if she was uncomfortable. He'd never cleaned a toilet in their entire marriage. He talked over her to the point where she wondered if he was deliberately fucking with her. But I needed more. Those all felt like normal, even quaint reasons to be frustrated with your spouse. I wanted her to tell me something darker, more sinister.

"Nick told me he needs two hands to hold each of my breasts now," I said, as a way of egging her on. "He said it while we were having sex."

She shook her head in disgust. "At least you're having sex," she said.

Bingo.

I slowed at a yellow light, carefully put on my blinker. Took a breath. "And you're not?"

"I wouldn't call what we do *sex*." She plucked crumbs from her jeans and the seat between her legs, dropped them into her cupped hand. "I don't even think I'm there most of the time."

I scanned through everything I knew about their sex life. I knew they didn't kiss during, but what married parents did? He once bent her over the sink after all of us got sauced at a barbecue a few summers ago. She had never, thank goodness, referred to what they did as *making love*. I always imagined they had a normal sex life. Once or twice a week. Rolling toward each other, completing the nitty-gritty, rolling away. Muffled but giggly.

Nick and I fucked four or five times a week. Sometimes I'd wake up, drooling onto my pillow, and he'd be holding on to me, pumping away. I couldn't bend over to tie my shoes without him coming up and rubbing himself against me.

"What do you mean, you aren't there most of the time?" I asked. I was already pulling into the parking lot, but I slowed down, pretended to look for the perfect spot.

"Oh, you know," she said. She looked into her hand where the crumbs were. She could look like a kid, like someone on the cusp of teenagerhood. Still a whiff of innocence. I wanted to touch it, that innocence, figure it out somehow. "I just go somewhere in my head. Like I'll meal plan or think about a dress I want to make Cece or something on television I just watched, and then I'll come to and his face is hovering over me, and he's dripping sweat into my eyes and mouth. You know? And I feel bad because he always has this look."

I pulled into a space in front of the Mexican bakery a few doors down from Get Skinny. I could smell the tortillas and the pan dulce. "What look?"

She rolled her window down so she could drop the crumbs out. "It was the same look he had when I was pushing with Cece, or when we bought the house." She brushed her palm with her other hand, then rolled the window back up. "Like we've done something special. Almost like he wants to high-five or something. He doesn't even see that I was distracted. For all he noticed, he could have been humping a hole in the bed."

I laughed. It's not that it was funny. Thinking about Adam, his need . . . I realized I was picturing me underneath him, me watching his face change as he got close. It made my skin crawl. I liked it.

There were two or three women who were much larger than I was, and a man who was so tall and large that he had to duck and turn sideways to fit through every doorway. Most of the other participants just seemed fluffed, like they'd spent a month or six letting themselves go, no biggie.

"Welcome!" A woman in a flower-print sundress and bright lipstick floated toward us. "I'm Pepper. I'll get you weighed and ready to go." She held a clipboard like a child holds a doll.

"Weighed?" I asked. That I hadn't prepared for. I hadn't looked at the scale in a very long time. I looked around and saw others being weighed, some with chagrin and some with shock. The man nodded stoically.

"That's right! And don't worry, it's private. Only you and I will know."

"Well, see, that's the thing, Pepper." I said her name like I believed it was fake, and immediately felt terrible about it. "I don't want to know."

"I see," she said, and I watched as she began to fill with the sort of gooey understanding and support that these places were famous for. She was ready to meet me on my level, go more than halfway to reach me, and I began to worry I might cry.

"I'll go first," Theresa said. She bumped her hip against mine and stepped forward. "Ha!" she said when she saw her number. "Really going for the gold there." I couldn't tell if she was alarmed or pleased.

"We try not to comment on ours or anyone else's truths," Pepper said, noting it all down on her clipboard. "We just accept them." She held her hand out for Theresa to take as she stepped off the scale. She was pretty, Pepper was. Very pretty. Her arms jiggled and her cheeks were full but there wasn't anything that would make you want to fix her. She smiled at me, her pink lips closed and her eyes serious.

"And then we work on changing the ones we don't like."

Later, after a woman in pants that drooped in the ass and crotch cried with joy that she'd met her weight goal, and the large man admitted that it'd been a rough week, that he'd lost track of some time, that he'd "entered denial and set up a picnic there," Theresa rose.

"Hi, everyone," she said, holding up a little baby wave. Her knees were still slightly bent, like she wanted to be able to sit at a moment's notice. "I'm here tonight because my best friend gave me the strength to be." She turned to me and held out her hand, which I took, even as I wanted to tell her to stop. I didn't want them looking at me any more than necessary.

That was my default, not wanting to be viewed. Just leave me be, let me be.

She went on. "The truth is, I've felt lost for . . . a long time now." Her voice broke and she coughed into her hand, as if her tears were dust. "When my daughter was little, every minute of the day was filled up with her needs, with entertaining and feeding and caring for her. I couldn't do anything without her tugging on me. I couldn't even pee!" I knew she intended this to lighten the mood, to give her a way out of the weeping she was holding in her throat, so I laughed loudly.

"Been there, girl," an older woman in a green polo shirt and octagonal glasses called out.

"Right?" Theresa said. "Yeah. But now she's older, she's fourteen, and the past few years, she doesn't need me so much. She doesn't want me, actually. You remember how it is. Your parents are the last people you want around. I get it, and we still have our nice moments, our bonding moments, like the other day we watched a movie together and we laughed so much." I squeezed her hand though our palms were starting to sweat. She'd told me some of how she was feeling, that Cece was locking her door more often, that she was asking for money for clothes from the thrift store and not wearing the dresses Theresa made anymore.

"And so, well, I filled that hole." Almost everyone else in the group nodded vigorously. "And I'm here because I want to stop filling it with food. I want to learn how to treat food like fuel, like nourishment, the way I'd feed my daughter, rather than something bad I do that feels good for a short while." She sat down abruptly, looked at me, her eyes wild, searching mine. I squeezed her hand again.

"Thank you," Pepper said. "Well done." She looked down at her clipboard. "Jackie, would you like to share? It's optional and no one wants you to feel uncomfortable, but newcomers often feel better once they've spoken. It's sort of an icebreaker."

"I feel better," Theresa whispered. Now she squeezed my hand.

"Sure thing," I said. I stood and tried not to pluck at my shirt the way I'd seen everyone else at the meeting do, removing it from between folds of flesh or patches of sweat. I folded my arms across my middle.

"So, my thing is . . ." I looked down at Theresa, who nodded at me. "I never told her this, because it felt like a shitty thing to say, but all of what she's talking about, which I understand and sympathize with, it feels like such a luxury." I looked down at her again, quickly, hoping she'd know I wasn't trying to shame her. "You know, worrying about your kid's every movement like that. Having time to think about what you'd say about whatever, having time to realize that your child is slipping away, that time is passing. I have four boys." I heard a gasp. The woman in the polo shook her head dolefully. "In my house, it's pure survival. That I get my boys fed and clothed in clean stuff, that the house is relatively picked up, that feels like a triumph at the end of every day."

"It is," Theresa said. Some of the others nodded.

"But no one sees it that way. It's *Where's my backpack, why don't we ever have any food, why is the bathroom so gross, why is there always a pile of laundry to fold, I need new shoes, a haircut, new clothes* . . ." I had started whining. I cleared my throat. "It's just an endless list of needs. No one, not even my husband, asks how they can help. Asks me how my day was. Asks me what I want to watch on TV. I'm just there, just a coat rack they fling their jackets and laundry and lunch boxes at. I eat because it makes me happy; it's a pleasure I have total control over." I sat down and my chair groaned. "Or at least, I used to have control over it," I said, hoping for a laugh. Theresa patted my leg. I could feel my heart pounding in my toes, all the way up in the part in my hair.

"Thank you," Pepper said. "What you're both describing is very common. I want you to understand that first and foremost. You're not alone." She placed her clipboard at her feet. "Some of us eat because we want to find a way of getting smaller," she said, nodding at Theresa. "We want to find a new way of fitting." Theresa nodded, swiped at tears on her cheeks.

"And some of us eat because we want to be bigger. More noticed, or even more respected. We want to be formidable. Impossible to ignore." Her eyes were boring into me, and it hit me that she, too, had once been at her first meeting. "It's all a way our imperfect hearts and souls search for meaning and deal with life. Think about it: We have to eat because it keeps our bodies alive. But if you're eating and you still don't feel alive, your instinct might be to have even more food. Because hunger has a lot of names: loneliness, boredom, fear, anxiety, trauma. All of those feelings are a hunger in search of satisfaction."

I was fucking *hooked*.

The rest of the meeting was about points and recipes and goals for the coming week, Pepper bestowing wise nods at each one of us. If there was such a thing as enlightenment, Pepper had reached it, and she had done so fueled by Easy Stuffed Low-Cal Peppers and Sugar-Free Lemonade and If It's a Big Enough Salad, It's a Meal!

On our way out she made a point of squeezing my arm. "See you next week," she said.

"You bet," I said, and it sounded flip, like I would never return, but that's how I had begun to sound. Maybe, if I too found enlightenment in something other than food, I could learn how to speak meaningfully, the way Pepper did.

The sky was baby blue on the way home, still not giving totally over to night. It was quieter, not so much traffic. This was the time of day when you could be convinced that where we lived, the sprawling same-old, same-old that is suburbia, could be beautiful. The streets were tidy, there were medians with wildflowers, a park we passed had an enormous magnolia. A newer drugstore, its yellow windows, even that seemed beautiful.

"That went better than I thought," Theresa said. "Right?" She looked at me. "It's just that I thought I would cry way more."

"It's true," I said, laughing. "We survived!"

"That weigh-in, though," she said.

"Yeah." I didn't know if she was trying to get me to tell her my number. I'd stepped on the scale and it had clanged, like an elephant had stomped it, and Pepper had murmured that the scale was old and that happened all the time. Then she'd moved the little weights, and moved them again, and kept moving them, and her nails were a peach color and her fingers were still slightly pudgy but overall her hands looked capable, and pretty, and filled with promise, like she could walk out of the building and right into the White House to take a meeting. And my number was 267. "There you have it," she'd said, and she waited until I looked into her tastefully lined, hazel eyes. "That's your starting point." I was trying my damnedest not to smash that scale to bits, not to sit down and wail. There was no way in hell anyone other than Pepper and I would know.

We kept the windows down and I could smell Taco Bell and Hardee's and Fazoli's but something must have gotten through because after I dropped Theresa off, after I parked in the garage and came in through the kitchen, I didn't even open the refrigerator. I breezed right past the pantry and into the living room, where the TV was on and where Nick and Douglas and Jayson were watching a baseball game, and I didn't dig my hand into their bowls of chips or take a nip of Nick's beer. I just went into the bathroom and closed the door behind me and looked at myself until I got a hold of whatever it was in my body I used to call hunger. "Hunger is often confused for so many other things," Pepper had said. "Give it a new name." I still had a nice pair of tits. I wanted someone other than me, someone other than Nick, to see them. Instead of hunger I'd call it desire. *That* was my starting point.

Nathan

Nathan was waiting for Douglas to go back inside so he could press his face to the hole in the fence and watch for Theresa. Sometimes she hummed to herself, arranged pebbles in neat patterns with Cece, drew butterflies with chalk on the concrete patio.

"Don't space out," Douglas said.

"I'm not," Nathan said.

"You're doing it right now." Douglas's voice had pitched into whining.

Nathan made eye contact, then bent to pick up Jayson's soccer ball. "Needs air," he said. He moved toward the garage, where the pump was.

She'd gone to the store with Jayson and Sammy, hadn't taken Douglas with, that's why he was in a mood.

"That's Jayson's problem," Douglas said, coming into the garage. "Let him pump up his own ball."

"Already finished," Nathan said. "Maybe we can do some drills."

They traded off playing goalie until Douglas kicked the ball too high and it went over the fence into Cece's yard.

"Go get it if you want," Douglas said. "This is boring." He was weird around Theresa, always interrupting her to get their mother's attention back on him.

Nathan considered hopping the fence, then decided against it. He walked through the house, so quiet without his brothers there, the television off for once, and went next door.

Cece came to her door holding the ball. "Your ball almost knocked the lid off my dad's grill," she said.

"Sorry," Nathan said. He tried to see behind her. "Where's your mom?"

"Reading a book about salads," Cece said. "Where's Jayson?"

"Getting new shoes."

"You want me to come over?" she asked.

Nathan thought about it. She'd probably kick the ball with him, but then what? "Can I just come over here instead?"

Cece had an ant farm in a big glass jar on the desk in her room. Nathan watched the ants working on a new tunnel, removing grains of sand one by one. "I can make you one," she said. "You just leave out a bowl of sugar, then when the ants come you pour it all into a jar of dirt."

"How do you feed them?" Nathan asked.

She stared at him. "They're pretty resourceful, my mom says."

Nathan decided to leave it. He pointed at a small television she had on her dresser. "Does that work?" he asked.

"Yeah, but nothing good is on right now." She opened a drawer in her desk and removed some paper and a set of markers. "I'm going to draw you."

He'd never been drawn before. He sat as still as he could, straining to hear what Theresa might be doing.

"You can breathe, you know," she said. Each time she uncapped a marker, she brought it to her nose and sniffed. He relaxed some. He maybe heard the toilet flush.

"Are those the kinds of markers that smell like fruit and stuff?" he asked.

"No, they all smell the same," she said. "Like marker. Why is your brother so weird?"

She could mean any one of them. "Who, Douglas?" he asked.

"No," she said. "Douglas isn't weird, he's just mean." She capped a green marker and uncapped a red one. "I mean Jayson."

"He's just really into soccer," Nathan said.

"I guess," she said. "Look." She turned the paper to face him. She'd drawn his posture, the way he had one ankle resting on his knee, his back curved and slouching. His hands gripped together in a jumble of sausage shapes. "I suck at hands," she said.

"Yeah, you do," he said.

"My mom told my dad she worries about your mom," Cece said. She folded the sketch into smaller and smaller rectangles.

Cece's dad ruffled the boys' hair each time they saw him, even Douglas's. He called them all *Champ*. He had a job that seemed both easier and better paid than Nathan's father's job. Nathan had once heard his father refer to Cece's father as *kind of a weenie*. "What did your dad say?" Nathan asked.

"He said your mom has too many kids, so of course she's losing it." Cece handed him the drawing. When she let go it sprung open, its folds refusing to hold. "He said your mom is going to eat herself to death."

Nathan thought of Douglas, the way Douglas said *I love you, Mom* over and over as she was leaving, until she was backing out of the garage and couldn't hear him anyway. How Douglas only seemed to smile lately when he was making her laugh. He pictured Douglas in the backyard right then, all alone, waiting for their mother to return.

"Tell your dad he's a weenie," Nathan said, dropping the drawing.

Theresa

She was trying to teach Cece about gentleness. "Look," she said, holding out her cupped hands. Crouched in the back corner of the yard, pulling dandelions out at the root, she'd found the wings of a butterfly. "See how they're speckled at the tips? Black and white polka dots, just like your favorite dress!" They were as thin as the tissue paper inside a present. "Here," she said. "Touch them. Feel how soft." A miracle. She thought about framing them, or nestling them inside the pages of a book.

Cece pushed her hands away. "Where is the rest of it?" she asked.

Theresa waited. "The rest of what, honey?"

"Mom," she said. "Something ripped those wings off of a butterfly."

Theresa looked. They were like bright petals of a rare flower. So precious, so vibrant. She'd never wondered about the rest of the creature, about its body. The lesson wasn't about being gentle. It was that beautiful things got destroyed. The bird that ate it was probably also beautiful. Theresa pictured something with a deep-red breast, gold-tipped tail feathers. She looked at her daughter. *Cece*, she was going to say. *Some creatures are stronger than others. Circle of life.* All of that.

"I bet it was Douglas," Cece said.

"No, honey, it was a bird, or something else that eats bugs."

Cece seemed to be thinking about it. Lately, she stood the way a child wanting to look like an adult would stand. Arms crossed, hip cocked.

"I think it was him," Cece said. "You know I'm right."

And Theresa could picture it, could picture Douglas in the back corner of his own yard, thinking how delicate the wings were, how easy it would probably be to— And then the wings were in his hand, the creature's body flung away. They weighed nothing in his palm. The slightest breeze disturbed them, threatened to carry them off. He hadn't meant to do it, had he? He held his hand up and let the breeze do the rest.

"Anyway," Cece said, "I'm pretty sure it was a moth."

Theresa sealed the wings behind the plastic sheeting of an old photo album. Years later, Cece pulled back the sheeting, hoping to hold the wings in her palm the way her mother had. The wings were stuck to the plastic, and when Cece tried to free them, they came away in bits that stuck to her fingertips. The wings were orange with black-and-white speckling. In her memory, they'd been blue.

Jackie

The food Get Skinny allowed was so boring. We could have popcorn with no butter or salt. Fat-free yogurt with water floating on its surface. Salad bowls of baby carrots because the thought was, the crunching occupied our minds and eventually became so arduous that being hungry was the preferred option. "If you're hungry, and it's not mealtime or the allotted snack time," Pepper said, "just brush your teeth!" It felt like I was brushing the enamel off mine. But she was right. The little minty burst and its sweet aftertaste often did the trick. We were told to drink a gallon of water a day, to flavor it with lemons or cucumbers or sprigs of spearmint. Chew sugar-free gum. "Cheat" by putting one tablespoon of natural peanut butter in our bowls of fat-free frozen yogurt that tasted like freezer-burned fat-free milk. Snack on dry cereal or celery because, again, the crunching. I was starving.

But it was working. My body began to shrink within that first week. After a month, none of my pants fit. I had to splurge on a new bra, then another new bra six weeks after that. One day, catching my reflection in the mirror of the boys' bathroom, I saw that the shape of my face had changed. I had cheekbones and a jawline. My shirt hung from my shoulders; my jeans sagged and billowed. It felt like only yesterday that I had nearly thrown those jeans out, so firmly was I convinced that I'd never fit into them again.

"Your mom's a toothpick!" Nick said to the boys. We were eating dinner, or rather they were eating the chicken and potatoes I'd made for them and I was chipping away at my faithful carrots, loving the *thock!* of the first bite of each orange nub. I laughed. I was proud. I had to stop myself from running my hands over my body all the time, feeling my hip bones and ribs and the small, firm muscles in my thighs. Loose skin dripped from my upper arms and belly, but Pepper told me it would shrink with time. It was just skin, it was no longer fat, and I felt myself waking up, confronting the world around me in a new way. It was a sense of belonging, of understanding that I had a right to look and be looked at. To take.

My hunger became my obsession, the way a lover sees her beloved everywhere. Clouds in the sky were like the whipped cream I used to pile on top of waffles or ice cream or spray directly into my mouth, and I no longer craved it. Now they were just clouds, it was just whipped cream. Butter lurked around every corner, and I proudly scraped it off my pancakes at Denny's with my family or asked for it to be served on the side, where it was left untouched. Nick brought good chocolates home from work, a gift from a repeat customer, and I let the boys devour them. I felt disgust at the brown glops moving around in their mouths, at the smudges on their lips and cheeks.

I began to feel more and more disgust. It seemed that there was a thin line between being in control of eating and being utterly powerless to food. Nick was always snacking, working his way messily through bags of chips and six-packs of beer, and the boys were black holes of hunger, needing meals and snacks and second meals and third meals and some kind of treat I was supposed to have prepared and waiting for them after school. Was I ever that person? The one who baked cookies and arranged them on a plate? I was. Only I also ate heaping spoonfuls of the dough until my stomach cramped. No more.

I watched Theresa. She shed her extra weight more slowly, and let herself indulge more often. She buttered her toast, she took Cece for ice cream—real ice cream, not froyo. At a Sunday barbecue I watched Adam hook his arm around Theresa's newly thinner waist and tell Nick, "I've even been able to cinch my belt a little tighter." He looked the same. Nick raised his beer and rubbed his hand up and down his own belly. I knew that Nick felt uncomfortable, that he often slapped his gut and said it was time to cut back, but he never did. I knew Adam was too careful with Theresa's new body, that he treated her like something made of glass. "I just want him to pound me," Theresa said, then threw her head back and laughed. I wondered if he was capable and shivered.

Eventually, Theresa stopped. "I don't need it anymore," she said. No more meetings, no more weigh-ins, no more conspiring to make our own sugar-free, fat-free hot fudge syrup. No more applesauce-instead-of-butter in cookie recipes. No more driving together in the car on Tuesday evenings, windows down, letting the smells of salt and oil and meat run over us as we drove past fast-food restaurants we no longer craved. She stopped, and I kept going.

Every waking moment, I plotted and planned and avoided and starved. My body was something I had made out of the rubble of four pregnancies and a twilight consciousness, everything low-lit and muffled. Now I was sharp-edged, brightly colored, the world loud and vibrant and mine. At the grocery store, I caught men looking at me, then looking again. On occasion I smiled at them or winked. Once, I held up a pomelo and asked a bearded man what it was. I rolled it between my hands and petted it with the tip of my finger. The man giggled and I had an urge, so strong that it took my breath away, to reach my hand down and cup his manhood in the same way. His cock would be thick, painful against his zipper. In the man's eyes I saw the beginning of something similar, but men are simpler, and he'd only gotten as far as *tit*. I gasped again. "Mom," Douglas said—I had forgotten about Douglas, always lurking, always checking on me, knitted to me in a way his brothers weren't—"it's just a pomelo." The man's wife drifted up behind him and tossed a loaf of bread into his cart. She wore a shapeless dress in a tartan pattern and I nearly laughed. I could have done it. I realized, or remembered, that we are one way to certain people and another way to certain other people. The way I was friend to Theresa and mom to the boys. Wife to Nick and stranger to the bearded man. It doesn't mean we are disingenuous or deceitful or bad. It is simply the bald truth. Ask any mother. She compartmentalizes as a matter of necessity. What mother sits on her partner's face in front of her children? We are many different women because we have to be. I winked at the man and pushed my cart away, my underwear wet even as I ran my hand over Douglas's head and told him he could pick out a frozen pizza.

I had emptied myself; now it was time to be filled back up.

Adam

A few times in his life, he'd thought, *Well, shit. So this is it.* As a boy he'd imagined his life as a grown-up: He could drink Sprite whenever he wanted and watch television all night long and buy magazines where the women forgot to wear clothes. That had been the extent of his imagining—the soda, the TV, the naked ladies, looped until he died. Then as an adult, fresh out of college, he'd wondered how his life would be once he'd started his career, really started it, like maybe had a secretary and enjoyed drinking coffee and started dreaming about the perfect lawn mower. That, looped. But the reality, the actual loop, was something more mundane and more bizarre. He settled into a routine: wake early, get some miles under his belt—it was roughly four miles round-trip from his apartment to the bridge he found that straddled what looked like a creek but was actually just a very skinny channel in a much larger river—shit, shower, shave, drive to work, get lost in work but for a few scattered moments throughout the day—first sip of coffee, a honk outside his window, that dreamy feeling in the last hour when the day was almost done and he'd be ejected back out into the world, where his time was his own—come home and have a beer and cook something easy in the microwave. If it was a Tuesday, he'd jog to the park for a pick-up game. If it was a Friday, he'd go out for that beer, plus three or four more. It was comfortable; it worked for him.

Then he met Theresa. She nudged in behind him at the bar one night, signaling the bartender. He could feel her against his back, could feel that it was a woman. He turned around and they were basically hugging, chest to chest, both fighting for space in the crowded bar. They laughed. She had a dimple and wavy hair and eyes that seemed to sparkle, even when she wasn't smiling. Later he'd discover that they sparkled even when she was angry, or sad, or bored.

"Sorry," she said that first night. "Is this okay? I can move."

"I'll buy you your drink if you promise me you won't move," he'd said back. That's how it began, his next loop. So easy, like they were coasting. There were no games, no holding back their feelings in order to control the situation. He'd been guilty of that plenty of times before. A girl seemed too eager, too aloof, too whatever. He picked up the phone or he didn't. His gut burned or it didn't. But Theresa. She was next level. He wanted to talk to her, and not just about how horny she made him. He wanted to ask her opinion on stuff at work, see how her day went. He even found himself talking to her about his family, how his mother was starting to remember things in a dark way, his whole childhood tinged with his father's neglect, while his own memories were good ones, pure. He felt loved by his father and it was a mindfuck being told he never had been. With Theresa, he found the words, and she listened.

Technically, he was still seeing someone. Missy. She was a first-grade teacher, and dressed like one—chunky jewelry and colorful blouses and flat shoes. She was there that night, sipping endlessly on her cranberry and vodka. Adam tried to include her in his conversation with Theresa. "I think I've got the sniffles," Missy said, and shook Theresa's hand as she left.

"Oops," Theresa said as they watched Missy push through the heavy bar door, her scarf blowing behind her. "I think we were rude."

"I'll bring her some tea later," Adam said. He never saw Missy again.

Sometimes, in his new loop, he looked back on his old loop and was baffled at how life used to be. Dinner alone in front of the TV, something chewy and burnt on a sectioned plastic plate, his jaw moving involuntarily, forgetting he wasn't holding his beer, he was holding the remote. His pile of wet towels in the bathroom that he only dealt with every other Saturday. His empty walls, his cursory bedding. In his new loop, he and Theresa cooked together. She encouraged him to buy things to hang on his walls, to frame his college diploma and hang that up in the bathroom. She was funny. He hung up his towels or he folded them and put them under the sink. There was still the jogging, the Tuesday evening basketball, the nights out with his friends. More often than not, Theresa, and now some of the other girlfriends, tagged along.

He still had those moments throughout his day when he'd check back in, when he'd snap to and realize that he'd been staring, for years, at the same section of ceiling above his office door with the small molar-shaped water stain, that he'd be staring at it for years to come. When he'd take his first sip of coffee and feel all the parts of himself rush in, assemble, become the person he was at work, someone who was *together*. When he'd look at the small, framed photo Theresa had given him for his desk at work, a picture of them from his most recent company picnic, both of them wearing T-shirts, looking at each other, smiling proudly, and he'd wonder how he'd ever lived without her. She was like that sip of coffee. His life before her was colorless, perfunctory, and she made it real. He had cloth napkins now. A toothbrush holder. A second set of sheets. He could see the use for such things and was grateful she'd shown him.

The first time he had sex with Jackie, his wife's best friend, the woman who treated Cece like a daughter, who folded his child into her own family like it was nothing, the woman who until recently had reminded Adam of his aunt Ramona, it was a total accident. Or, it felt that way. It needed to feel that way.

He'd been lost in his longest loop yet. Work home family. Family home work. Repeat. Repeat. Repeat. There were glimmers of the loop breaking—Cece's sudden silences, her retreats into her room with the door closed. Theresa seeming to brighten, and much as he didn't want to be the kind of man who noticed, the fact that she'd lost weight appeared to be the reason. At work, he had a nemesis. A young buck named Fletcher. Fletcher, for God's sake! He sometimes wore bow ties. He was quick and had an Ivy League education. He was handsome, sexuality impossible to discern. Adam's boss, Glenn, a woman who spoke in three-to-four-word directives, ate it right up. "I have to disagree with Adam," Fletcher said during a meeting just the previous week. "That's an old-school way of looking at it. What we need is freshness. Innovation. I mean, Glenn's always saying that, right?" He looked around with his wide, serious eyes, his jaw barely containing the glee. His gaze bounced off of Adam like maybe he wasn't the Adam Fletcher was talking about. Glenn looked like her underpants were vibrating. She used to look at *him* that way.

What happened was this—Adam caught Douglas being a Peeping Tom. He had a neon-green pair of binoculars and he was pressed up against his bedroom window trying to see into Cece's room. She was in the shower, which bought Adam

some time to just watch Douglas. Little shit. Also, *Cece?* She
was barely fourteen.

The window was all foggy. And where was Douglas's
other hand? Adam knew it was his job to do something, to
walk over and let Jackie and Nick know, but discreetly, because
he remembered his own pubescent years, how everything had
felt loaded, how he had wondered if he was weird for how many
things he was willing to stick his dick into. And Douglas *was*
weird; he once lost a game of HORSE at a barbecue and went
inside, grabbed a knife, and stabbed the basketball until it
flattened. Then he wept on Jackie's shoulder, allowing her to
lead him inside.

The kid had issues, and Adam wasn't looking forward
to ratting him out.

Jackie answered the door. She had on a tank top and little
pink shorts and she was tan. Her collarbone . . . He couldn't
stop staring at it. It was the key to something. He wanted to
find out. Had he never looked at her before? She looked like
someone's girlfriend, and he suddenly felt jealous. The look on
her face, she knew this was the first time he was really looking.
She waited and she let him.

"Hi, Adam," she said. Her toenails were painted bright
purple. He could smell her body lotion. It drugged him, that
was the only explanation. He walked right into it.

"Jackie," he said. He somehow had to explain what was
happening, that her son was a pervert, but it seemed like too
many words. If he had to say all those words, he didn't know if
he could get them all out before creeping forward and touching that collarbone. That shoulder. She brought a carrot up
and snapped a piece off in her jaws. Chewed and watched him.
He marveled at how carrots sounded exactly like they tasted.
It was powerful.

Later, much later, he saw that he was making a choice, there on her doorstep. He wasn't drugged, he wasn't hypnotized. He wanted to feel helpless. He wanted her.

"*Jacqueline*," she said. "I prefer *Jacqueline*."

"Jacqueline," he repeated, but it sounded like a question. Like, *You?* He was a dumb dummy, a flabby idiot. He pointed up, opened his mouth to start explaining about Douglas.

"Adam," she said, before he could begin. "Can I show you something?" She hooked a finger at him. She tossed the carrot stump out the door, over his shoulder, into her yard. Then she grabbed his arm and pulled him in. He was immediately hard. Fleetingly, a joke about being hard as a carrot came to him. He followed her, saw Jayson flat on his back in the living room, the TV on low, saw dishes on every surface in the kitchen they breezed through, saw the little kids out back wrestling in the grass through the sliding glass door in the dining room. Then they arrived at the master bedroom, and they walked in, and Jacqueline closed the door behind them.

"You're a handyman, right?" she asked. She stood close, holding her elbows. Adam looked around. The bed was unmade, the sheets in a twist on one side of it and neatly slept in on the other. The closet door was open, a pile of shoes tumbling out. The countertop in the bathroom was crowded with bottles, tissues, globs of toothpaste. He and Theresa were in sync when it came to tidiness, joining together to make sure that everything had its place, that the trash went out on Thursdays and the dishwasher got emptied promptly and the clutter got handled. And he was grateful for that kind of easy partnership. He couldn't imagine if one of them didn't care about those things. If both of them didn't care, had maybe stopped caring, and then add four boys to that. Jacqueline's room smelled like her, and like her and Nick's sleeping breath had saturated the walls over the years, and like shoes and socks and half-empty bottles of peach-scented body wash.

"Something need fixing?" he asked. He'd never been in this room before. Had he? He searched his memories of Christmas parties, barbecues. All the doors usually remained closed. And now he was behind the closed door. Jacqueline's bare feet were doing something to him. He still had an erection, but now he was blushing, his whole head hot.

"I think so," she said. "Nick's not very good at those kinds of things." She grabbed his hand and pulled him toward the closet. She bent and swept the shoes out of the way, her ass a blossom opening before him.

"I've seen you in your garage," she said. "With all your tools. I figured I'd ask." She pulled him into the closet with her, a walk-in just like the one in his and Theresa's bedroom. They had their backs to Nick's clothes—polos hung in with trousers, button-downs jammed in, truly a madman's closet—and were facing Jacqueline's side. There wasn't much, a couple of dresses and shirts with the tags still on, tons of wire hangers, her wedding dress in a plastic garment bag shoved to the wall.

She pointed at the space above the clothes. "I need a shelf," she said.

"A shelf." Her shoulder brushed his arm. He wondered if he could convince Theresa to have sex with him when he got back, if he could just pull her into their bedroom, if she was wearing a skirt or one of those crappy dresses she used to wear, the ones that looked like a T-shirt for a giant, and he could just pull it up and get in there, Jesus God he needed to get in there. He wondered if he had been gassed, what the hell had gotten into him, hard as a carrot in his neighbor's closet while she mused about needing a shelf.

"High up," she was saying. "I need somewhere to put stuff I want to keep high up."

"Simplest thing in the world," he said. He just wanted to get out of there before she noticed the distress he was in. He could see the closed bedroom door; why had she closed the door? He heard Nathan or Sammy shout, *Ha! That's what you get!* "I could have it done for you this weekend. I'll come back later to do some measuring." He started to edge out of the closet.

"Thank you. You know," she said, stopping him, that hand on his arm again, "it's nice to talk to someone who says yes."

He stared at a wad of underwear just behind her, so he wouldn't look into her eyes in such close proximity. His heart felt like a tennis ball being whacked against a wall. "Oh?" He cleared his throat.

"It's just that"—she stepped closer to him—"Nick's default is to say no. To be suspicious of me, or to worry whatever I'm going to ask is going to make it harder for him to just sit on the couch with a beer." She touched his other arm. "He's tired of me, you know?"

She didn't sound sad, or like she wanted him to contradict her, assure her that her husband wasn't tired of her. She said it like a fun fact, something offhand, easily accepted. What the hell time was it? He suddenly felt desperate to know.

"You're not tired of me," she said. "I can see that for myself."

Now his heart was an alarm bell, clanging so desperately his whole body was stunned. He felt light move through him from head to toe and out through his fingertips. It hurt. He needed to get out of there, get home, find the Tums.

"Marriage is a marathon, not a sprint," he said. Something his father had told him on his wedding day years ago. Looking earnestly at Adam, his bow tie askew and light from the window reddening the tips of his ears. "Everyone gets tired," Adam said, but she had moved her hand at that point, was palming his erection through his pants. He gripped her shoulders; he let one hand drift over to that collarbone.

"You can touch me anywhere," she whispered. Her breath smelled like cinnamon. He was having trouble closing his own mouth. "I like to be touched."

As a teenager, when his erections had first become a problem for him, he sometimes felt gouged, mournful, so sad he wanted to scream under a bridge somewhere, that there was nowhere to put this turgid, insistent nuisance. He knew there was somewhere, someone, if he was just given a chance. Using his hand, even lying on his stomach and sort of rubbing it around, it wasn't enough. He spent years feeling desperate. He got close senior year, naked with his girlfriend Abby in her darkened bedroom, but right when he felt brave enough to push in, she hissed, *Stop!* She wasn't ready, she said. It wasn't the right time. She grabbed it and sort of clenched her hand around it, clench, release, clench, release, until he told her it was fine, she didn't have to. He walked home and tried not to cry or scream. It was lonely, this utterly fixable problem, a grieving sort of lonely.

He hadn't felt that way in years. Eventually there were women, one after the other, and finally Theresa. But he felt it again in that shitty closet with Jacqueline, only now he was a man, and he knew things. He rubbed his thumb over her nipple; he cupped her ass in his other hand. There was something about how they were touching each other through their clothes that made it even hotter. Like they were kids, just figuring bodies out, not knowing how far it could go.

She raised up on her toes, brought her mouth close to his ear. Her breath there sent a shiver down his back. He had both hands on her ass now. "Adam," she whispered. "Do you want me to put your cock in my mouth?" He made a noise like she'd sucker punched him. It was beyond him, nothing he could have controlled. His penis felt like it could burst from his pants, like it was ten inches longer. Already, he was negotiating with himself. He'd go along with this just once. He'd see it through and then they'd both agree it was wrong and couldn't happen again. He'd feel the appropriate amount of shame and rededicate himself wholly to his family. No one would ever know.

How many moments in his day went unexamined? Did Theresa know everything about him? No. And he didn't know everything about her. These thoughts came to him in bursts of imagery as he braced himself in the doorway, the tip of his penis inside Jacqueline's warm mouth. It took all he had not to thrust; he knew, somewhere in the blizzard happening in his mind, that that would be rude. "Oh wow," he whispered. "Oh." She was playing with him, never taking him fully in. He nearly said, *Please*. He was that close to begging. He touched her shoulder and knelt so they were face-to-face. He still had all his clothes on; she'd simply unzipped him and fished out his penis. For a moment she had a look of woundedness, then panic, and then she pulled him toward her until they were on the floor among the socks and shoe polish and dust balls. He unbuckled his belt and she pushed down her shorts and then it was happening. They were fucking, stomach to stomach, Adam's face mashed into the toe of a tasseled loafer, trying not to moan or shout *Hell yeah*. He wondered if he should turn her over, if she'd want him to switch positions, but then . . . But then. "You can come inside me," she whispered, that breath on his ear again, and almost immediately, he did.

Theresa was in the driveway, bringing in the groceries. "You were at Jackie's?" she said, tucking a second bag under her arm so she could grab the jug of milk. Adam grabbed the milk from her, and the bag under her arm.

"Yeah," he said. He wanted to look down at himself, see how rumpled or stained he was, try to catch a whiff of the bleachy, salty smell of sex. He swallowed, trying to keep his voice level. He was giddy. He felt like laughing, like dropping the groceries on the driveway and grabbing Theresa and spinning her in the air. "She asked me to build her a shelf."

"Huh," she said. "She never told me. A shelf for what?" She pushed her sunglasses to the top of her head, studied him. "Never mind. Must be one of her whims."

"Right," he said. Was he also one of her whims? And was that good news or bad?

Later, in the shower, he could see how he'd been seduced. And he'd fallen for it. Nick wasn't his best friend, but he had to be able to look the man in the eye. What exactly was going on over there? Then again, he told himself, these things happened more often than anyone talked about. He knew of at least two friends who'd had affairs. One friend, Sean, dropped one lover and picked up another right after, all the while planning his tenth wedding anniversary trip with his wife. Humans were animals.

It enlivened things. He saw everything anew, as if he'd been wearing the wrong prescription. He saw how Theresa lined their bath products so neatly, keeping his shampoo and body wash together in a little basket. He'd always taken that for granted. Who'd bought that basket? His wife. She was so thoughtful, so organized. He loved his wife! Her body wash smelled like apricots, he discovered, and he fought the urge to squirt some into his hand and touch himself. For the first time in a very long time, he could go twice in one day if he had the opportunity.

It had happened. No turning back. But it never had to happen again. He and Jacqueline had needed something, a little jolt to remind them they were alive. The whining noises she made and the way she was bald down there, *bald!* Oh God oh God. And now they'd never forget it.

"I'm going to hop in the shower," he said to Theresa once the groceries were put away. He'd expected her to say something like *Now?* Or *Again?*

"Okay," she said, placing the apples into the fruit bowl, one by one.

He dripped onto the bathmat (also purchased by that magician, his wife) and looked at himself. He was aging. He was the same age his father had been when he'd begun spending hours watching golf on television, sending out for VHS tapes of men giving golf tips, murmuring to the viewer like they were on their deathbed. Men did strange things because time passed and it passed very quickly while you looked around thinking how slowly it was passing. He wondered what Jacqueline's reason was. What was she doing over there, at her house? Was she still on the closet floor, her boys bored out of their minds? With a start he realized he'd never mentioned Douglas. He'd install blinds in Cece's bathroom window, talk to her about how boys were idiots, morons, so she needed to be more careful.

"You're not into kissing," she'd said, after. She was straddling him, rubbing herself on his spent penis like a cat. It felt like a challenge and he grabbed her and kissed her, his hands in her hair, his abs engaged from holding his head off the floor. When they parted she licked her lips like she was tasting something and said, "Me neither."

As he was leaving, picking his way through all the clutter, Jayson muted the TV, turned to watch him go. "I'm going to build a shelf for your mom," Adam said.

"Oh," said Jayson, and unmuted.

Douglas

Later, a lot later, Douglas would think about what he did and didn't know, and when. What, he wondered, is a child aware of? His childhood, when he looked back, was a stream of sharp and muddled images, one-sided memories, strange defining nothings that when put together only made sense as a sort of collage, a symbolic bewilderment that had meaning he couldn't put into words. But that was how it looked later. What did he see then, what did he know then? Did Douglas know about his mother and Cece's father? He knew enough.

He knew that his mother was gone a lot more now, and that she didn't want him going with her so much anymore. This was a relief, the way a stab victim feels relieved when the blade is pulled from the wound, only to watch the blood begin to gush. He knew that she started talking about going back to school, maybe becoming a nurse, that she bought a word-of-the-day calendar and tried out words like *ambivalent* and *punctilious* on them, that she now wore red-brown lipstick and circles of rouge, that she pulled her hair back in a girlish ponytail and visibly enjoyed swinging it back and forth as she walked. He saw the way men noticed her, edged closer to her, found reasons to talk to her. Worse, his mother liked it, encouraged them with little slaps on their shoulders and peals of laughter and with the way she rubbed the palm of her hand across her breastbone.

For a year now, Douglas had been taking daily baths, an activity he knew he was too old for, but the sound of the water and the locked door offered him his only opportunity to masturbate, to close his eyes and use his soaped-up hand on himself, to think of Brittany Schmidt in that striped sweater she wore every week, so tight, the way she jogged from class to class, her breasts moving up and down . . . or Cece, how she didn't seem to be aware of how long her legs were, or the way she looked up at him from under her hair, the way she always seemed a little afraid of him, her small breasts the perfect size, little plums he could weigh in each hand, and in his fantasy she cried out a little, scared of his touch, but unwilling to back away, and he would come into his hand and cover his mouth with his other hand so he wouldn't make those little noises he sometimes made. But she'd also been there. His mother. Blurred, standing some distance behind Cece, watching him touch her. He'd masturbated to a fantasy involving his mother. And he'd ejaculated into his hand. That was another thing he knew. It—and he was unable to name it, being a teenage boy, but *it* referred to *sex*—was in the air. It was contagious, shimmering all around the house, an energy that flowed in velvety waves from his own mother. He didn't want to give up the baths. He needed them. But he couldn't risk closing his eyes, turgid in his own hand, and seeing her.

One night, lying on his stomach in bed, he saw Cece's light come on. Instantly he was hard. Her shade was drawn, and he could only see an occasional shadow as she moved around her room. He began rubbing himself gently against his mattress, envisioning her underneath him. Would his weight be too much? Would she be able to breathe? This had always mystified him, when thinking of sex. How not to crush the woman underneath him? In his fantasy, Cece gasped, holding tight to him. He came against his own stomach. In the morning his dick was stuck to his abdomen.

Watching Cece, even a glimpse of her—moving through her house, or knowing she was in the bathroom—that became Douglas's only safe haven. If he kept his eyes on the house, on a brief sighting of her hair, or her arm, or the handful of times she looked right back at him, then his mother never entered the fantasy. It was just him and Cece. He locked Jayson out of their room. He began sleeping on his stomach at all times. He wanted to hump the bed—to *fuck it*, a phrase he'd heard in a porno at a friend's house, a woman with thick black liner around her eyes, dressed in a white lace bodysuit, saying *Fuck me, fuck me*, in an angry voice—but he couldn't risk giving himself away. It was a pleasant kind of withholding, the never letting himself move as roughly as he wanted to. It became—his therapist would later explain—his kink. Always, he walked around with it pent up inside him. A churning, a flame that roared into a blaze. His heart pounded against his chest. He could hardly breathe. It was ecstasy, and it was awful.

One early spring day, the sky a washed sort of blue, the grass still yellow, the ground soft, the smell of cold, wet soil drifting on the air, Douglas watched his mother let herself into the Lindens' backyard and sit on Cece's swing. She had on her ugly winter boots, shit brown with fur sprouting out the tops, and she pushed herself with her toes. He knew it would be creaking, a ragged, groaning *uh-uh, uhhhh-ohhhhh*. She was slumped the way Cece often was, dreamy, her coat clutched close in her fists.

He'd been watching for Cece, hoping to see her come outside, bend over Mrs. Linden's garden, touching the crowns of the yellow tulips that had sprouted the week earlier. She talked to herself back there, wandering with her arms crossed tight. Girls at school liked Douglas—he saw them watching him, the braver ones smiling, and once he'd been beckoned over by Cherise Daniels, her bent finger wiggling at him. "You going to ask me out or what?" she said, snapping her gum. She had long brown hair and strong thighs, freckles across her nose. She gave him a hand job at the movies, a bucket of popcorn on his lap to hide her hand, and after fifteen minutes she yanked her hand away and hissed, "What the fuck?" He hadn't come and he knew he wouldn't, not there. Now Cherise ignored him at school, and her friends snickered behind their hands when he passed, but he didn't give a shit. There were other girls, shy girls like Rebecca Sharp, who talked to him with her shirt visibly moving from the force of her heartbeat, and freak girls like Shay McMillan, who wore black lipstick and ripped tights and sometimes met him under the stairwell by shop class, where they stuck their hands down each other's pants and breathed hard into each other's mouths but never kissed. None of them was Cece, who'd become his angel, her disinterest in him a sort of protective bubble around him. When he watched her in the yard talking to herself, he imagined her saying, *I need your cock* or *Take me from behind* or *Just do it*, in a voice so desperate it broke his heart.

But she didn't come out that morning, just his own mother, hunched on a child's swing. Even in her coat she looked too thin. Her hair seemed to be pulling away from her scalp, and from his vantage point Douglas could see what looked like a bald spot at the back of her head. Jayson pounded on the bedroom door. "I need to get changed for soccer, man," he hollered. Douglas ignored him. Since he was a kid, he could read his mother's mind. His brothers saw her as food-bringer, comfort-giver, birthday-planner. Generic mom shape. But Douglas spent a lot of his childhood trying to figure her out. Who was this sad woman they called Mom? Why was she sad? When she was happy, why was she happy? There were tricks he discovered along the way. If he named her emotion correctly, she drew him to her and held him there. "You feel like crying, huh, Momma?" he'd say, and be nestled into her soft arms and belly. "You're so tired, right, Momma?" and she'd pull him down beside her to nap. He never heard his father talk this way, and it was so easy! It was so obvious. She just wanted to be noticed. Now, after years of noticing, Douglas couldn't stop. Looking at her on the swing, he knew she was waiting. Excited. Probably humming to herself. Douglas had nearly turned away from the window, so very tired of noticing, when Mr. Linden came out the back sliding glass door, carefully closing it behind him. His mother rose and turned, letting go of her coat, letting it slip off her shoulders. She was nude. Douglas saw her used-up belly, how it hung in wrinkled folds, saw her scrawny legs, her flat ass with its small dash of a butt crack. Mr. Linden rushed to her, pushing her shoulders back, trying to lower her to the ground, but his mother got on her knees. Douglas watched. He watched all of it, saw how Mr. Linden threw his head back, his hands useless in Douglas's mother's hair, how rapidly her head moved—did it hurt?—how she reared back, letting him drop from her mouth, waiting for him to look down, and then turned over onto all fours, how Mr. Linden pushed himself into her, bent over her so he could hold her breasts in his hands as he thrust. Douglas watched as Mr. Linden came, then watched as his mother turned around and pressed him down onto his back and pushed him back inside her. Douglas was erect, and he hated her, and he hated Mr. Linden, and he hated Cece, hated her calm and quiet life and calm and quiet mother who had chosen this monster, this flabby man who was holding on to Douglas's mother like she was trying to take all of him inside her, hated that he knew this, had to know everything about her, and he hated how badly he wanted to touch himself. He thought of Cherise, of her *What the fuck?* He thought he understood but he didn't, or he didn't want to, or he no longer wanted to. He turned from the window and stared into his room, so dim compared to the outside light, and waited for his bed and Jayson's bed and their narrow, shitty desk to come into focus, then he opened the door and pushed past his brother and locked himself in the bathroom to take a bath.

Cece

Cece woke. Took a breath. She could still smell it. Or not smell it exactly, more like she could sense it in a way that felt like a smell. Like how you knew someone was going to have bad breath before they leaned in and whispered and old coffee and sleep smacked you in the face. More and more, she was having these kinds of senses. The kinds she didn't want. Her friend Victoria claimed to be psychic, said she could tell who liked who before they even knew, and Cece had once watched something she'd found, flipping through the channels in the middle of the night, where a man could levitate items just by looking at them, and both of those examples seemed like much more useful abilities. Instead, she was stuck with the one she had, which she had begun thinking of as *the dread*.

Sometimes, she also felt it in her crotch. She looked out her window toward Jayson's house, at the sliver of his window she could just see without sitting up, but it was dark.

Downstairs was quiet. She stood in the kitchen in her T-shirt and underwear, the tile freezing cold through her socks. Her father cranked the air-conditioning as a matter of principle. She wasn't hungry; lately she couldn't even remember what it felt like to be hungry. Eating? What was the point? You'd just have to do it all over again in a matter of hours.

Her parents' door was closed. She imagined her mother, curled under the thin quilt, her fists bunched at her chin, protecting herself even in unconsciousness. From what? That's what Cece couldn't put her finger on. In reality, her mother was probably tightly cocooned against Cece's father, their fingers intertwined. Cece had stopped trusting her father shortly after he'd shaved the beard.

She settled on dry cereal so she could pick at it for as long as she wanted without worrying it'd get soggy, and settled on the couch with the bowl between her thighs. The sun was level with the sliding glass doors, flooding the family room with light the color of butterscotch. Their house was a mirror of the Stinsons' house, the same floor plan and everything, though Miss Jackie's style was bolder, while Cece's parents seemed to buy sets from the furniture store, right down to framed geometric prints in blues and grays. Miss Jackie had hung a headdress above the television, a dreamcatcher in the bathroom.

Cece had started to wonder why they were best friends, her mother and Miss Jackie. When she was younger, it was a given. If they were going someplace, to the park or to mini golf, to the McDonald's or just to sit in the driveway kicking a ball around, they were going together. Miss Jackie and her boys and Cece and her mother. It was all Cece could remember. People often asked if they were sisters, though Cece's mother was fair and small and Miss Jackie had dark curly hair and big shoulders and big thighs and a big mouth. They linked arms and put their heads together and roared with laughter.

Now, though . . . Cece didn't have a sibling so she didn't know for sure, but it seemed like what happened when siblings fought, when there was a break that wouldn't mend. Douglas and Jayson were like that, had been since Douglas had turned thirteen. One couldn't say anything right to the other. Miss

Jackie was always rolling her eyes, Cece's mother crossing her arms and sighing all the time. It had something to do with the husbands, Cece figured, because when the men were around, Miss Jackie and Cece's mother faked it, nudging each other and screeching like always.

The sun had crept upward and Cece's face held a tired ache, like she'd splashed it with cold water. She heard the toilet flushing in her parents' bathroom and hoped it was her mother awake and not her father.

Jayson knew, too, Cece could tell. About the dread. They were so careful with each other now. She imagined Jayson on his own sofa with his own bowl, and she had to stop there because imagining the bowl against his bare thighs made her hands shake. She got up to look at herself in the mirror her mother had hung in the foyer. *Was* she pretty? She had okay hair, thick and wavy, but the color was whatever. Kind of brown, kind of red. A small gap in her teeth she'd begun hiding when she smiled. Cute nose, some freckles, normal lips. Her best feature was her eyes, which were green, genuinely green, deep jade, even. She turned her head to the side and looked at her own profile. Should she look at Jayson like this next time?

"See anything you like?" her father asked. Cece whipped around, filling with shame at being caught in a moment of vanity, and with disgust at her father's bare legs, disturbingly hairless and muscular, his boxer shorts that hit three inches above his tan line. He held up his hands like she was charging at him. "Just a joke, sweetheart." She refused to turn to see what look she had on her face. She knew it was something hard, possibly ugly.

They just no longer knew what to make of each other. She'd read the books about disaffected teens and their raging or sorrowful or negligent parents. She'd seen Douglas and now Jayson, how their dad didn't play catch with them anymore and no one hugged. It was happening here, in her own home, too. She could trace it back to the day she'd gotten her first period, how her mother told her father as soon as he walked in the door, how he looked at Cece like she'd just farted in church. Should he laugh? Should he warn her? Ignore it? Soon after that she grabbed his hand standing in line at the food court in the mall, something they did all the time—hold hands—but he shook her off. She got the message. She wasn't his little girl anymore.

"We're learning about skin cancer in Bio," she said. "I thought I had a spot."

"Gotcha," he said, already making his way into the kitchen. "Come talk to me, kid," he said, but she was already following him, and that was something she hadn't read in the books before, how families just naturally fell into rhythms despite themselves, how they tried and tried again to relate even when they were messing it all up. Like right now, Cece was annoyed with herself, sick of her conflicting emotions. He was gross but he was her dad.

He was humming to himself, tinkering with the coffee maker. He'd become obsessed with the perfect cup. Before that it was wine. Before that it was gardening. Before that it was stereo equipment. Before that it was bicycles. The man had to have something to perfect.

"Are you singing—" Cece stopped herself. "What are you singing?"

"I don't know the name of it," he said. The sunlight streaming in from the window lit his face and made his eyes sparkle, but his hair, now the color of the cocoa powder her mother baked with, was flat. She wanted to find a way to tell him, to help him understand that the cheap hair dye wasn't doing him any favors, but she ached at the thought of him feeling ashamed. "It's on the radio all the time, though," he said. He leveled the coffee scoop with the flat edge of a butter knife, the excess grinds falling into the sink. They'd stay there until Cece's mother came to wash them down the drain. Proof that he didn't notice *everything*.

"How do you even know that song?" Her voice was bitchier than she intended. The song was huge at school. Everyone believed it was a poorly veiled ode to blow jobs. That her father was humming it in his boxer shorts, that he was cheerful, that he didn't remind her to speak respectfully, all of it was ick.

"What do we have on the agenda today?" he asked. *The agenda.* He loved to talk like he was lording over some office.

"I don't know. I have a paper to write, but it's easy." She knew he'd suggest she ride her bike, get outside. "It's too hot to do anything."

"Maybe we can play catch later," he said. It was like he was worried that if she sat still for too long, she'd turn to dust. "Before I have to leave."

She'd forgotten. He was leaving for California for a week, some conference where he'd pass out his business cards. As a kid, she'd loved them, how they were so thick and textured, how they said his name in bold print, how they almost felt spendable. At the conference, he would throw his head back to laugh at dim jokes and roll his shirt sleeves up immediately, because it made him feel both approachable and hardworking. She'd seen him, watched him, over the years, at office picnics, Christmas cookie exchanges, the annual take-your-kid-to-work days. He was a guy who saw himself from the outside first.

"Sure," she said. It could happen. It probably wouldn't, but leaving the possibility open seemed to help ease whatever shittiness hung in the air, at least for the moment. She reached over and grabbed the loaf of bread on the counter, tossed it to him. "Will you make me your toast?"

"She eats?" he asked, clutching the loaf to his heart.

"Toast tastes better when someone else makes it for you. It's a fact."

"I see." He hummed again while he toasted the bread, and while he slathered half a stick of butter on. "Jelly?"

"Of course." Cece heard her mother walking around upstairs, gathering her pilled yellow robe, standing at the sink with the water running while she brushed her teeth. She'd come downstairs and take a bite of Cece's toast, and Cece's father would offer to make another piece.

It did feel good, every once in a while, to have a family, people who knew you, the rumpled, unadorned you, and loved you no matter what. Sometimes it was like they were each whipping around a skating rink, flying past each other, a waving blur, and sometimes they slowed down at the exact same time and glided together for a while.

Jayson

The days in summer were dry and the red clay sent up eddies of ankle-high dust. The sun rose quickly, the asphalt shimmering with heat. In the afternoons a gray sheet blanketed the sky, teasing rain, quieting the insects that clicked and hummed in the scrubby grass. If it did rain it was a short burst, not enough to saturate more than the top layer of clay. Then the gray sheet rolled back, the sky pale blue with a white sun. The house was dark and cool, the TV always murmuring softly from the living room.

That day, Saturday, it was Jayson's turn to bring the snacks to soccer practice. Jackie never remembered the snacks. She once showed up twenty minutes late, with eight Happy Meals and a two-liter of Mountain Dew he knew she'd brought from home. No cups. The other boys—Richie with that stupid rattail and his buck teeth, Griff with his tight curls and slobbery lips—looking at him with that revolting mixture of pity and fear. There were ten boys, so he went without and he prayed that someone—Andre, whose voice hadn't changed yet, or quiet Jeff, whose father forced him to be on the team, even though he clearly loathed it, spent practices staring off at the highway—would agree to share.

This time, he had reminded her last night at dinner—grocery store rotisserie and Kool-Aid, no sides. "It's our turn for snacks, Ma."

She'd winked, chewing her food and spitting it into her napkin. "I got you," she said. She'd lost the weight, was still losing, and her face had shadows and planes now, angles, her eyes larger and harder to see into. She'd taken the family photos off the walls, leaving dim rectangles where the frames used to be, tossed them into a box and shoved it into the far corner of the garage. "We can't have anyone thinking your mom is a fatass," she said, laughing, but it did seem to Jayson that they were two separate people, this thin woman with hair the color of buttercream at the tips and the mom in the photos, with her mousy bob and enormous glasses and fat cheeks. She'd sung to him, the old mom did. This new one forgot to buy milk and listened to the radio station with the popular music, not the stuff he knew she really liked.

Also, she was pretty. She wore bikinis and makeup, and that was a hard pill to swallow.

He'd chewed and swallowed his chicken, delicious in its utter familiarity. He had begun to hate Kool-Aid, though; drinking it felt like he was agreeing to the narrative she was demanding of them, that she was a cool mom who served cool foods, and not a mom who did the bare minimum. He must have had some look on his face, because she flared her nostrils and said, "Don't worry so much about the friggin' snacks. Snacks are optional in life, it's time you learned that."

Saturday morning, she told him he would have to walk to practice because she had errands to run. He gaped at her. The walk was almost a mile, the day already stifling. She was wearing her glasses, something she only did in the mornings. She wiped crumbs off the counter and into her palm, sprinkled them over the trash can. "Beat it," she said, wringing the purple dishrag into the sink.

Jayson walked up their block of tidy homes, some trees lush and shady, others too new and of no help to him. He made his slow, sweaty way past the shaggy boxwoods at the front of the subdivision and out to the main road he would take all the way to the high school. There was something else, and he had no choice but to think about it on his way, the heat sapping his will to beat it back. He'd seen things, events that could be nothing but added up to something in the gross private world of adults, a world he wanted no part of.

One. Two months ago, at his brother Nathan's birthday party, he'd seen his mother and his neighbor, Mr. Linden, hip to hip in the laundry room, heads bent toward each other, whispering.

Two. His mother took late-night phone calls in the yard right outside his window. More whispering, some giggling, an occasional moan. Also, she was maybe smoking.

Three. Mr. Linden shaved his beard and Jayson was pretty sure he'd also dyed his hair, because suddenly it was a weird, flat brown color. Or maybe it had always been that color and Jayson was just paying more attention. Regardless, the beard was gone and Mr. Linden had taken to cutting the grass shirtless, his nipples the palest pink and disturbingly low on his chest.

Jayson had watched Cece Linden closely, but he couldn't tell how she felt about her dad's hair, newly smooth face, or if she also heard him outside her window murmuring like a teenager. Douglas noticed Jayson watching Cece. "You love her," Douglas sang at breakfast one morning, eating his Pop-Tarts like a sandwich. Nathan and Sammy watched, waiting to see where their loyalties should lie. Douglas gasped, held his hand to his heart. "You want to touch her boobies."

Jayson's whole head got hot. He'd never even considered it. But now it was all he could think about. He'd played naked in the baby pool with Cece and there were pictures to prove it. He'd picked his nose in front of her. Farted. Cried! *Boobies? Cece?*

Boobies. Cece.

If his mom and her dad were doing it, wouldn't that make it, sort of, incest? If he did touch her? He felt the heat in his mouth, his tongue thick and gloppy. Since then, he'd had a hard time looking Cece in the eye.

Finally, he rounded the corner and there it was, the high school, the soccer field just beyond the parking lot. It was hyper-green, sickening, the color of a sour lollipop that'd sting your tongue. His teammates' parents sat in camp chairs in a semicircle of knobby knees and Tevas and coolers. They nodded at him but he knew they'd whisper about his mom, this new version of her, as soon as his back was turned.

"Aw, fuck, it's your turn today?" This from Anthony, the only Black kid on the team, the only Black kid Jayson had ever seen play soccer. When it was his turn, Anthony's mom brought orange slices, so cold and juicy, and sandwiches she cut into triangles and icy Capri Suns in the right flavors. Anthony wore a bandana around his neck, his hair in short braids; he could run up and down the field and never get winded. Nothing ever tumbled out of his mom's car when they rolled up. Rumor was he had a girlfriend and they'd *done it*. Jayson wasn't sure if *it* meant *IT*, which only added to the myth of Anthony, the only Black kid on the team.

"Chill," Jayson said, pretending to mess with his shin guard. It was stained, smelly, no longer white, but he knew he couldn't expect the same attention from his mother as the other guys on the team got from their mothers, knew she just didn't have it in her. His mother would tell him to wash it himself, but how? *How?* "My mom's on her way."

"Shit," Anthony said, walking in a small circle. "I knew I should have brought something." Anthony did a header and the ball whiffed just past Coach.

"I could run to the Circle K," Jayson offered. "I've got a twenty in my bag, I think—"

"What?" Coach said, distracted, obsessed as always with the cones, with anyone approaching the cones before he'd given the okay. He looked wounded and tired; even the thick hair coating his legs seemed matted. It often occurred to Jayson that no one was ever where they wanted to be. He looked around and didn't see one person who wasn't drifting in and out of boredom. You had to make up things to care about, like soccer, and then you either had to be naturally amazing at it, like Anthony, or you had to have what his father called *heart*, which seemed to be a way of ignoring how bad you were at a sport. His father was always talking shit about the other salesmen at the dealership, how they couldn't even keep their trays of business cards stocked, how it was his idea to offer a year's membership to the gym along with any convertible sale, how no one appreciated him, his drive, his commitment, his purpose. All of this said while he was picking a toenail or ignoring his cell phone or moving his balls from one side to the other. Jayson knew it was all horseshit. The other guys at the dealership probably said the same stuff about his father. Or worse.

Jesus *Christ*, it was hot. His neck hurt from squinting down at his cleats, and from the slouching his mom was always on his ass about. But it hurt more to stand up straight.

"There go your mom, Jay," Anthony yelled. She was pulling up, the minivan lumbering across the dried clay. He could see her ashing her cigarette out the open window. Sometimes she did something he knew she'd believed looked cool when she was in high school, and in those moments, he wanted the world to neatly, tidily, quietly, end. "Hope she brought some food."

"She didn't," Brian said. He was a shitty goalie and they all knew it and he had to take his shots where he could get them.

"I bet it's some old potato salad or some shit," Anthony said, already folding into the set of burpees he knew Coach would give him for swearing. "Some stale-ass white bread and a scraped-out jar of peanut butter." He was cracking himself up, the other boys' laughter like clapping at a parade, all of them winded from laughing.

Jayson walked to the driver's side and stood before his mother. He tried to think of something mean he could do or say that would feel satisfying to him but go unnoticed by her. He studied her loose tank top, its pattern of triangles in various sizes, her bologna-colored bra fully visible under her armpit. "You wore that last week," he said.

She pulled her sunglasses down. "What's up with you?" she asked, her voice the same as always, just short of sarcastic. The worst times were when he could see the old her, almost, in the inner corner of her eyes, the way she studied him without blinking or looking away. "I brought food, worrywart."

He leaned slightly to the side so he could see around her, thinking there'd be bags on the passenger seat, but it was Douglas. Something about the way Douglas was sitting seemed off, the way he gripped his knees, how he was staring out the windshield and not taking the opportunity to dole out some shit for Jayson to eat.

"Why the hell's he here?" Jayson asked, loudly, so the guys could hear him swear in front of his mother. She no longer cared about that stuff.

"He's got to help me with something." She winked at Jayson and pushed her sunglasses back up. "Jealous?" The motor was still running. She hadn't even put it into park. Jayson felt outrage, then relief.

Douglas was always helping her with stupid stuff like making returns at the store or using an expired coupon at the oil change place. She called him her lucky charm but really people just liked to look at him, his wavy golden hair and turquoise eyes and bobbing Adam's apple. They didn't see how he picked his nose with his pinky finger. How he barely ever brushed his teeth. How when it was his turn to say grace he stumbled over words and his ears turned blood red. They saw the Douglas she wanted them to see, the gum-chewing flirt, the hair-flicking, quiet jock.

Coach blew the whistle. "What'd you bring?" Jayson asked. She reached behind her and handed over an enormous shopping bag and he could smell it immediately. "You got Auntie Anne's?" He didn't know if he should feel impressed or worried. Would hot pretzels keep until break?

"Told you," she said. She waved at the other parents, all staring openly at her. Some of the moms returned the gesture, tiny little fluttery nothings that meant nothing. "Told you I'd remember."

"No drinks?" he asked. Coach blew the whistle again.

"Use the water fountain," she said.

The water fountain was all the way on the other side of the school, but it was useless to remind her.

"Hey," she said. She reached out and pulled him closer to her. Her hands were ice cold and bony and her fake nails pushed into his skin. Douglas still wouldn't look at him, some stick up his ass as usual. "Listen up."

He was so close to the van that he was probably smashing the pretzels, and Coach blew the whistle a third time, so loud and long that Jayson wanted to yell *Stop!* only he didn't know at whom. "Mom. What?"

She ran her tongue over her front teeth, another thing he was sure she'd seen in a magazine or on one of her talk shows. *How to look sexy anywhere, even sandwiched between two of your very own sons, you utter freakazoid!* He couldn't see her eyes through her sunglasses, only two small reflections of himself. Even there, he had enormous ears. "Jayson," she whispered, squeezing his arm tighter. "Fuck 'em."

She released him and drove off and she made a left at the road instead of a right, so he knew she wasn't headed home. He had an okay practice, lending an assist to Anthony right before he scored a goal, Brian crumpling to the ground in his shittiness. At break Jayson handed out the pretzels and the small cups of dipping sauce and offered to fill everyone's water bottles at the water fountain and he felt useful. Liked, even. Still, though all of it went fine and there was a breeze on the walk home, Jayson's arm felt hot where she'd gripped it and he kept seeing her face, kept seeing how she wanted him to understand her, how *fuck 'em* was a hidden message from mother to son, yes, but also from human adult to still-a-child, a hand reaching down to him from some later step he'd take in life, and it gnawed at him, because he didn't want to take that step. He didn't want to understand her. He didn't want her to think she understood him. In fact, he wanted the opposite of all of that. He wanted her to see what a mess she made even as she believed she was making it all—making herself—better. And yet, he knew, watching Anthony and the rest of them bust on him and his mother and their dirty-ass van, that *fuck 'em* was correct, too.

Jayson's cleats were dusted ochre, his shin guards dyed rust, his kneecaps smudged. He smelled ozone and looked up to search for signs of rain. A graphite-colored line of sky seemed to be thickening toward him. He was thinking of his mother, of Mr. Linden's ugly new hair, of how after practice he'd made Anthony laugh by doing an impersonation of Coach drinking from the water fountain, arching his back as he bent to make his ass look bigger. And he thought of Cece. His mother said they were born a day apart in the same hospital. It had never seemed interesting to him before. Sometimes she sat next to him on the bus, going over her homework in her binder or staring out the window. Occasionally she asked him how his weekend was, how his soccer game went. All the girls preferred Douglas. Did she?

"Fuck 'em," he whispered, his sneakers slapping the sidewalk. Fat drops of rain hit his neck and slid into his jersey.

Jackie

Adam sometimes wanted to talk about how guilty he felt. "I was thinking," he said, still breathing heavily after we'd fucked in my garage, "maybe if both of us try a little harder. I was thinking I'd ask Theresa to have a weekly date night." His hairline was sweaty; his dick dangled between his legs.

"It's just," he said, bending to pull up his pants. "Eventually this has to end, right?" I felt him watching me, waiting for me to thank him for such a great idea, release him from the dead end we were hurtling toward.

A secret is like a loophole, a slim opening in which other possibilities in life become available. My friendship with Theresa existed outside that opening. Inside it, there was another facet of me, one I'd forgotten about or had simply never met. She—we—needed to have sex like an animal.

"She'd love that," I said. I pulled him to me in a hug, pressing my pelvis to his. I breathed gently on his ear. Quickly, he unzipped again and we went another round. It was that easy.

I wouldn't have been upset if they did start having date nights. If they started going to the movies or Chili's or just out for a drive. She was my friend. I'd have been happy for her.

*   *   *

Adam wasn't my only secret. I had friends I'd visit all over town. Not for sex. For something much more taboo. My friend Dana worked afternoons at McDonald's. She let me sit as long as I wanted, filling and refilling my cup with ice and crunching through it as I watched families make their way through Big Macs and fries and hot fudge sundaes. My friend Sheryl worked evenings at Taco Bell and let me sit as long as I wanted watching families share tacos and nachos and hot, soft burritos. No cup, no ice, though. Sheryl was afraid of her manager, what he might say. My friend Thomas worked at Pizza Hut, my friend Mavis worked at Olive Garden. Those were harder to swing, because you had to be seated, and someone inevitably came and asked what you wanted to order, but Thomas and Mavis knew to leave me alone. To all of them, I said I had cancer, that it was terminal, that I could no longer enjoy food but just wanted to be around it, smell it, watch people enjoy it. All of that was true save the cancer part. It fascinated me, watching people chew and swallow. I couldn't remember a time when I could let that happen. Didn't they know what they were doing to themselves? Didn't they know how dangerous it was? I knew if I started eating again, I'd never stop. Watching all those families, those lonely men eating alone, the teenagers clumped at tables swiping each other's fries, I knew I'd reached a level of power most people never do. My feet barely touched the ground. I skimmed instead of walked. Nothing fit me; I'd started wearing Sammy's T-shirts. I was barely there, just a whisper, just the barest hint of a body. I stood, and I hitched up my pants, and held them cinched as I walked out, leaving all those slobbering fools to their disgusting hunger.

*   *   *

Nick and I still had sex. If anything, what Adam and I did made me want it with Nick all the more. I was fucking him to cover my tracks, to distract him, but also the sex with Adam heightened my desire rather than sated it, the way eating a French fry would only make me want a thousand French fries. A million. I licked his stomach, I twisted his nipples, I bit his earlobes. I rubbed against him in the kitchen, then ran to the bedroom, daring him to chase me. He came quickly, then watched me, sheepish, to see if I was mad. I used to get mad. Now I reached down, touched myself, and brought my finger to his lips. "Oh my God, Jack," he said. "Who are you? What'd you do with my wife?"

"I'm right here," I said. We laughed. We'd been together so many years. I knew he'd been bored, that he was worried about me, that he sometimes thought about how he'd ask me for a divorce. I knew all of those things because I thought about them too. *You know I love you*, he'd say, *but you know as well as I do* . . . It's funny how sex fixes things.

"How's work?" I heard myself ask him. I stared at the light patterns on our ceiling as he spoke, the setting sun melting through the leaves of the maple tree outside our window, making and remaking butter-colored shapes that danced around the light fixture. Nick turned onto his side, drew swirls and spirals on my abdomen with his fingers. He played with my nipples as he talked about meeting his monthly quota for minivans sold. I felt my body tuning in, enlivened by his soft voice and his fingers, the pretty shapes on the ceiling. I moved myself down, threw my legs over his so we were crotch to crotch. An invitation. He was talking about Jerome, his manager. His breath was stale; his dick stayed soft. "Mmhmm," I said.

So many couples these days just give up. But to me, divorce seems like a lot of work. Adam and I would not start a life together. He talked too long, kept himself going by laughing at his own jokes. Sometimes when he spoke, I watched Theresa tune out. Drift away. I liked to imagine she was envisioning pushing him off that dumb new decorative balcony they had off their bedroom. Nick was still talking, something about a recall on a fancy two-door he always knew was trouble. Tuning out, the special skill of every wife. Suddenly, I was sick of it. Nick with his petty work issues that could be solved by a single conversation with his boss, and Adam with the way he needed to bring Theresa up every time we met, so I, what? Wouldn't forget what we were doing to her?

In my most exhausted moments, the solution was always murder. Nick, Adam. Round them all up. Joe down the street and Phil from the cul de sac. Have them step one by one into concrete molds, drive them to a body of water, and kick them in.

"You know," I said, pushing his hand away. "You're not the only one trying to keep it all together." I untangled my legs from his, rolled off the bed. I looked down at him, my naked husband, at the little grubworm penis hiding in the bushy shrub of pubic hair, and I laughed. I put my arms around myself so I could feel the way my ribs contracted, could feel my bones. How I loved my bones! My collarbones, my hip bones, the delicate fan of bones reaching out from my breastbone. I took pride in my bones the way I no longer did in anything else. I wondered if Nick noticed that there was a layer of grime on the windowsills, dust furring the small television on our dresser. Could he smell the mold at the bottom of our bathroom trash can? For months I'd needed a new toothbrush, the bristles of my old one yellowed and frayed, but I kept finding other things to spend the money on. Jayson needed new shin guards. Sammy needed pants that fit. The household budget whittled down to nothing, week after week. Why didn't he notice? Why didn't he ever bring home things we needed? It was a bargain we'd made long ago. I was the one who noticed.

"I need a new toothbrush, goddammit," I heard myself say. Nick pulled a pillow under his head, crossed his ankles. He had a look on his face like he was watching something unfold, but at a distance, like a man watching an actress perform the part of Crazy Woman on a TV show.

"You think," I said, bending over him, "I want to fuck a man who can't buy me a toothbrush?"

"I think," he said, sitting up, taking my wrist delicately in his hand and pulling me on top of him, "you need to eat something." Obediently, because all I was anymore was bones and sex, I crouched, started to take him into my mouth. "No, Jack," he said, covering himself with his hand. "I mean actual food."

"I eat," I said. I was thinking about all the food I watched people eat, how it also felt like mine, like something I'd taken into me. "I eat all the time."

"No, you don't," he said. "Sammy asked me if it was okay to swallow his food the other day." His eyes with their thick lashes searching mine. I could see his pores, the spiky black hairs coming in, the small red patches he'd begun to have on either side of his nose. One of his bottom teeth jutted up above the rest, and when he wasn't talking his tongue often poked at it, played with it, and it was doing that now as he waited for me to say something. Douglas had that same way of watching me. I wondered if he was on the other side of the door, listening, the way he used to do as a child. Adam never mentioned my weight, never asked me to meet him somewhere for a meal. "They're all watching you," Nick said. "They need a healthy mom." His hand closed tighter around my wrist.

I pulled free and stood. "So, stop looking at me," I said. I was trying to whisper, sure Douglas was listening, my voice ragged and hoarse. "You, the boys, all of you can stop looking at me." I threw a robe around my body and opened our bedroom door. There was no one there.

Women age. Our bodies loosen. Our skin gets dry. Some of us fare better than others. Theresa's hair was still shiny and her cheeks still blushed a girlish peach when she was happy. Happiness was simple for her. But see, that's a story I tell myself. Theresa was just an average woman, guileless, blameless, unaware. I hated the pity in Nick's eyes, and here I was showering Theresa with the same. My body was my fault no matter what I did. *How could you?* the world seemed to ask, or I felt sure they were asking. *How dare you?*

I was thinking about all of that—about how being a woman is a zero-sum game—as I had Adam's penis in my mouth. And yet I also had a feeling of accomplishment, of triumph and skill, of being genuinely appreciated. There was something wrong with me, wasn't there? Nick was right. That this—this, frankly, sour-smelling gag fest backed by Adam's helpless gulping—gave my day meaning.

"Okay," Adam whispered, "okay, now." I knew what that meant. He was going to come unless I slowed down, gave him a minute. Sometimes, in the early days, Nick would take a walk around his room, holding his head back like he was trying to stop a bloody nose, before charging back and going for another 120 seconds. And I would laugh! And pant and pretend to come because what was coming, anyway? Wasn't it just the end to things? The loud, sweaty end? I could do that.

I sat up, letting Adam have his moment. We were in his car, parked behind the Whirligig, a children's play place I knew would be dark and empty by six p.m. I told the boys I was going to Get Skinny, and Adam told Theresa—who knows? I touched myself, idly, watching him try to pull it together. He shot his cuffs, wiped his upper lip with the curl of his index finger. That men ever thought a woman could experience an orgasm simply by dogged thrusting! It was true that just the thought of such a thing used to get me all hot and bothered. He wants to put it where? Inside? I could go on that for hours, flat on my back in my childhood bedroom, my body frozen on the outside but throbbing and aching all over, thinking of the plunging, the humping. So animalistic! Need, laid bare! It was a wonder people didn't drop everything and go at it in public. And here I was, in public! Adam put his fingers where my fingers were, leading with his nails. He thought of himself as a very good guitar player, brought his acoustic with him to barbecues and block parties and played the same Dave Matthews and Jimmy Buffet setlist time and time again, and he had clearly come to believe that a clitoris should be plucked, nails-first, like the strings of a guitar.

He looked at me, gathering himself. "You want to get in the back, or . . . ?" Was there a moment in my life when a male wasn't asking me, "Blah blah blah, or . . . ?" They waited to be told what to do. They grew angry if the instructions didn't materialize. But could I say, out loud, "Yank me over until I'm straddling you but we're both facing forward and ram yourself in while applying enough pressure on the hood over my clitoris that I go temporarily blind"? No, I couldn't, because once again I'd be instructing him, when all I wanted was for one man in my life to fucking figure it out.

"Bend me over the car hood," I said, grabbing his wrist and guiding the heel of his hand so I could vise it between my thighs and lightly grind.

"No," he said. He craned his neck to look out the back window. "Are you serious? No."

"Okay, Grandma," I said, and did a little curling rotation, like a dog, so I ended up on all fours, my knees on either side of the gear shift and my ass in his face. "Do it this way, I guess." He did, muttering to himself like I'd asked him to carry me across the Sahara, and then he went silent, holding his breath as he seemed to be racing to the finish line, and then he came onto my lower back and honked the horn with his flailing elbow.

"I can't help myself," I used to say, my plate slopping over. *I can't help myself*, a fool's lament. I looked at Adam, head back against his headrest, dick slumped over like it'd been bludgeoned, ankles together but knees apart. He looked helpless, too. We had that in common.

Bird's-eye view, we were two middle-aged humans with dull hair and sensible shoes. And yet. There was something addictive in the combination of the wrongness of it all, how much he seemed to want it, and my perpetual throbbing horniness that hung in the air like a weather system. In some ways, I was falling for him. I couldn't help myself. To be needed like that? I had to have his need every day. Every single day. This former fatso enslaved by my appetite, all of me just an emptiness.

Cece

"**Y**our brother watches me," Cece said. For as long as she'd worried about saying this very thing to him, it was amazing how easily it spilled out of her mouth. Douglas was a shithead but all the Stinson brothers were weird about letting anyone say that. Even Jayson. Like the one time she'd seen him almost get into a fight, it was with Shad Fitzsimmons after Shad accused Douglas of being the one who'd stolen money from the other track team members' lockers during practice. "We all know it was you," he yelled, loud even over the din of the lunchroom, his face red and baldly self-righteous, swallowing over and over, Cece feeling opened, wild, like she wanted to laugh and point at how absurd it all was, but secretly agreeing with Shad, whose mother had ovarian cancer and who assuredly wouldn't be taking on this kind of problem unless he knew he was right, unless he knew it'd be a win for him, which he probably desperately needed. Douglas was definitely the dick who was stealing the money. He barely tried to hide it. He always had dollar bills for the Pepsi machine; he came to school practically dripping in McDonald's. Still, Jayson pushed a chair at Shad, who hurdled it expertly. Douglas had his hands in his pockets, like he was trying to hold on to what he had, or push it deeper, and then Mr. Enriquez yelled and came stomping over and everyone scattered off.

That was the thing. Everyone knew he sucked but no one was allowed to say it.

Jayson had taken her hand. It was just a normal, stupid Wednesday. They were in the yard between both their houses, where his had a high window that was chemically fogged for privacy and hers had a window that looked directly onto the fence. The only way she and Jayson could be seen was if someone was upstairs in Jayson's room and knew where to look. It felt intimate, secret. They'd been talking about the McRib, how it was overrated. And he'd taken her hand. Inside Cece, it felt like *finally*. And then, movement in Jayson's window—maybe just the sun glaring off the glass, or maybe *he* was up there watching them, and she'd blurted it out: "Your brother watches me."

"I know," he said. He looked away but squeezed her hand tighter. The back of his neck was tan; when had it started looking so manly? He had blond hairs leading up to his dark hairline. His neck atop his suddenly broader shoulders. She shivered. She really could look and look, all day if she was given the chance. Then she realized what he'd said.

"No," she said. "I mean, like, watches me from the window." He nodded, still not looking at her. Their hands were starting to sweat and even that felt good, like something they'd normally try to hide, something illicit and wholly theirs. "To see if he can see me getting out of the shower or whatever."

"I know, Cece," he said.

He sounded tired, not mad or shocked or apologetic. Just resigned. She waited. She could hear her mother inside, taking pans out of the cupboard, turning up the little yellow radio she had in the kitchen. They'd been eating piles of soggy vegetables and a cheese substitute that smelled like feet, and Cece's father had been farting loudly in protest, asking Cece if all this so-called healthy eating made her gassy too. But her mother was happy, it seemed to Cece. She didn't walk around looking like she should apologize for her presence all the time, or like she'd just woken up and wasn't a hundred percent on what her function was. Her parents kissed on the mouth in front of her now. They were planning an elaborate road trip for the summer, Cece's mother trying on two-pieces every time they were at Target and her father studying the L.L. Bean catalog like there'd be a test later. Something was different, better. Watery broccoli and flaccid green bean "spaghetti" seemed worth it.

Cece put her other hand over Jayson's and he finally looked at her. "I'm glad we're holding hands," she whispered. His eyes were the color of a pond. She could still see the old Jayson, the boy with the yellow slicker who always waited for her to catch up when they rode bikes. His face, his body, his hand in hers, she knew that as well as she knew herself. She'd had crushes before, and she still did have crushes. She basically wanted the entire water polo team to touch her boobs, but Jayson was hers, and she was his.

"I don't like that he does it," he whispered. "I tell him to stop and he says he will but then I catch him again."

She nodded. She reached out and touched his neck, the part with the blond hairs. There was nothing surprising there; it felt exactly as she thought it would, but still something ran through her and it ran through him too. Their faces were so close now, their foreheads touching. His breath never smelled. How did it never smell?

"Isn't there a movie like this?" she asked. He put his hand in her hair. "They're, like, aliens and they touch heads, or something." She laughed, not because it was funny but because she wanted him to laugh, his face so deadly serious that she was worried he might cry, and that's how he kissed her, directly onto her open, laughing mouth, with the sound of her mother humming to herself and the smell of garlic and far, far off, the wail of a siren. When they parted, they did laugh, both wiping their mouths and then laughing again.

"You taste like something," he said.

"Oh my God," Cece said, scanning back through what she ate that day—peanut butter toast, orange juice, what else, what else? "Something bad?"

"No," Jayson said. "It's something good, I just don't know what it is." He held her hand again. "It's something good."

Her mother called for her, asking if she knew where the saucepan was. It was clear she thought Cece was in the house, upstairs in her room.

"Why did you hide your mom's saucepan?" Jayson whispered, and that was it, they lost it, hunching over with their hands on their knees, heaving with laughter. Cece lay on the ground, her back on the grass, giving herself fully over to it. The clouds stretched across the sky like the hair in her biology teacher's combover, and that made her laugh harder. Jayson lay beside her and she tried to explain but she couldn't get the words out. It felt good, necessary, to laugh like this, to push past how hard her heart was beating. She rolled over and kissed him again, letting her tongue find his, surprised at how easy the whole thing was.

"That was my second kiss," she told him.

He picked a leaf out of her hair, held it up for her to see. "Mine, too."

"First tongue kiss, though."

"Oh, tongue kisses?" he said, rolling over so his face was above hers. "I've had hundreds of those."

It was incredible, a feeling so good it was crazy to think people didn't just kiss all day, didn't probe and question and answer with their tongues. He kept his body by her side, didn't roll on top of her, but she knew that was an option for further down the road, and that felt like the secret to everything. One day, he'd lie on top of her oh my God oh my God! Inside, her mother shouted, "I found it!"

She peeked, wanting to see if *he* was peeking, and she saw the curtains in the window Douglas watched her from, how they were cinched to the side by his hand. He was there, watching his own brother. Cece kissed Jayson harder, willing herself to feel only him. No one else.

Nathan

He knew when Jayson was thinking of her, could tell because his entire being changed, as though an essential part of him escaped the room and left his body there to chew or sharpen his pencil or paw through his sock drawer. She had that kind of power over him and it mystified Nathan. She had breasts but he tried not to think of them; it was her long, slender fingers that did the trick for Nate, how capable and womanly they seemed, how she absentmindedly cracked her knuckles or snapped an aimless rhythm. She was nice to him, asking him about school and waiting for his answer. He'd seen Jayson and Cece kissing in the yard, seen Jayson put his hand on one of her breasts, seen Cece put her hand over that hand. Even then he knew it was tender, new.

There was a girl at school, Amber Skeen, long reddish-orange hair and freckles just a shade darker and pale-blue eyes. She hadn't been pretty all the years they'd been in school together. She'd been gawky and timid, bookish, not all that interested in anyone outside her tight circle. Then one day, not long after he'd seen Cece and Jayson, he noticed her long, pale legs, her pink, dewy lips, her balletic, slender fingers. She was gorgeous and no one knew it. He could claim her, plant a flag. Hard to know whether or not he understood that in thinking of her that way he was being a jerk, a typical dopey teenage boy, but he liked imagining her as something he could call his. He was filled with self-awareness then, which he later recognized as self-loathing, a belief that he was shittier than most people, sometimes just a hair shittier and sometimes the shittiest.

One day, he handed her a poem he'd copied from a book at the library, folded up into a triangle and heavy on the virgin metaphors, though he didn't quite grasp that at the time. Really, he just thought her beauty was being compared to the springtime, forget all that crap about flowering. Walked right up to her as she was stuffing her clarinet case into her locker and scratching the back of her calf with the toe of her sneaker.

"Here," he said, jabbing the note at her, dropping it without meaning to. He pointed down at it and said, "It's for you," and walked away, as though he had nothing to do with it, was just the delivery person. Cece was at her locker, across the hall and two classrooms down. He hoped she'd seen, hoped she was curious about what was happening, maybe even jealous.

"Nate," Amber called. "Is this from you?"

The hallway was filled with chatty students and teachers and announcements and scuffling. Cece was plugging book after book into her frayed purple JanSport, the one she'd had for ages. "Of course," he called back to Amber. "Of course . . . It's for you."

Amber smelled like clementine. He thought of her reading the note all through algebra, his heart pounding in his ears. "Seventeen," he answered the teacher. "I mean, sixteen." After school it was as though they'd agreed to meet in the center of the starburst where all the hallways converged, walking slowly toward each other and grinning like they were getting away with something, nobody noticing a thing, and he carried her clarinet for her because he needed something to do with his hands, and they walked together to her bus. Number 264.

"It's okay with me that you didn't write that poem," she said.

It never occurred to him to pretend he'd written it or not. His heart pounded harder but her face was neutral. She genuinely didn't care.

"Here," she said, handing back his note. "My number's in there. We can watch *Jeopardy!* over the phone together if you want."

Nothing was nerdier. He knew if he did that Douglas would stand behind him making fart noises or, worse, the rapid jackoff noises he made by grabbing his cheeks and pulling at them quickly.

"Or," she said, taking her clarinet back, "we can just talk. I watch *Jeopardy!* so I can do better on the SATs or whatever."

As far as he knew, Cece didn't watch anything on television. He couldn't think of a single time she'd mentioned an episode of something. She, for a semester, had also played the clarinet. He noticed that Amber had a small hole in the toe of her sneaker. Earlier he'd noticed a scab on her elbow. These sorts of things were becoming increasingly embarrassing, these small evidences of their fading childhood, their burgeoning, unavoidable humanity. He thought of his mother, how she'd cut her finger sometimes in the kitchen and just suck the blood away. His father had a black toenail and had for weeks.

"I'll call you," he said, heat rushing up the back of his neck. "I'll try to think of stuff to say." In his head it seemed like a normal, fine thing to say. Out loud it seemed like calling her would be a burden, something he'd have to endure, something he didn't actually want to do. But again, her face was neutral.

"Okay, cool," she said. "Me too."

"TGIF," he said.

"It's Thursday," she said.

"TGIT," he said.

"TGIF," Amber said, standing at his locker.

"Yeah," he said. He turned to make sure Douglas was long gone.

"That was a joke," Amber said. "Since it's Monday?"

They'd talked on the phone over the weekend; he'd successfully called her and ducked Douglas by bringing the cordless into the bathroom with the lock. They talked so long Nathan's ear began to grow hot. He watched himself in the mirror as he chuckled at stuff she said, as he made listening *hmms* and *huhs*, and he tried to see if he was normal. That was his one desire in life, his baseline hope, to just be normal. Not weird, not stupid or angry or mean. Amber was telling him about the time she'd dropped her tray in the lunchroom and he was pretending like he hadn't seen it, hadn't felt his own face flush with shame on her behalf, hadn't walked the long way around to his table so he wouldn't have to make the tortured decision to help her. She was different then, though it had only been the previous year.

"No one even helped me," she said, laughing, but Nathan felt ashamed all over again. "I smelled like lasagna the whole rest of the day." She didn't seem to have that thing he had, that constant worry that he was an idiot, that he needed to edit and review everything before it flew out of his mouth, then review it again. She just seemed to be herself. Was that normal? It should be normal but Nathan had the feeling it wasn't. She even burped, a quiet pip of air, and excused herself, said she'd had a sip of her father's Sprite. His gut swirled. Her voice was so close to his face that it felt sexual, but also absurd. She had to go do her homework and they hung up. It was a total success, nothing to torture himself over, and Douglas simply raised his eyebrow at the phone as Nathan placed it back in its dock. Had he been quieter lately? He was never where he should be. More and more, Douglas stayed in his room at meals, or out late with his friends on school nights, or driving off somewhere to help their mother with some errand. He was more fidgety, less aggressive. Nathan watched as Douglas blinked rapidly, staring at the TV. Nathan sat next to him and watched a show about teenagers traveling back in time. Douglas laughed through his nose as one of the teens tripped and fell, papers flying everywhere. When it was over Douglas said, "That blew," and went up to his room.

Now, at his locker, Nathan felt mildly sick. Confronted as he was with her actual person. He smelled tomato sauce, or was that just in his head? Her lips were glossy and pink. She had three freckles that, if you connected them, would make an isosceles triangle. It seemed like something he could say, some future version of himself that had already kissed her, had held her hand in the hallways.

"I like your spots," he said, interrupting her. "Wait, what were you saying?"

Cece and Jayson had already passed, making their slow, oblivious way to first period, which they had together.

"My spots?" Amber asked. She burst out laughing, her hand landing on his shoulder. "Are you trying to say *freckles*?"

He nodded, smiling, a doofus, but proud he'd made her laugh. After that, he called her every night. Walked her to and from her bus. Sometimes walked her to class. Tried to play a note on her clarinet, almost burst something important in his neck. Always, she laughed. They shared each other's lunches, he taking half her peanut butter sandwich and she taking his carrot sticks, which he hated and she liked fine. She once cut something out of the comics section of her father's newspaper for him, a three-panel series with no dialogue bubbles in which some sort of fluffy animal scared a nearby spider with its fart. She'd cut this out! Taken the time to fetch the scissors and work them methodically around each corner! Stored it in her three-ring binder! Handed it to him already laughing! There *was* something funny about it. The fluffy thing was resolute, and perhaps ashamed in the final panel. They walked with their arms linked, and he'd grabbed her hand a few times. She was a rush of happiness, perhaps the only uncomplicated relationship in his young life.

One night, his ear hot and the side of his face sweaty, he realized they'd been silent for some minutes. Just going about their lives, alone together. He was rereading a paragraph in his chemistry textbook, finally beginning to understand, and she was working on her diorama project for English. Every now and again she hummed to herself, but other than that they just listened to each other breathe as they worked. The silence began to feel heavy, as though it was something he should attend to. He couldn't hang up, didn't want to, but he couldn't think of anything to say. Was something wrong with them? This silence, and also they hadn't kissed. He'd had chances, seeing her off by her bus in the afternoons, or getting a quick one in as they shared lunch sitting at their corner table, but although it had been possible, it had never felt right. Shouldn't there be music playing, or stars overhead? He thought of Cece less and less, now that there was Amber. Cece didn't laugh nearly as much. She hated carrot sticks. Jayson and Cece kissed all the time, right there in the yard, although they probably thought no one was watching. They held hands and touched each other. It seemed natural. Passionate. Again, Nathan worried. Where was the passion? Why was it so easy to be around

Amber? He looked forward to telling her something, like when he caught Mr. Zirelli, the US History teacher, picking his nose thoughtfully. He did an impression of it, right down to how it looked like Mr. Z wiped it on his mustache. She choked on the smoothie she was drinking, trying to catch its dribbles in her cupped hand as she laughed. When, though, would he want to touch her breast, kiss her with tongue? Cece and Jayson laughed and talked. But they also groped and moaned. He just wanted to be around Amber, the way he felt about a new friend.

He did think of her, at night, in bed. He imagined kissing her, but if he went further than that his heart pounded so loudly he heard it in his ears, and a lump rose in his throat, and he thought of her horrified face if he touched her all wrong. Too hard, or in the wrong place. He started to believe she'd merely wanted a friend. He was her friend, and she was his friend. Why did it make him feel panicked, a surge of rage gripping him? He couldn't tell what was true, what was real. If people wanted to kiss, they kissed. That seemed simple enough.

"Amber," he said. They were walking slowly to their after-school obligations, she to track practice and he to soccer. Her arm squeezed his and he could smell the banana-flavored taffy she was eating.

"Yes," she said, mimicking his serious tone. She turned toward him and he could see the bright-yellow candy clinging to her teeth. She smacked her lips and swallowed and it seemed like more evidence that he was merely her friend.

"Why don't we ever kiss?" He forced the words out, buoyed by his hurt certainty that he was nothing to her, nothing special. They stopped walking and looked at each other. A smile started at the corners of her mouth but then she coughed, hard, bending over and dropping all her bags onto the ground so she could use both hands to cover her mouth. She hacked and gasped, tried to stand up only to double over again. He pawed through her things, looking for the water bottle she sometimes had with her, then gave up and patted her back.

"It's okay," she managed to croak before another surge overcame her. She pointed at her throat. "The candy," she said. He stopped hitting her and stepped back, toeing her things into a pile. People walked by and laughed, elbowing each other and pointing. Finally, she calmed, was able to stand and wipe her eyes and breathe, use the back of her wrist to wipe her nose. He watched her giggle, her bloodshot eyes and wild ponytail. The light was a deeper yellow, autumn descending, and she was shaking her head at herself as she flung her backpack and gym bag over her shoulder. It felt like something already written, something he was rereading, something he wanted to reach out and touch simply because he couldn't, not from where he was seeing everything. And that's why he chose that moment to step close, to get her to look at him, see how serious he was, and kiss her. Their noses bumped and his lips landed on her teeth and once it was over she began to cough again, but just before she did she smiled at him, a big Amber smile that made him want to pump his fist, run and tell someone. They began to walk again, holding hands now, and when he left her at the door to the locker room she said, "Okay, Nate," and he said, "Okay," and they stood there grinning and holding hands.

He couldn't remember, later, as an adult, why they'd broken up. It seemed to him that time had simply passed a damp cloth over them, back and forth, until their connection faded. Surely there'd been a tortured conversation, maybe even tears, but he just didn't remember. The memory wasn't there; there wasn't even a void where it used to be.

Maybe, he sometimes thought, Amber Skeen lived in the Before, and she didn't travel with him to the After. Maybe she was back there in her four-point sprint start, forever about to explode in a rush of speed and power. He was the blur that watched her, the taste of chemically flavored taffy fading on his lips.

Jayson

There was fresh asphalt on the road right outside their houses. Mr. Delmonico—their neighbor on the other side, with his shiny bald head, elaborate gold wedding ring, some sort of fingernail fungus he didn't appear to have any shame about, so often did he reach out and pull a coin from behind their ears or tousle their hair, leaving them crimson and disgusted, the other kids pointing and laughing about how they had ear/head/cheek fungus now—had worked for the township for decades, still had some pull, and he was able to get a crew to come out and pave over the potholes that had been there since Jayson could first remember weaving his bike around them. Kids jumped skateboards over them, dared each other to pop wheelies, ride over them without getting snared and thrown to the side. After about a day's work, they were gone, the road black and even and new.

"Smells like ass," Nathan said.

"Smells like *your* ass," Douglas said.

They were at the end of the driveway, all four of them, a rarity. Their mother was at some meeting, or shopping, or driving around, whatever it was she did now that she seemed tired of being their mother. Douglas never sat around with them, preferred to spend his boredom locked in his bedroom or out of the house. Today he couldn't sit still, cracking his knuckles and adjusting his T-shirt so it lay flat against him, looking down the street like he was waiting for a taxi.

"You should come over tomorrow," Cece had said. They'd been lingering in her backyard at dusk, playing a game where they only touched each other fingertip to fingertip, then leaned in as their hands flattened and pushed away as their fingers curled in. Their faces got closer and closer until he could smell that she was wearing the strawberry lip balm he'd told her tasted good. "My mom's going to Zumba later and my dad's at some work thing."

"I will," he'd said. She'd looked up at his window, checking for Douglas, then turned and kissed him. He could feel that her heart was beating as hard as his. They had never been alone in the house before.

And now he didn't know what to do. He couldn't tell his brothers his plan and he wasn't sure if Cece's mom had left yet, the garage stubbornly closed and silent. He kept glancing at the dining room window, hoping he'd see some sort of signal from Cece, the curtains twitching or, like, a little mirror she'd hold so it could catch the sun and flash at him. She could come out and pretend to check the mail, wink or nod or something.

"Why do you keep staring at Cece's?" Douglas asked. "You obsessed with her or something?" Jayson didn't know why they played this game. Douglas knew about them, knew where they went to make out, probably even knew that Cece saw Douglas trying to see her naked. Yet he pretended like he was still trying to catch Jayson doing something embarrassing, Jayson with his guard down, Jayson letting Douglas in on something valuable he could use to foul up the little life Jayson had to himself. "You little freak."

Why do you keep staring at Cece's? This was something Jayson wasn't free to say back to Douglas. And that was the stupidest part of the whole thing. Douglas could give him shit all day, but the minute Jayson threw it back at him, he'd go nuts. Once, when Jayson asked him if he was still planning on asking Sarah Harvey to the movies because Sarah Harvey was kissing Harry Whitcomb in the parking lot, Douglas had gotten so wild he'd ripped his shirt off like some kind of steroidal bad guy in a movie.

"Mom's in there," Samuel said.

"Mom drove away," Douglas said. It always seemed like he was talking from his chest, from something bigger and more hateful than his mouth. "You waved at her and told her to bring you back a surprise because you're still such a baby that you don't get that she just grabs whatever she sees near the register at the 7-Eleven."

"I saw her," Samuel said.

"It's cool, Sammy," Nathan said. "You're just thinking of another time you saw Mom go in."

"This is so boring. I just want to go somewhere," Douglas said, but he didn't, just turned his face away, as if that were enough, as if he had found solace in the way the cherry blossoms fluttered from the Mickelsons' tree. A green Mazda drove by. A white delivery van coasted through the stop sign and screeched to a stop outside the Delmonicos'. Jayson had the feeling Douglas was also waiting for Cece, waiting for the house to send him some kind of signal. He thought a lot about what Douglas might be thinking or doing, he realized. Douglas wasn't someone you could ask. Mainly, Jayson wanted to know what he was in for. Was Douglas in a joking mood? A hitting mood? A quiet, no-idea-what mood? Then he could set himself accordingly.

Always, it was hard to see Douglas beyond the way his shoulders filled out his T-shirt. Same wide shoulders from when he was six, ten, thirteen. Girls liked him, looked at him and looked away, giggling together, but he never had a girl-friend. Jayson guessed he was intense in a way that made girls feel uncomfortable. The way he joked without blinking. The tips of his ears always red.

"You think they ordered porn?" Douglas asked, mean-ing the Delmonicos. The boys watched as Mrs. Delmonico signed for her package and offered the delivery man some change from her apron pocket. He declined and jogged back to the van.

"It looks like a letter or something," Jayson said. Imme-diately he felt like a fool. Why engage?

"Yeah. It's a special-order nude photo," Douglas said. Douglas had a shoebox under his bed, taped shut with thick packing tape. Every now and again Jayson checked on it. Often it had been slit open and retaped. He held it, weighing it in his hands, and shook it softly. Impossible to tell what was inside. It wasn't all that heavy, definitely less heavy than the pair of shoes it had once held, and it sounded like any normal thing sliding around inside. It didn't sound like rocks, or jars, or money, or jewelry. It sounded, maybe, papery. Whatever it was, Jayson was convinced it was pornographic. Shameful. In need of several rounds of packing tape. Yet treasured. That space between his shoulders, where his T-shirt clung, that was where Douglas held the part of himself he was hiding. It was palpable, odorous, deafening. Jayson wanted to put his hands on those shoulders, push back a smidge, see his brother's body take form. He straightened his own posture, felt his traps settle. He looked back at Cece's house. Still nothing. Maddening stillness.

"Don't they have the Internet?" Nathan asked. "You can see whatever you want on the Internet." This made the broth-ers laugh, all at once, all of them with their father's jet engine *haw-haw* except for Samuel, who tended to snort like their mother, and who wasn't all that sure what was so funny in the first place.

"You're darn tootin'," Douglas said, in sneering mimicry of their mother, who was herself mimicking her father when she said it. "You sure can see whatever you want on the Internet, young man!" He laugh-coughed into his fist, a tough-guy thing he'd picked up from somewhere.

Did Cece look at porn? Jayson had googled *boobs* and then *big boobs* and, once, *sex*, but he'd also seen his fair share of shitty cop shows where they pulled up the perp's Google history, and he worried Douglas might do that to him, might print it out and put it up on the fridge, so he stopped, only every once in a while drawing a pair of boobs (two circles, two dots) to think about.

A cloud passed overhead, and the afternoon light turned blue for a moment, their street dimming, and Jayson knew today wouldn't be the day. He wouldn't get to lie with Cece in her bed, wouldn't get to see what happened. He'd allowed himself to hope in fleeting images: kissing her jawline, his hand on her breast (over the shirt), his fully clothed body on top of hers, each pressing into the other. It felt like they had all the time in the world. He was nearly fifteen years old. He didn't have a clue how to do any of the things he knew he would want to do, if they were in that bed. And he knew Cece didn't know either. Something pulled at him, an ache from his throat to his sternum, but he was also happy to have it.

Jackie

The sex was becoming mean, gross. A cudgel. *Suck this, fuck that, eat my, let me, do this.* We were animals. Starved, frightened, raging animals. *I don't want to do this anymore*—we said it when we meant it and when we didn't. We said it to hurt or to end or just to get out of the car. But always, always, there we'd be, waiting for Nick or Theresa to leave, waiting for the school bus to chug off. We were like magnets, powerless against the force of what I had come to think of as *the need.* Once, I stripped Adam's shirt off in his driveway, his fingers in my underwear, and we stumbled into my house, where he was inside me before we'd even collapsed in the foyer. We no longer kissed so much as fused our open mouths together, teeth clashing. I kicked the door closed right as Adam came, letting loose a sound like he'd been sucker punched. We said goodbye by pawing each other and sometimes I'd end up bent over the arm of the couch, inhaling the scent of my boys' socks, my face ramming into crumbs and coins. He put his dick in my asshole, nearly his whole hand inside my vagina. I sat on his face and licked semen off his stomach. We were driving somewhere but the road just kept stretching on and on. I bit his nipples. He choked me. I dragged my nails down his back, wounds he had to hide from Theresa for a week. We stared into each other's eyes with hatred flaming our irises. We begged each other. One night, I had a dream Adam threw me off a cliff. "That's what we want," I said to him, grinding his face so hard that his nose swelled up. "We want to kill each other."

We were loud and not all that careful, and one day there was Theresa, watching Adam with his face between my legs on the floor of Cece's bathroom. He'd told me to not shower for days. That's what I was thinking about when I opened my eyes and saw her. Theresa. My best friend. *Will she think I'm the kind of woman who smells?* And then: *She better not think I'm the kind of woman who smells.* And then rage at being caught, at Adam for allowing us to be caught, for not being more careful, for falling for it, for falling so easily for it, when he should have fought harder, been better.

Adam was still slopping around down there, the tip of his finger in my anus. Theresa looked sick, like she was seeing something that was going to make her vomit. The disgust in her face. We deserved that.

"Get up," she said. Her purse flopped off her shoulder and she caught it with her hand, then let it slump to the floor.

"It's not what it looks like," I said, and I almost laughed as it flew out of my mouth. It was *exactly* what it looked like. I was pinching my own nipples.

"Hmm?" Adam said, looking up. His nose was sheened with me; he still hadn't caught on. He was impatient, annoyed, thinking I had one of my requests again, some elaborate position or game I wanted to play. We were in Cece's bathroom because I'd asked him to play hide-and-seek. Every time he caught me, he'd try to get me into position, but I'd escape and hide again, until he was furious. Finally, in Cece's bathroom, I let him push me to the floor, my head smacking the toilet, and then I wrapped my legs around his head.

"Jesus Christ, Adam," Theresa said.

Adam. Sometimes I think—*Adam? Him?* I watched it dawn on him, his hair mussed like a little boy's and his wrinkled shirttails hanging over his shrinking cock. He was coming to. He'd been drugged, tricked, led astray. Ignore the fact that he fucked me at Cece's birthday party, both of us stopping just before climax because we'd heard Theresa calling for him, it was cake time; ignore the fact that he begged me to pretend to take the trash to the curb so we could finish up against Theresa's car in the garage; ignore the fact that it was just one example of how he'd begged and begged me. Now he was stunned, looking around at all the rubble, holding the detonator in his hand.

"I'm sorry," Adam said. He stood, pulled his pants up and buttoned his shirt and tucked and patted and swiped at his hair. Theresa picked up her purse. "We never meant . . ."

"We both love you so much," I said. I was looking around for a towel. In Cece's small cupboard she had a pyramid of toilet paper rolls and a bottle of pink mouthwash. A white fluffy towel drooped from a hook by the door, but I would have had to walk toward Theresa to fetch it.

I wanted to go home, rewind the day to the morning, never meet Adam after the kids were at school. My head ached and my vagina felt raw, vaguely itchy, what was the point of all of it? It had been exhausting. Adam slouched, hung his head. I imagined his dick doing the same inside his pants, and I laughed.

Theresa rushed at me, swinging her purse. I knew she had a thick set of keys in there, an extra deodorant, sometimes a water bottle. I held up my hands but I let her hit me, over and over. I had earned it. With my head down like that I could smell myself, smell the sourness of Adam's mouth and the earthy odor I'd cultivated for him.

"He threw me on the floor," I heard myself saying. "He slammed my head into the toilet." The purse blows slowed and stopped. "I had to do what he told me or he was going to hurt me."

I looked up. Theresa stood over me panting. Adam had a hand out like he would try to stop her if she got five to ten more blows in. I crawled away from her, slid up the wall to standing. "I have a knot on the back of my head if you don't believe me."

Sometimes, I'd yell at the boys or grab them by the arm and drag them inside, and Adam and Theresa would get these looks on their faces. I didn't like it. It was like they were embarrassed for me, like there was a better way and I was too dumb, too crazy to know it. They looked at me like that then, in Cece's bathroom. Adam inched closer to Theresa. The air was cold on my naked legs and ass. She looked like a stranger, suddenly, like I was just meeting her all over again, thinking I had her all figured out just by looking at her. She was young, I saw. Younger than I'd ever felt in my whole life. Her hair was frizzy and the color of the pale part of a peach. She'd gained some of the weight back and it looked nice. Her cheeks were full. She hated me, this sudden stranger. I edged along the wall, trying to get closer to the door. My head really was throbbing. I wasn't lying about that.

"I won't involve the authorities if you let me leave," I said. I could see the twist of my pants at the foot of Cece's bed. The frilled bed skirt, the stuffed elephant on her pillow. We had been fucking in the domain of a child.

Theresa stepped aside, clearing the doorway, her shoulder bumping into Adam's chest. He burst into tears.

"If you want me to move out," I heard him say as I made my way out of Cece's room.

I walked barefoot from their front door to mine. It had been hot and dry for weeks. The grass felt sharp under my feet. Clay dust plumed with every step. I stood inside my door for a long while, the house so quiet, the air-conditioning kicking on and off with a sigh. I waited. The phone didn't ring; no one came to the door. I started a load of laundry, carefully separating the lights from the darks, the towels from the clothing. I thought maybe I'd change the sheets on the boys' beds, something I hadn't done in months. I sprayed Windex on our front window, wiped it off in slow, thorough circles.

He didn't mean it, would never move out. I wondered if Theresa would call Nick, or stop by his work, or leave an anonymous letter in the mailbox. Adam didn't know, had never known, how much power Theresa had, if only she'd wield it.

The boys came home from school. I waved to Cece as she walked up her driveway, watched as she let herself in and closed the door behind her.

"Mom," Douglas said, holding a pile of his neatly folded shirts. "Everything okay?"

Theresa

She felt an energy flowing through her, a pleasant blooming that surged at times, helped her to make quick decisions without being bogged down in options or regret. It was anger. A clean rage. She called her sister.

"Babe," Carissa said, and paused, letting out a breath, like she wasn't sure she should say what she was about to say. "Every man cheats. Just look it up. There are a hundred books that will tell you the same thing."

She hung up. Adam had left, dragging his feet out to his car, still in his rumpled, disgusting clothes, and backed slowly down the driveway. She watched until his car was out of sight, her heart slamming around inside her, then she closed the door and stood in her home. She'd come home to get the sack lunch she'd left on the counter, didn't want to pick up fast food or starve until dinner time. Adam's car was still there, and a woman's voice was drifting down the stairs, sounding like she was in pain. Theresa followed the sound, into Cece's bedroom, over to the bathroom door, and there they were.

Jackie had become a chore. She was too skinny, terrified of getting fat, and it made her bitter. Nasty. She couldn't have fun anymore. She didn't want to go to the movies with Theresa because of all the snacks; she couldn't sit still long enough to just have coffee. Theresa thought Jackie was trying to outrun herself. She wondered if Jackie ever slept.

In reality, Jackie didn't want to be around Theresa because she and Adam were fucking.

She gathered a bucket, some rubber gloves, scouring powder, disinfectant. Cece's bathroom looked the same, no obvious globs or puddles, but still Theresa scrubbed. How long had it been going on? She thought of Nick, how he always seemed to be playing a part, affable-yet-bawdy neighbor, brusque-yet-proud father. She could drive to the dealership, walk in, and tell him. Maybe they could have sex in his office for revenge. She pictured his naked torso, his paw-like hands grabbing at her. She could take pictures and text them to Adam.

In the mirror, she saw that she was crying. This enraged her more. She considered pouring the scouring powder into her eyes, rubbing vigorously.

When she was done with the bathroom, she moved to Cece's room. She made the bed, fluffed the pillows, stacked books on the desk. Cece would come home, ask what was for dinner, when her father would be home. Theresa sat on the bed, exhaustion pulling her down to Cece's pillow. Forever after, there would be a Before in Cece's life, and an After. Theresa closed her eyes, trying to force the After to look promising, even better than the present. Cece proud of her mother for not taking any shit. Cece deciding to shun Adam. She and Cece moving to a town close but not too close to Carissa, starting over. Eventually, Adam would be allowed to call Cece, to visit her. He'd be shriveled, fired from his job, working as a bag boy at the grocery store. Theresa would bring him a glass of water. Pat his shoulder. She would feel nothing for this stranger, but she would perform graciousness, and he would feel the pity.

Theresa slept, a deep blackness crowding in.

* * *

A pressure on her shoulder, a sound like a voice. A lovely heaviness holding her down, her head cradled, her limbs deliciously tired.

"Mom," the voice said. The pressure was a hand, shaking her. With regret, Theresa opened her eyes.

Cece stood over her. "Why are you in my bed?" she asked. She had that look she got more and more, a look of amusement and annoyance, each emotion fighting the other in the set of her mouth, the narrowing of her eyes. "Are you sick?"

Theresa sat up, remembering. She still wore the rubber gloves. They felt fused to her hands with sweat. She peeled them off, let them tumble to the floor. "Kind of," she said.

"Did you clean my bathroom?" Cece asked. She looked toward her closet, then quickly back at her mother. *Ah*, Theresa thought, *her hiding place*.

"I did," Theresa said, a lie forming easily. "I figured I'd better make good use of this day off."

Cece stood back, folded her arms. "You're still in your work clothes, though."

Theresa looked down at her slacks, the way they bunched at her hips when she sat. She rubbed her eyes, ran a hand through her hair. Behind Cece was the door to the bathroom, the sharp scent of bleach. Eventually, she'd have to tell Cece some version of what happened. She would have to start divorce proceedings. Find an attorney. Figure out how to pay for an attorney. Find a new place to live. Pack them up. Drive them wherever they were going. Get Cece settled in a new school. Unpack. Find a job. Go to that job. Buy groceries from a new store. Do all of it without demonizing Cece's father, so that Cece could grow up and trust her future partner, build a life with them, be happy. But somehow also prepare her for the possibility that her partner could make mistakes, or one big mistake, could handle her heart roughly and only feel regret once found out.

The easiest thing would be to never tell Cece. To go to therapy with Adam. To shun Jackie and her family, to move. Wait until Cece was an adult, then divorce Adam. She could make it a few short years, couldn't she?

"These pants already have a stain," she said, standing. "I figured it was no big deal to just keep everything on while I cleaned." She felt herself swaying a little. Her head felt thick, her heart thudding. "I think I'll go lie down in my bed," she said. *My* bed. Not *our* bed. It was already happening.

"Want me to make you some soup?" Cece said. She put her arm through Theresa's. "Chicken and stars?" It was what she made Cece when she was sick. Chicken and stars in a plastic bowl with a faded alligator on the bottom, her favorite when she was little.

"I don't think I'm all that hungry," Theresa said. "Just tired." She pictured throwing Cece over her shoulder, running out the door. Buckling her into her seat and speeding down the street. Or on a ship, nothing but water around them, water and the sky and the line of the horizon. Or squeezed into the cheap seats on a plane, holding their elbows in tight, both of them looking at the sky out a tiny window. Cece would have questions, and Theresa would have to have answers.

"I'll come check on you before I leave," Cece said. "I'm going to the library to study with Jayson." Theresa's heart quickened; she wanted to tell Cece she could never see Jayson again, that they were leaving and never returning. But now wasn't the time.

"Don't worry about me," Theresa said. She gathered the bucket and cleaning supplies and left them at the top of the stairs. In her room she closed the door and sat in the chair by the window, the one they never used, and watched her bed. Surely, they'd fucked there; where else? She heard Cece leave and felt a deep relief.

She had never been jealous of Jackie, never caught Adam looking too long or finding reasons to get close to her. If anything, the things he said about Jackie were disparaging. She was too loud, she lorded over Nick, her house was filthy. She pictured them talking about her, laughing. She was aloof, cold, a bore. They gave each other what they needed. With Jackie, Adam could be wild, and with Adam, Jackie could feel desired, needed as a woman and not as a wife or mother. Theresa was just a conduit, a speed bump they stepped over as they crashed together. They nurtured these secret selves and in so doing humiliated her, and it was all part of the fun.

She could approach Nick. Or Robin, the new hire at work who wore sweater vests and bow ties. Her boss, Angelo. She could push her face into his neck and smell his cedar cologne. Mr. Delmonico's son, who visited every few weeks and wore an open track jacket no matter the weather. She could approach Douglas. He was nearly eighteen. She could ask him to come over and help with something, looking past the way he'd sigh and try to find reasons why he couldn't. She could seduce him. It would be easy. He was probably watching the house that very moment. She pictured his pale-blue eyes, his Adam's apple bobbing up and down, his nervous habit of picking at his sharp jawline. When he was little, he'd cling to Jackie's legs. He'd follow her into the bathroom, sit on her lap when he was way too big to do so. Someone already loved Jackie the way she wanted, a desperate yearning obsession. Theresa began to vomit and raced to the bathroom in time for it to erupt from her.

* * *

In the morning, she felt better. The rage had burned off to a clear sense of purpose. The thing was to get away. Distance was essential. Carissa would help; Cece would adapt. Adam had returned home in the middle of another of her cleaning binges. It was easy to tell him, even easier to walk away from him with the kitchen trash in her hand toward the dark mouth of the garage door, where he didn't follow. He slept on the couch and Theresa woke on the bedroom floor, hearing him leave in the early hours. She pulled herself onto the bed, which she'd stripped to its mattress the night before, the sheets in a heap on the closet floor. When she woke again the light was brighter and Cece had left for school already. She showered, the water at its hottest setting, pummeling the ache in her muscles to nothing. She dressed in a loose blouse and her favorite slacks, already writing her letter of resignation in her head. Angelo was old-school, he never asked them to recite how the company made their lives and the world better; he just wanted them to show up on time and get the work done. He wouldn't take her quitting personally, just wish her luck and offer to give her a reference.

Theresa had some money in savings; her car was paid off and the rent in her sister's part of the country was cheap enough. Carissa said Cece's new school was called Newbury, which sounded dignified, a place where kids built electrical circuits and flew weather kites and played instruments. Theresa felt impatient, wanted to skip all the steps it would take to get to that moment when she and Cece were installed in their new lives.

She toasted a heel of bread, dotted it with cold pats of butter, and left them to soften while she gathered her shoes and purse, then she walked into the garage and closed the door behind her. She'd forgotten the toast, had turned back to retrieve it when a hot burst of light exploded before her.

She held her hands up to touch it, to push it away from her. Through the colors and sparks and pain she saw that it was Douglas, that he was sorry but he wasn't going to stop. She felt her ribs crack, she felt bits of her teeth on her tongue. The blows came faster and faster, Douglas grunting and sobbing. It was hard to figure out where to place her arms, how to protect herself. Finally, he stopped, left out the side door, closing it quietly behind him. She rolled to her side, watched the dust twirl and shimmer in the shaft of light coming in from the window. The light dimmed as a cloud made its slow way past the sun. By the time it was clear, dust glittering in the beam, she was dead.

PART II

The Crime Scene

She hadn't shown up for work, hadn't answered the phone. Something like that. The husband made some calls, asked around. We have a recording of him. You can hear how he sounds a bit hysterical, like he already knew. We all thought about that possibility.

The house was nice. The whole neighborhood was. You know how sometimes there'll be two or three nice homes and then a whole block of nasty ones? The neighborhood either on its way up or down. This house was on a street of nice, tidy houses. They had some shrubs, some flower boxes, newer windows. After a while on the job you notice those things. You feel thankful for them. That's not to say I haven't seen shit go down inside some of the nicest houses you've ever seen. I have. But it's a breath you get to take when you make visits to nice homes. Maybe what I mean is happy homes. Nothing extreme. No toddler in a soggy diaper stomping around, all the dog shit ground into the rug. No teenager with a black eye, no panting stepfather. Just normal families doing normal stuff.

Now that I'm saying it, I realize the irony. Because, as you know, when we got into that nice, normal home, through the back door because the husband said it'd be unlocked, which quite frankly felt like another red flag, it was just a short walk through the kitchen before we saw her. The garage door was open and the overhead light was on and there she was. Even from where we were we could see how her fingers were mangled, how her arm bent the wrong way at the elbow, how her face was swollen and pulpy. A sheet of blood under her. Classic blunt force trauma. I read in the paper later that the medical examiner said he had never seen such severe injuries in a beating before. Said it was like she'd been dropped fifty stories. Said it was overkill. We called in homicide and backed out of there. That's when we saw him. It was weird. My Spidey sense got all tingly. He was just standing there by the trash cans, this young adult male. He looked kind of out of it. I couldn't see any blood on him but I thought, maybe he changed, threw his bloody clothes into that trash can. I approached.

"You live here?" I asked. He was still looking over my shoulder, at the vic's house. Looked like he was looking up, toward the windows on the second floor.

"I live here, yeah," he said. He pointed at the house behind me, the one next door to the vic's. He was good-looking, reminded me of a baseball player, someone who eats a PB and J every day at lunch, even the crusts. Wholesome.

Listen, the more I'm talking about this, the more I'm seeing my own weird assumptions. We're taught not to do that, not to contextualize. Just to take information in and spit it right back out. Maybe it's because I'm sitting here, not in uniform, drinking coffee and shooting the shit. Or maybe this case stuck to me more than I realized.

"You see anything strange?" I asked him. I moved my head to block his view, so he'd have to look at me. "Anything out of the ordinary?"

"Why?" he asked me. Now I had his attention. "Why are you here? Is something wrong? Did something happen?"

At this point, if I'm being honest, I was less suspicious of him. He was standing next to the trash cans, yes, but he didn't seem like he was trying to stop me from looking in them. It was more like . . . maybe he'd taken out the trash and noticed our squad car, and now he was trying to puzzle something together. But again, the contextualizing is a no-no, so I just kept going. "What's your name?" I asked. Sometimes it helps to get people talking if you just ask them an easy question. He said his name was Jayson and that his friend Cece lived there, in the vic's house. Actually, he might have been about to say his *girlfriend*. That got me interested. How many stories you hear about the daughter's boyfriend getting mad and doing in the parents? I can think of at least three.

"Why aren't you in school?" I asked.

"Strep," he said. I backed off a little. I could hear the sirens approaching, knew the whole kit and caboodle would be there in under a minute. My partner was still in the back, making sure no one went in or came out. I just wanted to get the measure of this guy, see what his deal was, and also get him to stay put until the detectives arrived.

Something was coming over him. Dawning on him. I watched it happen. First his ears perked up. I'm not joking. I watched them sort of tune in. Then his whole face opened up. He finally looked at me. "Did you find Theresa?" he asked.

That was her name, the vic we'd found. Did we find her? Why was he asking that? I played dumb. "Theresa?" I said. Again, get him talking and staying put is my only goal.

He started edging around me, trying to head toward the house. "Is my mom in there?" he asked. I'll admit, it took me a minute to work it out. Now he was asking if his mom, who didn't live in that house, was in that house. I stepped in front of him to block him.

"Why do you think your mom is in there, Jayson?" I asked.

"Because we can't find her," he said. "Sometimes she's at Theresa's." He looked at me. Steady. He was a good kid. Sometimes you can just tell. He was swallowing a lot and sometimes that's a sign of lying, trying to choke down the truth so it can't get out. Or sometimes it's a sign that you're a teenage boy and you don't know shit about the world and you're doing all you can not to piss your pants, talking to this lady cop in the driveway of your girlfriend's house.

The contextualizing, I know. I know. We can't help but be human. That's the rub. I was looking at him squinting at me, probably seeing himself reflected in my sunglasses, nearly as tall as I was but kind of scrawny, not filled out yet, and I was seeing Mike Cobb. Mike Cobb was a boy in my US History class, senior year of high school. An all-around decent guy. Wasn't popular, wasn't bullied. That was the year I didn't have my shit together, the year I got suspended for fighting, the year I kissed Julie Dukes behind the lunchroom and she smiled at me and ran off and told everyone. I didn't know what *dyke* meant, but they yelled it at me, wrote it on my locker. They suddenly hated me, pushed me from behind, flipped my lunch tray, stomped on my homework. The shitkicker of it is that Julie Dukes and I started kissing regularly, meeting after school or sometimes skipping together, and then at school she'd be sneering and spitting with the rest of them. We all have our thing, I guess. Now she's a cashier at the Dollar General. She's got three kids and no partner. She looks exactly the same. I went in and bought a pack of gum and she never even looked at my face. Just swiped the gum, took the money, held out my change pinched between her fingers. She had no idea who I was. She was the best and worst thing that ever happened to me.

Mike Cobb. During all that crap, he just said hi to me, talked to me like I was a normal person on a normal day. Laughed at my jokes. Offered me rides home. It wasn't like he wanted anything from me. He wasn't into me and he didn't want to ruin my life. He was a friend and he acted like a friend, a true friend. One time in the hall when they were all screaming and laughing at me, he walked up and said, "Hey, Alicia, can I see your notes from class yesterday?" Like none of it was happening. He ignored them and changed the subject. It was like he turned the spigot and the water stopped rushing out. The bell rang and we all went our separate ways. He wasn't my savior or anything. If I'd felt like he wanted to save me, I'd have been ashamed. Somehow, he knew it. He just did what he could when he could. He was decent. Do you know what a relief it is to meet someone who is decent?

Here was Jayson, a decent kid in a shitty situation and I knew it even if I couldn't prove it. See what I mean about being human? We take what we've learned and we apply it and we can't help it. All that blood in the garage, that devastation and horror. No way that kid did it. I'd stake my career on it.

Just then is when they all rounded the corner, the detectives and the squad cars and the ambulance and the coroner.

"Jayson," I said, putting my hands on his bony shoulders. "We have to get out of the way." I steered him into the back of my vehicle and closed him gently inside. I told the detectives about him, pointed him out, and then I got swept up into the nitty-gritty of the scene, mainly staying out of the way until I was needed. At some point we were released and I saw that he wasn't in the car anymore, and I figured he'd been let out, and we headed to a call about a man urinating outside a Taco Bell.

He said *we*. *We* can't find her. I've always wanted to know who he meant. His whole family? Maybe. But it was just him standing there by the trash cans. By now I know where she was, and the reason they couldn't find her, but by now I also know that kid was very much alone in his big family. They all were. But he still said *we*.

Jessica Blender

Jessica Blender got her period the morning of the day she was supposed to meet up with her boyfriend and have sex on his parents' bed. It wasn't a lot of blood, but she knew he'd still be freaked out, that she couldn't hide it, be all like, *Hang on Mikey, gotta just* and then yank out her tampon and whip it over the side. Though she'd heard of girls who did that. In the locker room she'd heard Danielle Suarez say her boyfriend *took out her tampon for her*. Mikey didn't have sisters and his mother was the type to put her hand to her heart if you mentioned, like, a cramp. She'd talk to him, though. Remind him today was go time, that they wouldn't have another chance for days, maybe weeks, that the last time they'd done it was so long ago she felt haunted down there.

She'd been planning on asking him if they could try doing it on their sides. It was something that came to her in a dream. They could start out spooning and work their way into full-on doing it. There was something in the desperation and convenience, like why roll over when we can just . . . ? It could fail but it'd still be hot, like that time he snuck into her bedroom and they did it in her tiny en suite shower, water in their eyes and mouths and everything slippery until finally

they'd tumbled out and finished in missionary on her cold
tile floor.

She was thinking about all of this, sitting on the counter in the school bathroom, her back to a mirror, staring at
the shoes of another girl who'd been locked in a stall forever,
Jessica was realizing. They were scuffed white Keds, no socks,
perfectly stylish at the current moment in their high school,
but the no socks was unique. Where had she seen it?

Oh, shit, it was Cece Linden.

Jessica hopped down from the counter, quietly, and hurried out. If the girl needed to sit in the stall and cry or stare
at the door or pinch the sensitive flesh on the inside of her
elbow until it stung—Jessica's preferred method of reminding
herself who was in control—then she deserved to do that in
private. It had been months since that whole thing had happened with her mom. But who knew how long it took to get
over something like that?

Mikey was waiting for her at her locker, digging his nail
into an old Chiquita banana sticker that had been there since
before it was her locker. When he concentrated on something
he could look really dumb, his lip pulled up and his nostrils
flared and one of his eyes squinched shut. It would be much
later in Jessica's life that she realized she didn't have to "put
up with" or "stand" or "get over" anything; she could just
move on until she found someone she genuinely liked, not
just someone who was hot or, and this happened all too often,
someone she felt sorry for.

"Jess," he said. He flicked his hair out of his eyes, rolled
the sticker between his thumb and forefinger like a booger.
"You want to just skip seventh?" Now he looked cute again,
his eyes wide, searching hers. Those lips. As if he'd read her
mind, he leaned down and kissed her. She could taste the
Doritos he'd eaten at lunch.

Over his shoulder Jessica could see Cece coming down the hall, given a wide berth by everyone. She kept her head down and her books held to her chest, walking slowly like she wasn't sure where to go next.

"I feel so bad for her," Jessica said. Mikey turned to see who.

"Yeah," he said. "But, you know, she probably doesn't want people feeling sorry for her. Like she, like, feels that and it makes her feel worse, you know?" He went back to the sticker, working on the goo it had left behind, but he looked at Jessica. He had that look he got when he said something he wasn't sure about, like that time he asked her if she knew what a blow job was. She did know but she pretended she didn't hear him.

"That's actually so true," Jessica said. She tried to see Cece from her periphery, not stare directly as she approached, but that in itself felt pitying. "Wow, Mikey," she said. "You're so, like, Dr. Phil." She touched his bicep to let him know she was only teasing. Cece passed them like a wraith. Only then did it occur to Jessica that she could do something, talk to Cece, help her out a little. It was like those times when she'd notice a problem, like her clothes hamper being full, and realize she was capable of solving the problem. A whirlwind of images passed across her mind—she and Cece driving around in Jessica's dream VW that she didn't own and couldn't drive anyway, she and Cece making prank calls from her bedroom, she and Cece somber, holding flowers, staring down at her mother's grave, she and Cece laughing about how during sex Mikey's voice got all high-pitched and he sounded like Michael Jackson, laughing harder when Cece yelled *Mikey Jackson!* She and Cece hugging goodbye, both heading to different colleges, Cece fully restored as a person and able to face the world, now that she'd had such a solid friendship with a pretty, popular (enough) girl who took the time to help her.

"So do you?" Mikey asked. "Want to go right now?"

She did. She really did. Kissing him, touching him, she was desperate for it. It was actually, at that point, the only way life felt real. Everything else felt like a dream. Algebra, chores, dinners with her family where her brother inevitably leaned over and farted while someone else was speaking. All of that passed like channels she was flipping through. Being with Mikey felt like a choice she was making, something she was putting into motion, her whole body awake and alert.

She'd read online that Cece and her mother had been very close, that they'd been best friends. Jessica pictured them shopping together, watching movies, laughing. Jessica's mother was always asking her how much she weighed, if she still fit into her clothes from last year. "I'm just trying to help you, sweetie," she'd say, drinking one of her endless cups of appetite-suppressing tea that she bought in bulk from the GNC in the mall, its burning-tires smell wafting from room to room. "It gets harder and harder to stay in shape as you get older."

"I got my period," Jessica said, ignoring how Mikey flinched at the word. "Just this morning. I know. I'm so bummed."

Jessica caught up with Cece, who looked like she was about to enter another bathroom, the one down the hall that led to the cafeteria. "Hey," Jessica said. "Wait up." Cece looked tired, like she could fall over and sleep right there. It was hard to think of what to say, now that she was standing there. *I'm sorry about your mom.* No. *What's your name again?* Fake.

"You want to get out of here?" Jessica said. Cece looked at her, ran a hand up her face to push her hair off her forehead.

"Here?" she said.

Jessica was unsure how to answer. What was she asking? "Yeah, here." She put a hand on Cece's arm, started gently pulling her along. "It's easy. You just walk out the side door. I do it all the time." Technically not all the time. She wasn't a derelict. But it was important for Cece to feel like she was in the presence of an expert, someone she could trust.

"Sure," Cece said. "I guess."

The first bell rang and kids pushed into classrooms, the hall they were in starting to empty out. They hurried, breaking into a jog as they rounded a corner. It was easy to leave, yes, but that didn't mean teachers wouldn't hassle you. "We'll have to take a bus," Jessica said, walking faster. She passed the door to her seventh period. Mr. Lutz had his back turned, probably giving someone a hard time about their hairstyle or piercings. "Let's haul ass," Jessica said. Mikey was in his seventh period, weightlifting. With a pang she remembered the hot dog smell he got after.

As they burst out the side door, Jessica stopped. She let the door swing shut behind them. Cece was panting a little. Her hair could definitely use an avocado-and-mayonnaise treatment at some point. "I'm Jessica, by the way," she said.

"Yeah," Cece said, looking around like she didn't know how she'd gotten there. "I know."

They ended up at the mall because that's where the bus was going. Jessica revisited the scene she'd imagined for Cece and her mother, giggling through the shoe section at Dillard's, splitting a hot pretzel, Cece's mother announcing she was splurging on the jeans Cece wanted so badly. But when she looked at Cece's face, it seemed like she hadn't been there before. She looked around blankly, still hugging her books. "You want to get a frappe?" Jessica said. Her mother forbade them. *A whole day's worth of calories, caffeine stunts your growth, who spends nine dollars on a milkshake?* "The coconut one is amazing but they have other flavors. Vanilla." Cece shrugged, then nodded. They made their way over to the escalator, Jessica walking slow, then slower, Cece trailing her like a sleepwalker. "Here," Jessica said, and linked her arm through Cece's.

Secretly, Jessica loved the escalator ride up. It reminded her of when she was a kid and her parents would take her to see Santa. First, they'd take the escalator so they could look down on the Santa's Village that the mall workers built every year. It was the only way to glimpse him. On the ground he was hidden behind Christmas trees and a serpentine, velvet-roped waiting area, always packed. But going up the escalator, Jessica could see him, his hair and beard fluffy white. Her favorite was when he was in his "workshop" clothes, green velvet shirt and pants and gold embroidered suspenders. Her mother would squeeze her hand and her father would say, *Can you see him, Jessy? He's a fat one this year!*

These were the kinds of memories that confused Jessica. They had good times, normal times. Her mom and dad made each other laugh, hugged Jessica, hugged each other. It was maddening to spend all her time wondering what had changed—if their family had been all wrong from the start, or if something had happened, maybe something she'd done—to turn their house into a place where she felt she hadn't been invited.

She looked over at Cece. They stepped off the escalator and Jessica tugged her toward the Starbucks. Maybe people just got tired of each other. Was she tired of Mikey? She thought of his body, his curiosity about hers, that sweet thing he said about Cece at her locker earlier. No, not yet. She thought of how he picked his nose, not hiding it, how he wore the same mesh shorts sometimes three days in a row.

It was hard to tell what the future held. This was something she imagined talking about with Cece. Like, *Hey, Cece, what do you think happened? Do you think if some things had been done differently, your mom would* . . . But that would all come later, once she'd gained her trust.

"What flavor?" she asked, just outside the Starbucks. In this one it was best to know what you wanted before you went in. All the baristas appeared to be snappish middle-aged women, and if you didn't have your shit together, they'd tell you to stand aside until you did. Jessica prided herself on reading people, on giving them what they required out of an interaction. Those baristas needed efficiency. Cece needed coaxing. "They have coconut and vanilla, like I said, but also mocha and caramel and sometimes they have mint . . ." Cece was finally paying attention, her face stricken, staring in. Jessica looked and saw a guy, normal looking, kind of on the skinnier side, his hair winging out at the neck and ears, like he needed a haircut. He took a sip of his coffee and winced.

"Oh," Cece said. "Oh, shit." Jessica looked again, saw the guy making the same face Cece was. Then it dawned on her. "Is that . . . ?"

Cece nodded. He was one of the Stinson boys. "Jayson," Jessica said, as soon as his name came to her. He played soccer, had a million brothers. And his mom had been Cece's mom's best friend. And all the rest of it.

"Let's go," Jessica said. There was another Starbucks, way back by a janitor's closet and a side exit on the ground floor. She linked her arm again, gently pulled.

"No," Cece said. She bent and put her books on the floor, shrugged off her backpack and went in, right up to the guy. They just looked at each other, kind of awkward, standing in the middle of the lane people used to exit or get to the creamer, and then Cece reached for him, hugged him, buried her face in his shoulder. Jessica couldn't help it; she blushed, felt rude for watching. She knelt and pretended to organize Cece's things. She put the books into the backpack, which was empty save for a few pencils rolling around. She put those into the small front pocket and zipped everything up and then she allowed herself a glance. She couldn't see them. She stood up, leaned in for a closer look. There they were, at the table way in the back by the bathroom, both of them standing, ignoring the stools. Jessica went in; she wasn't sure what the protocol was here. Would Cece want her to be close by, in case . . . in case anything? Did she want privacy? Jessica tried not to feel slighted that Cece seemed to have completely forgotten her. *It's not about you, Jess.* The thought was calming and made her feel adult. She positioned herself a few tables away. Cece had her hand on his arm, like she was afraid he'd bolt.

One of the baristas began wiping Jessica's table down. She had strong forearms, almost mesmerizingly so, but she looked right at Jessica and said, loudly, "Honey, if you aren't going to order, you need to step outside." Cece looked over and Jessica waved, gestured at the backpack. Jayson looked and Jessica waved at him, too. It was at that moment, her arm helicoptering around in the air, the barista shaking her head and hustling off, that Jessica wondered just what on earth she was doing. None of this, literally none of this, had anything to do with her. She'd had this idea that, what, just her presence would be healing for Cece? What, that she could be her mother, or something? She of all people should know there was no replacement for the real thing. She thought of her own mother painting her nails in front of the television every Tuesday night. Paper towels laid out on the coffee table, the sharp smell of acetone. The perfect filed curve of each fingertip. And then she'd apply a color called "Raisin Dreams" or "Brown Is the New Brown" or "Depress Your Daughter." She thought of these things, these Patricia Anne Blender–specific details, with a mixture of disgust and intense love that left her feeling the need to protect her mother, who was defenseless against these thoughts.

Jayson and Cece had moved closer together, practically whispering into each other's faces. Something about it gave Jessica the impression that she'd had it all wrong. Cece didn't need a friend. She needed Jayson. She needed the world to drop away, everyone to shut up and everything to stop, so she didn't have to grip his arm so hard. Jessica went to the counter and ordered an iced chai. It felt right. She was on a different level now. "Babe, can you make sure my friend gets her backpack before she leaves?" she said to the other barista, a woman in lipstick and glasses so large and thick and ironic that they were LIPSTICK and GLASSES. Jessica had never called anyone *babe* in her life, not even her boyfriend. She took her chai, the ice in it chattering pleasantly, and headed toward the Victoria's Secret on the first floor. Her aunt had given her a gift certificate. "For the lotions," she'd said, but please. Mikey deserved to see her in a thong. Black, with lace. Maybe purple. She rode the escalator like a queen descending.

Nick

He got Manuel to help with the move. Everything he wanted to take with him fit into six boxes. It had to. That was all he'd swiped from the loading dock at work on his last day. Manuel would make the drive with him. They'd do it straight through.

Did he know? He felt the question underneath his every interaction now. The way Manuel was careful around him, said he could do most of the driving if Nick just wanted to rest. Jerome offered to get him a job out West, a buddy of his that ran a dealership in Nevada owed him a favor. Really Jerome just wanted him off the lot, far away from the customers, the freaks who'd begun showing up just to catch a glimpse of the man whose son had murdered the neighbor. The man whose wife had been fucking the neighbor's husband.

Did he know? How could he not know that his wife was fucking that drippy little shit?

He ran over and over it in his mind. It seemed so obvious now. She got skinny. She started wearing tight clothes. She was hyper, full of energy, always running errands that he now understood weren't errands at all.

"It's not your fault," Manuel said. He said it over and over. Nick wondered if some part of Manuel believed he did have something to do with it.

*   *   *

They stopped at a motel that promised a pool and cable TV. The place was L-shaped, with an office and small cafe in the short part of the L and a row of a dozen rooms with bright-orange doors in the long part. A woman with bright-blue eyeshadow and a beehive stood behind the counter. When he got closer, he saw that she wasn't nearly as old as she looked, was maybe no more than twenty-five. She handed him two room keys on heavy gold keychains, the same lightning bolt on the sign outside printed on each key.

"I'm Mabel if you need anything," she said, smiling warmly. "Just dial zero on your room phone." Nick wondered what her real name was. He could spot someone playing the part from a mile away. Behind her, a space-age-style television showed the news in black and white.

Outside, it was full night. The road by the motel was quiet. Further off, he could hear the hushed roar of traffic on the highway.

"I'm going for a swim," Manuel said, grabbing his duffel from the trunk. "Meet you at the cafe in an hour?"

Nick tossed him a room key and took his overnight bag from the back seat. The key didn't slide so easily into the lock and he had to jiggle it to get the door to his room open, but inside it was clean, a double bed with starched white bedding and a small bathroom that looked freshly scrubbed. He was pleased to see that a more modern television than the one in the office was bolted to the wall. Maybe he could watch something later, though he'd have to be careful. Too many times, he'd switched on the set at home, or walked into the break room at work, only to see his son, his wife, a picture of Theresa from the previous summer, her arm linked to Adam's. He'd taken that picture.

He opened his bag, looking for his toothbrush. In between his change of clothes and underwear, he found a folded piece of paper with *Dad* written in Sammy's handwriting. *Come back soon*, it said. He pushed it down to the bottom of the bag. Something jagged caught in his throat. He coughed and it freed itself, turned into hot tears that coated his face.

The cafe had waxed gingham tablecloths on the tables and chrome stools at the bar. There was a jukebox, but when he got closer he saw it was just for show. An older couple were at the bar, drinking coffee and staring at the television mounted in the corner. Nick found a table next to the window and sat with his back to the TV. He saw Manuel walking barefoot across the parking lot toward his room, a towel slung over his shoulder.

Mabel came and wiped down his table. As she bent he saw that there were bobby pins holding the beehive in place. It looked painful.

"You want something to drink?" she asked. She took a pencil from somewhere in her hair, licked its point. He thought of all the days when he'd have to approach someone and pretend to be the confident, no-bullshit salesman people seemed to like. All the jokes he used and re-used. All the laughing, his throat raw at the end of each day. He wondered if Mabel was sick of playing her part, or if she was still having fun. "We have egg creams," she said. She winked at him. Underneath all that makeup, she was pretty, genuinely pretty. All-American girl, that's how he'd describe her.

"What's your real name?" he asked.

She pointed at her name tag. *Mabel* in cursive. "After my great-aunt," she said.

He was supposed to be able to read people, see through the guards they put up, glimpse their real desires, their actual budget. It was something he thought he was good at, really good at. Maybe her name actually was Mabel. Maybe she liked to dress like a midcentury alien in her everyday life. Maybe Jackie had never loved him. Maybe Douglas was just a cold-blooded murderer, not the mixed-up teenage boy he remembered himself being.

"Just coffee for now," he said.

The coffee was hot and rich and Nick sipped it slowly, enjoying how its warmth spread through his whole body. The shades were drawn in Manuel's room and the light was off but Nick could see the flickering of a television. He drank a refill of his coffee, noticed that Mabel had a lot of ear piercings, kept his eye on Manuel's room. He never emerged.

"Can I have a waffle?" he asked when Mabel came around for a third refill.

"You can have two," she said. "Back in a jiff."

He watched as the older couple left, the man helping his wife with her coat and she turning to do the same for him. The man nodded at him as he passed. He watched as they made their way past the row of rooms, let themselves in at the last door.

"Aren't they cute?" Mabel asked. She set a plate the size of a cafeteria tray before him. His waffles were swimming in butter and syrup. "They're on a road trip for their forty-fifth wedding anniversary," she said. "They were here on their honeymoon, way back in this place's glory days." She darted to the counter, brought back a cereal bowl full of whipped cream.

She waited, hands folded in front of her. There was no one else in the cafe. He sawed at the waffles, took a bite. "Mmm," he said. It was delicious. The syrup had been warmed and the butter was salty and he could taste the vanilla in the waffle. Mabel tidied up where the couple had been, balancing their cups and saucers and disappearing into the back.

He'd given Jackie a waffle maker for Christmas one year. Months of Saturdays when they'd make waffles for the boys before he had to go to the dealership. But one morning he spilled coffee on it and it fritzed and they never bought another one. Had it been as simple as that? Family breakfasts, cooking together? He closed his eyes, tried to remember better. Nathan hated syrup. Sammy wanted to cut his own. Burnt waffles, waffles that fell on the floor, Douglas layering three waffles together and saying, *Look! A waffle sandwich!*

He pushed his plate away, went back to his coffee.

In his room he undressed until he was in his boxers and undershirt. He had forgotten toothpaste so he ran his toothbrush under water and quickly scrubbed his teeth. Tomorrow, they'd make the rest of the drive, and then he'd drop Manuel at the airport the next day, send him back home. It didn't feel possible; his body ached from exhaustion. He spat. Wasn't his toothbrush purple? The one he held was blue. It was Jackie's, he felt sure of it. He rinsed and spat, rinsed and spat. Opened his door and threw it into the parking lot.

He could hear the TV on in Manuel's room, and underneath that the low rumbles of his snores. He decided to risk it and switched on his TV. The late show was on, an actress with stick legs wobbled out in spiky black heels, took the host's hands in hers like they were at a funeral. He muted it and got into bed. He dozed. He dreamed he was at home in his own bed. Sammy shook him awake, was trying to get him to look at something. Finally, he did. There were clouds on the ceiling, swirled with pale colors. He looked at Sammy but it was now Nathan. Nathan bent to tie his shoe, stood and was Jayson. A knock at his bedroom door, but he couldn't get up to see who it was. *Who is that?* he asked Jayson, but it was Douglas. The colors from the ceiling washed over his face. He opened his mouth and there was a knock. The knocks were coming from inside him. His face was green, now purple, now the pale pink of the inside of a shell. *It's Mom*, Douglas said. *It's just Mom.*

Nick woke. The TV showed a commercial for a truck that could drive through the mountains, through a shallow body of water. A boy grinned at his dad. The commercial ended with them fishing, the truck parked nearby. The alarm clock on the nightstand read 2:34. Someone was knocking on his door. He'd had a dream where there was knocking, hadn't he? He remembered Douglas, the colors washing over his face the way they had in the lights of the police cruiser.

He stood, made his way on stiff legs to the door. Through the peephole he saw the old man, the one from the cafe. Nick opened the door.

"I can't get anyone in the office," the man said. He had a voice that seemed strong, younger than the man looked, with a slight twang. "I need a little help."

Nick wondered if the man was drunk, or if he had one of those diseases old people get where the mind starts to go. He looked around for the wife but the parking lot was empty. The lights in the office were out. "You want to come in?" Nick asked. It was eerily quiet, not even the sighs of the highway.

The man grabbed his arm, his hand warm and strong. "I need you to come along with me," he said. He looked desperate, a little panicked.

"One sec," Nick said. He backed into his room and closed the door. He stood for a moment, then checked out the peephole again. The old man was still there. Nick put on his pants, grabbed the room key. At the last second, he dialed Manuel's room number, heard it ring and ring next door. He tried again. Then he dialed 0 but no one picked up there, either. He found a can of pepper spray in a zippered pocket of his overnight bag, tucked that in the waistband of his pants, and pulled his shirt over it. He felt stupid doing it. But he felt stupid not doing it.

He opened the door and the man grabbed his arm again, pulled him down the row of rooms. The old man's door was propped open with a woman's shoe, a bright wedge of light spilling out onto the sidewalk, the TV blaring. They stopped just short of the doorway and the man let his arm go. "My wife is a good person," he said, his voice quiet. He had bushy eyebrows and one wild hair hung down and touched his eyelid. His eyes were wet and his mouth made clicking noises as he spoke. He had strong hands and forearms, and his back was straight, his shoulders broad, and Nick saw that he had probably been handsome in his day.

"I'm sure she is," Nick said.

The man looked down, rubbed the back of his neck. "I just mean that she has had a difficult life."

"Haven't we all," Nick said. The pepper spray was digging into his back. He could see clouds of bugs hovering around the light above the door. He was about to tell the man he needed to get back to his room, needed sleep, that he'd help in the morning, or find a way to rouse Mabel, when the man pushed open the door. He beckoned for Nick to go in first. The man's wife was spread-eagle on the floor outside the bathroom, nude but for a pair of white underwear, sound asleep.

"I need help getting her into bed," the man said. "If she wakes up like this, she'll be—" He stopped himself. "She can't wake up like this," he finally said.

"You don't think she needs a doctor?" Nick said. The TV was too loud and he nearly had to shout over it. He looked around for the remote but didn't see it.

"I'm a doctor," the man said. "She just takes it a little too far sometimes."

Nick crouched beside her. In the bathroom trash can he saw miniature bottles and tissues stained with lipstick. Her tried not to look at her tits, which melted toward her armpits but were surprisingly plump. "I'll take her arms," he said. "You get the legs."

The man cinched his robe tighter, rubbed his neck again. "I am no longer able to lift her," he said. The words came out choked, like they hurt to say.

Again, Nick thought of Manuel, of pounding on his door and waking him up, getting him to help. He did not want to carry this woman alone.

He opted for the fastest thing. He grabbed her by the armpits and gently, slowly, dragged her to the bed. Then he knelt on the bed and reached down and lifted her, pulled her up inch by inch. The dragging had pulled down her underwear and he looked away, looked at the TV, where they were showing footage of his house, of Nathan and Jayson getting home from school, Jackie waiting for them in the doorway.

"We're hearing reports that Nick Stinson, Jackie Stinson's husband, has left town," a woman with a voice the texture of wood said. They showed a picture of him, his Salesman-of-the-Month photo in which he had worn a velvet blazer and slicked back his hair to make the guys laugh. He looked like a shithead, the kind of man who'd abandon his family, leave his boys with their scheming mother.

The old man was hovering, his back to the television. The woman's legs were half off the bed, but it was good enough, and Nick just wanted to get out of that room that smelled like a bar.

"Okay, take care," he said, edging toward the door. He saw that the wife had been lying on the remote and he wanted to grab it, mute the television before he left.

"They've been running that story all night," the old man said. He sat on the bed, put his wife's head in his lap, began stroking her hair. "When I saw you in the cafe, I wondered if it was you." He tugged at the blankets on the bed, trying to get them out from under his wife. "Now, I'm sure. I bet those boys of yours are mighty confused."

Nick walked toward the man and raised his fist. The man flinched, put his hands up to protect his head. "I mean you no harm," he said.

Nick turned to leave. They were showing a picture of Jackie next to a picture of Adam now, the flash making Jackie's eyes look red. He reached behind the television and yanked out the power cord. The room was suddenly silent. The wife whimpered softly in her sleep.

"This your kink?" he asked the old man. "Get your wife wasted and then watch a stranger touch her?"

"I can see why you might think that," the man said. He nodded at the television. "But no. She does what she likes. I learned that a long time ago." The man leaned over and switched off the lamp. Nick tried to close the door but the shoe was still there. He kicked it and it disappeared into the dark room.

In the morning a different woman waited on them at the cafe. Her name tag also said *Mabel*, though she was short and squat and probably fifty years old. She swayed as she took their order as though she were rocking a baby. Manuel ordered in Spanish and she giggled.

"I slept like a dead man," Manuel said, shaking salt over his home fries. "Woke up still in my trunks."

The maid's cart was stationed outside the couple's door. She brought out a twist of sheets, a bag of trash.

"Hey," Manuel said. He nodded behind Nick, where the television was. "They're showing a picture of you." The men looked around. Some truckers had parked in the lot and come in for breakfast, but they ignored the television, their faces gray. One ordered pancakes and slept on his arms while he waited.

"You think this is the right thing?" he asked Manuel. He'd ordered scrambled eggs and toast and they sat untouched on his plate. "You think I should have stayed?"

Manuel dragged his hand over his face, wadded his napkin and dropped it on his plate. "You know I can't make that decision for you."

"I'm not saying go back to Jackie," he said. He thought of the way Jackie told him, sitting at the police station after Douglas was arrested, when all they knew was that he'd attacked Theresa. *Adam and I were fucking,* she'd said, impatiently, like he should have caught on a long time ago. And then, when he explained how he needed to get away, to set up somewhere else so he could keep working, she had that weird smile on her lips. Like he was doing exactly what she thought he would do. That girl, dancing at the party, the mother of his children who could get them all laughing, even Douglas, she was gone. He was just the last to know. "I'm saying go back home and be there for my boys."

He had lied to Sammy, lied to Nathan and Jayson. Said he was going on a short trip to make some money so he could get them all a place together. He hadn't planned on returning. "Or maybe I can convince them to move to Nevada with me," he said. He picked up a triangle of toast, dug at his eggs with it.

Manuel nodded. "It'd be good to get them away from all those cameras," he said. He signaled for a refill of his coffee. As Mabel poured, he asked her to switch the channel to golf.

*   *   *

They kept the windows down in the car as they drove. The air grew dusty, then cleared. He tasted grit in his teeth. Manuel fiddled with the radio, bet that he could find a Michael Jackson song every hour. In Nevada, the land was barren and the light seemed filtered through a prism. Manuel's buddy had found Nick a furnished apartment in a cream-colored building with a warren of staircases. It was hot everywhere, the air dry and stinging. It took ten minutes to bring all his things inside. His bedroom had a view of sandstone cliffs just beyond the highway and he could see the lights from the dealership where he'd work.

"You good?" Manuel said, leaning in the doorway. "I'm taking a shower."

Alone, Nick couldn't decide where to put Sammy's note. He needed it to remind him, but he didn't want to see it. In the end he put it in between his mattress and his box spring. He'd forgotten all about it a year later, when he moved to the other side the highway, closer to the blood-red beauty of those sandstone cliffs.

The Investigative Journalist

The homes looked smaller than they did in all the news coverage. Jackson was used to that but there was something else, something he hadn't yet identified, that was making him feel like he was in a wax museum, or a dream in which the coffee in his hand was more real than the house he was approaching. He'd taken a red-eye that was delayed to a normal takeoff time, the hours in the airport sludging by, his mild anxiety about canned air blossoming into something hotter, sharper, his body tense and aching and the small boy across from him sneezing so richly and thoroughly that his whole face was wet. Jackson had let fly on his producer over the phone, sitting in the smokers lounge just to breathe something different and calling Marty a *little dumb shit* and then apologizing to the point of (forced) tears and generously acknowledging that Marty was both ten years younger and half an inch taller before hanging up and gagging in the Men's. Maybe he was just tired. It was a thankless job. Sure, he'd mention what he did to various barflies in the hopes that the person he was talking to might get that *aha!* look and say his own name to him out loud, clapping him on the back and offering to buy a drink or scooting closer and brushing his arm or knee, depending on their gender and/or sexual orientation. He was comfortable

with whatever. He was a modern man, goddammit. But after
that initial *aha!* came the inevitable letdown. It wasn't *that*
impressive. He talked to criminals and murderers for a living
and sure, there were cameras and a national network involved
but it was kind of strange, wasn't it? That he knew so much
about truly despicable things done by truly despicable people,
in the loosest sense of the word?

He could still work it into sex or, at the very least, groping and fondling and hot breath in each other's faces, but it
took work. More and more work with every passing year. His
hair was nearly all silver, now. He *was* tired.

And he'd been accused, in the past, of flirting. He was
from the upper Midwest! Was it his fault he'd been raised to
be friendly? Polite? To show some common shitting decency?
Flirting was, in fact, a defense mechanism. Also a tool. A sharp
little digging tool that let him slowly break through. He was
old-school, was how he put it. *You can't touch people so much* was
how it was put to him. *They don't like it. You look like a lonely
old man.* Well. He knew who'd complained, that dusty, plain-
faced baldy who'd buried all those women under his porch.
Jackson had a hunch about that man. He practically begged
Jackson to mount him, begged him right through those foggy,
scratched-up granny glasses perched on his nose. And it had
worked! Jackson had only to grab the man's freckly paw and
squeeze it a bit before he was a heap of tears and heaving.
Camera zooming in dutifully. Everybody loved it, just read
the message boards! And please. As if he would ever stoop. In
that man's dreams!

And now he was here, on Hot Springs Drive, about to
come face-to-face with Jacqueline Stinson. He'd do what he
was paid to do. The lawn was patchy and the door needed a
new coat of paint and in general the house was as tired as he
was. He had a brief shitfit about being quite possibly sucked

into something that was going to freeze him in amber as he was in that very moment, which was to say not at his best, not winning the fight against aging, not even the sort of spry you'd want in a digestive yogurt commercial. Something was going on in that house, quite possibly the entire street. These people with their bed hopping and bloodshed. It screamed of boredom, the kind that went beyond the normal suburban malaise and into something darker, something that raged to be set free, but from what? From whom? It longed for a target. He could feel it sizing him up, or maybe *she* was watching him, though that tacky enormous picture window remained empty aside from a small gel snowman in the corner. He shivered. Clatters from the assorted vans rose up behind him. Had Wickman ever in his fat little life *not* dropped something onto his fat ankles upon exiting the passenger side? "Wickman!" he called. He mimed zipping up. He meant it figuratively—as in pull it together, you pink-cheeked buffoon—but also literally, because his parka was flapping around him like he was a four-year-old at recess. Wickman had attended Georgetown, a school that had rejected Jackson two decades prior, and admittedly he hated the man's polite guts for it.

In fact, he had a muddy memory of telling Wickman exactly why he hated him, at one of those post-interview happy hours everyone loved, where inevitably Maria would do an impression of a widow sobbing or a criminal shifting up a smidge to fart (as had happened more than once!) and everyone laughed dutifully until the empties multiplied and the laughter became real. *Wickman,* he'd perhaps said, *nobody thinks of you unless you're right there in front of their uncomprehending eyeballs. And that's a problem, son.* But had it happened? Or had he only wanted to say it, but still had a modicum of decency left or at the very least too little energy to deal with the emotional fallout, of which there would assuredly be a large one, because Wickman bore his entire existence on his beach ball of a head.

Jackson was tired. He was on, perhaps, his third midlife crisis.

Well. Back to it. He tossed the coffee back like a shot and slapped himself across the face. He turned to his assistant to indicate that she should be the one to knock, to greet, to intro-fuckin'-duce him, as he was the star here! He could afford suede, he'd been asked as a goof to present an award at a youthful award show, and he expected his staff to acknowledge that he was a star. That was it, the sum total of his life's aims! Three crisp knocks, Andrea, and let's get going!

She answered the door. That was how he knew. She opened the door wearing a loud sweater that flopped to mid-thigh and leggings with some sort of sheen, bare feet, and the artfully messy hair of someone much younger. She looked as if she'd just come in from raking leaves or picking apples or chasing someone who loved her, something wholesome but cloaked in chill, and Jackson felt it grip him as well as he stood there smiling that furrowed-brow, amused-but-not-giving-an-inch smile. It was his signature, and it fought on despite the freezing maw of death that she carried closing delicately around him.

"I know you," she said.

You don't, he wanted to say, but it wouldn't suit his purposes. He wanted to wipe off his shoulders and arms and he looked at Andrea to see if she had some sort of towel, a rag, but why would she? Briefly he considered the decorative kerchief on her head before he realized there was nothing to wipe off, it was just a feeling, *just a feeling,* like his therapist was always saying. *Just a feeling?* he dreamed of saying to her during sex. Therapy felt like something he had to win, only his therapist in her velvet highback didn't give a shit about the rules.

"Jackson Schafer," he said. Neither of them held out their hand. Andrea edged inside to find and secure the bathroom. He had standards when it came to that sort of thing. A lock on the door, enough toilet paper, an unflecked mirror. Utterly normal, acceptable expectations! "Shall I come in?" he asked, because Jacqueline still hadn't moved aside. Andrea had ducked under her armpit. He began having doubts about the mirror.

"I was just putting some snacks together," she said. Her eyes glittered and he wondered if she had a fever.

"I don't eat," he said. He had meant to say, *I already ate.*

"Not for you, smarty," she said. She opened the door wider. "If I don't feed the animals they start to push my buttons." She grabbed his elbow and ushered him through. Even in shoes he could feel the grit in the carpet, could smell the settled essence of other people's lives. It was in the corners, lurking in the sofa cushions, throbbing gently from the curtains. Here, in Jacqueline Stinson's home, it was in the carpet, wafting foully up and tendrilling in through his nostrils. Dust. Tears. Sweat. Blood? He was already writing his intro—dreamy transitions from the front of the house to the interior, his voice deep and thoughtful, playful, even loving. *Dust. Tears. Sweat. Blood?* His eyebrow nudged up into his forehead, pulling the corner of his mouth along with it.

He hadn't expected the children to be there. Where else would they be? If what people said was true, what friend on earth would she have left to send them to? He knew their names. Jayson, handsome in a way that looked startled and then punchable; Nathan, already in glasses, full cheeks like his father; and Samuel, who in pictures looked like any kid brother on earth, one step behind or grinning blank-eyed to match his brothers, but who now seemed like he might be on the verge of a long career in cat burglary. He'd seen that certain things no longer mattered, and while Nathan and Jayson might have gravely accepted that but stuck to their burgeoning moral codes to get through, Samuel would be taking a different path. Jackson knew it by the way he tried too hard to ingratiate himself, sticking out his scrawny hand and then, when he thought no one was looking, letting the smile fall off his face and replacing it with pure raging focus.

They were ignoring bowls of Doritos and yogurt-covered pretzels. A plate of browning apple slices shoved first by Jayson and then by Nathan.

"Douglas is the one who likes apples," Jackie said. "I forgot." The boys looked at her, quickly, as shocked as Jackson that she'd uttered his name. "You like oranges, right, Jayse?" She turned and grabbed one from a bowl, began peeling it.

The crew was moving furniture around. Someone found the vacuum and turned it on. "I hope this is okay," Jackson hollered, sticking his thumb over his shoulder. "It's probably off-putting, isn't it? Seeing all your stuff out of place." He made eye contact with each boy, skimmed past Jackie's face. Had they heard the word *off-putting* before? He'd done his research into this area of the country, what sort of education they were all likely getting. Columbus discovered America; math was for sissies. Andrea still hadn't emerged; the bathroom must have been a war zone. He wanted to send her a text to forget it, he could powder his face in his sleep.

"Will your husband be . . . ?" he yelled. The vacuum was giving off a hot-foot smell. He came around the cluttered peninsula to work on cracking the window above the sink. It helped him achieve his aim of being both familiar to and in charge of his subjects, to act as if he was utterly at home in their home. He'd once snapped at the college-aged daughter of a man who'd been caught in a murder-for-hire to go upstairs and brush her hair, put on a different shirt. She'd been intent on ruining it for everyone, it was clear. Rage with nowhere to go just darts around aimlessly, he'd noticed. She came back down the stairs cowed, unrumpled, sullen yet compliant, and she'd even teared up despite herself, during the part where he asked if her father was her best friend. *Good girl*, he nearly said.

Jackie plopped the orange down on the countertop, peeled but unwedged. "No," she said. The vacuum switched off. Samuel was openly picking his nose, watching his mother. Perhaps Jackson could finagle solo interviews with each boy. Samuel would speak out of turn, or start yelling, or punch something. Jackson knew a star when he saw one.

"I'm sorry to hear that," he said, though he wasn't. He'd done his research there, too. A regular old meathead, was Nick Stinson. Annoyed that he'd be asked a question he didn't immediately have a rote answer to. *How are you? Good, good, can't complain. How's business? Good, good, can't complain. Tell me what happened the day Theresa was murdered.* He'd beef up, grow red, threaten to pummel Jackson about the head and body. Dramatic, yes, but not all that good for television.

Although, Jackson was getting up there. He was considered old-fashioned now. Maybe that's all anyone wanted anymore. Mess.

He leaned against the counter, crossed his ankles and his arms. He looked from face to face to face to face. Andrea drifted by, holding aloft a thumbs-up, on her way to grab his bag and sundries. "Tell me what you all are thinking," he said. His voice edged with concern, with genuine empathy. Of course he felt for these people, in all kinds of ways. He'd been a young boy himself, trapped inside his mother's world, with her blaring television and her raw-onion smell and the way she appeared to be counting down the days until he fucked off into adulthood and she could clock out. He looked at the boys, at how they watched their mother. He remembered that he also loved to make his mother laugh, that she'd sometimes lay her hand on his head and keep it there, so gentle. Things were complicated. But how to get that across in a forty-three-minute segment on national television?

He'd considered murdering exactly once in his life. So he could empathize there, too. What human television viewer couldn't?

"Um," Nathan said. He was the one uncomfortable with silence, with a question just hanging out there. Jackson nearly licked his chops. "I feel nervous, I guess." He looked at his mother. She looked down. Uh-oh. "I mean, I guess I don't know what I feel."

"Is this part of the . . . the interview thing? Are we being recorded?" Jayson, the heartbreaker. He was the easiest, for Jackson, to consider. In fact, Jackson had let himself get lost on a few occasions, meditating, trying to get inside the boy's head and heart. Young love, cut violently short. He'd been trying to get an interview with the girl, the ultimate victim in all of this. He'd hoped they'd be next door, watching the crew drive up, dash in and out of the house, that he'd see the white curve of her cheek as she looked out her window. Silly. The house had been empty for months, a FOR SALE sign gone a bit crooked on the front lawn. It'd be all spiffed up in there, clean as a whistle. Companies that did such things were a dime a dozen. He wondered what that said about the world. Maybe there was a morning show appearance in that. One of those quirky opinion slots. America ate that shit right up.

"No, son," he said, grandfatherly now, "I'm just interested in what you have to say. Whatever it is." He kept his eyes on Jayson a beat longer than the boy was expecting.

She noticed. "Boys, go on up until I tell you to come down," she said. She held her arms out as if she was herding them. They jumped up and filed out.

He watched her shoulders relax once they were out of earshot. "I'm only doing this because my lawyers said it was a good idea," she said. She leaned against the counter opposite him, adopting his posture.

"Uh-huh," he said, noncommittal, maybe validating her, maybe not. "And why do they think it's a good idea?" A text came in from Andrea: *Place gives me the creeps, you want a latte?*

"It's the only way I get to have my say," she said.

He pretended to get another text. She was on the verge of spilling her guts, either genuinely or via the rehearsed and practiced format she'd likely ironed out with her attorneys, and he did not want her to waste that on him when no cameras were rolling. He typed, thumbs circling each other: *Have I ever wanted a latte? We go on in twenty.* "Hmm?" he said, looking up. She opened her mouth to repeat and he looked down again. He added a smiling emoji. Andrea was of the generation where all emotions had to be translated through sprinkle-sized yellow faces, and/or all texts without emojis meant he was disappointed in her, angry, annoyed. He added the smiley even when he was all of those things.

"I read about these societies, way back, where the women were the rulers, the ones in power," she said. "Like, the men didn't say boo without the go-ahead from these women." She nodded at the phone in his hands. "I think we're going to get there again."

"Oh?" he said. Now he really needed Andrea, needed the disk of powder and the hairspray and the chairs facing each other. Jacqueline wanted to talk.

"Every man I know gets sucked into his phone. They're blinded by their phones. Do you know how easy it would be to just"—she mimed ripping something out of his hands—"poof, now it's mine." She folded her arms, looked at him. He was beginning to see. Some people were simply more alive, their eyes lit from the inside, their hearts beating an extra beat every second. It was alluring, frightening. You wanted to get closer to figure it out, but you also wanted to hold something out in front of you, to shield yourself.

"You can have it," he said, offering his phone.

"I'm not talking about your fucking phone," she said. There was mirth in her voice. He'd misunderstood her, and it proved something to her. This woman was gorgeous, he could see that fully now. But it wasn't the type of beauty that was apparent. It revealed itself bit by bit, as if a shadow slowly peeled itself off of her. Her wild hair, the single dimple when she smiled, the big, white American teeth. She could have him if she wanted him. He realized it and knew it was important to realize it. He succumbed because he had to. For the interview. If she believed she had power over him, her defenses would be down. He smiled back, let his eyebrows drop sheepishly.

"Then what *are* you talking about?" Andrea blurred by, leaning over from the weight of his duffel on her shoulder. He wanted to signal to her, to anyone, that they should be watching this.

"I'm talking about power," she said. "You—all you men— you've stopped paying attention." She turned and filled a short glass next to the sink with water, drank it down in one quick gulp. *Odd*, he heard his own voiceover say. She smacked her lips. "Power comes from paying attention," she said.

Didn't he know that? Paying attention was what he was paid to do. He watched her be lured into the canvas makeup chair Jodie had set up in the dining room, where the natural light was the best. He paid attention as Jackie waved away the offer of lipstick, eyeliner, gel. He paid attention as she declined to put on socks or shoes. He paid attention as she shapeshifted from what he'd glimpsed in the kitchen to plain housewife— scrubbed face, little vanity, peeling cuticles, hair shoved behind ears. It was armor; he was watching her prepare for battle. He wondered how many mothers had mastered that trick.

Rumbling from upstairs, the footfalls of boys. She tilted her head imperceptibly toward it. There it was, the pull. That innate thing she couldn't hide. Had his own mother felt it? He thought of her laughter, quick and light, a cascade of bells. He thought of the fear in her voice as she shouted at him that he was in danger of becoming a nothing. That fear meant she loved him, was bound to him. Correct? He had so many questions. *They said Theresa's head had been caved in, that she'd fought ferociously. That they never found her other shoe.* He simply wanted to say the boy's name and see what happened.

"Douglas," he said.

"He's at the other one," Jodie said, rubbing the ends of Jackie's hair between her fingers, misunderstanding. Douglas was the name of a crew member who was at the strip mall parking lot where the Get Skinny group met, shooting B-roll.

"No," he said, but the moment had passed. They were being ushered through the kitchen and into the family room, everything darkened and simplified and lit and ready. He felt off. He'd felt something similar recently, when was it? As though he'd forgotten to brush his teeth, or worn his underwear on his head. Occasionally, in the night, he'd get up to pee and jolt awake in the act, worried he was actually in bed, wetting himself. Was he awake, or was this the dream? He needed to slap himself, pinch the delicate skin behind his knee, something, anything. He was Jackson fucking Dawes goddamn Schafer. He was old and tired, yes, but he had his ways. He'd been told the lawyers weren't allowing any questions about Douglas, that because he wasn't there with his attorneys to defend himself, it was unethical if not illegal. Of course the network had its own lawyers, who had their own lawyers, and he knew how to get away with it. One of Jackie's attorneys settled just behind her client, tottering on a child-sized wooden stool, her suit jacket angling out all over as if it had sprouted elbows. It was the show's thing to use what furniture the subjects had at hand, but sometimes it invited the absurd.

"Jacqueline, remember our escape route," the attorney said, at the same moment as she leaned over and handed Jackson a card. *Debora Blickmann*, it read. He wanted to edit it, that name, add an *h* at the end of *Debora* and strike an *n* off of *Blickmann*. He handed it over his shoulder and someone plucked it from him and he'd never see it again and they both knew it. A business card! As if he needed to know her name! As if he'd even be able to see her once the lights were fully lit, slumped back there with her ankles akimbo like a friendless child! "Up and out of the chair, through the foyer, out the front door, and into my car. Okay?" she said, already dimming into the background.

He smiled, coaxing his face into that relaxed, all-knowing smirk everyone loved. He'd let Jacqueline have her say. He'd let her say all of it and more. Crossed one leg over the other. More and more it was hard not to feel as if he'd vised his privates when he did it, but it looked intellectual, unrushed, trustworthy, and it was another one of his things. He practiced the breathing exercises his therapist had taught him that time he'd called her during a teeny tiny panic attack inside the M&M's store in the airport and mentally fixed Andrea in the room somewhere, the way a laboring woman might her hand-wringing mother-in-law.

"And three and two and . . ." They were rolling.

"So," he said. "Tell me."

The shadow had reapplied itself fully; she was simply a mother again, practical and harried. She was ladylike in her girlishness. "I lost my best friend," she said.

He made a humming noise. His eyes had done that thing they always did, which was to put the subject at the end of a long, dark tunnel, so all he could see was her, but she was also hard to see. He didn't need to hear what she had to say in order to know the truth. He'd known it as soon as he'd walked in, as soon as he saw her sons' faces. When he was a child his father told him stories about monsters, how they lurked under beds or in the dark corners of his bedroom. As an adult he knew monsters were as common as dandelions. He'd interviewed plenty. They were bankers, plumbers, city workers, fast-food workers, even presidents. They were mothers. And as long as you pretended like they weren't monsters, they'd leave you alone. You had to play along, and Theresa had stopped playing along. He made another noncommittal noise, performed that famous furrowing of his brow.

Jayson did his best not to look out the window, because she wasn't out there. He kept forgetting. Sometimes she smelled like spearmint. Didn't she? "I forgot," he whispered to himself. His brothers nodded. Downstairs, their mother was yelling. They each took a breath and shared it. The window showed the sky, bright blue but yellowing at the horizon. They yearned to join together, to absorb one another into a being powerful and giant. In the end they held hands.

Douglas

They were in Common Room II, which had the window. Outside, the sky was the color of the drain water that gushed into the slop sink in Laundry. The trees were just bones, no leaves, not even an old squirrel condo to look at. Douglas knew there was a road on that side of the prison, but the window was too high for him to see, which sometimes felt like an especially creative cruelty and other times felt like mercy. The Pepsi machine kicked on, kicked off. None of them had shit to spend, never did. They all helped themselves to the tepid, sludgy coffee, holding the paper cups in their rough, dirty hands like ladies at a book club, pretending at cozy, at normal. Riley sometimes brought her own tea bags to share, but you had to use tap water, and even then, you had to keep it running a good two minutes before it got hot enough, and then what you had was tea that tasted and smelled like the pipes under the prison.

Javi was talking now, forming the words with his hands before speaking them. Grand larceny plus breaking and entering and assault. But he seemed like such a shy man, unable to make eye contact, rubbing his hands over his face over and over as if he could wipe it off.

Riley was always asking if the men had sexual dreams about their mothers. "It's completely normal, you know," she said as if she hadn't said the exact same thing again and again. "There's so little we know about the human brain, actually," she'd add, and maybe she should do some more reading herself, get another degree, to find out why she repeated herself so much yet acted like she was saying everything for the first time. "Some people believe this is all a simulation put on by our unique minds. That there's a multiverse and we're all living beside each other, that there's no physical realm, and thus everything is possible, and also impossible." No one, not a single shaven-headed, grim-faced inmate, nodded along. Riley was a doctor, or at least she'd introduced herself as one on Douglas's first day in Group, but he was beginning to wonder if she'd gotten her degree from some college inside her own simulation.

Douglas did have dreams about her, his mother, but preferred not to talk about them. From the time he was a boy he knew dreams were nothing but commercials his brain made and then watched, little bits of absurd quilted to lurid sewed to banal and run through a weed whacker. He pinned no hopes upon them; he did not attempt to figure out what signal his brain (his multiverse) might be sending him. She was fat in his dreams, always, the way she was in his earliest memories. He didn't know she didn't want to be fat until she started going to her classes and weighing her food and pointing out mothers who were fatter than her.

"Douglas," Riley was saying. "Did you hear what Javi just said? About how he had a dream about killing his mother with an axe?"

"With a hatchet," Javi said.

"The point is," Riley said, "nothing in our heads is real. Nothing. Not a thing. You have power over all of it." Riley was hard to read sometimes. At first she'd seemed like a perky cashier type, but lately she seemed almost deranged, with her ponytail always off-center like a little girl's and the drawstrings of her favorite hoodie getting crimped and dingy.

"If nothing in our heads is real," Douglas said, "then what part of us has control over it?" He rarely spoke up like this. But he was sick and fucking tired of this conversation, the one Riley initiated at almost every meeting. He thought of his brother, Jayson, how he had that business that helped people do cool shit, "realize goals," "actuate a new reality," "see more, do more, be more," and a bunch of other lowercase slogans in the brochure he sent with almost every letter, which seemed to Douglas like it was nothing more than a travel agency with positive affirmations you paid to use. But even that seemed more useful—an actual tangible journey where at least you had the pictures to prove it—than this bullshit about both ignoring and embracing the shitty thoughts that had gotten them all where they were.

"What part of you do you *think* has control over it?" Riley asked. Pete laughed into his fist. Pawel and Tim rolled their eyes.

He knew what she wanted from him. She wanted him to give up the goods, talk about Jackie. When his mother visited, he'd often catch Riley looking at them through the window dividing the visitation room from the smaller conference room. She had that bright, expectant smile. Sometimes she nodded at him encouragingly, as though he was supposed to do something, perform something.

"That your girlfriend?" Jackie asked once. She was always looking for ways to tease him, talking shit about his "prison hairdo" or the state of his fingernails or the fact that the other men weren't up to her standards. Nothing had changed. As a child he rarely brought friends home. *Why's he always wearing red? Isn't his mother a little snooty? Don't you want a friend more your size?* That last one was about cheerful, fun Kevin Mooney. She couldn't tolerate chubbiness. She couldn't help herself from noticing, from saying something.

"My point was," Douglas said now, shifting in his seat so the other butt cheek could get numb, "that the mind is what controls everything. Without the mind you're just a body."

"Talk more about that," Riley said. She was struggling to keep her clipboard and a stack of file folders from slipping off her lap. One of them was bursting out all over, curled Post-its marking every page. He knew that one was his.

He was the only inmate in Group who'd been convicted of killing. The others were in for drugs, theft, assault, rape. Riley had a thing about murder. Douglas had seen a news story about how murder was popular, especially among women, how they basically started fan clubs for Ted Bundy and other psychopaths.

"I think it's somebody else's turn," he said.

"I'll go," Tim said. He was in for rape, though he refused to call it that, called it "the date from hell." He was a wide man from the front, thin from the side, with deep grooves that ran from the outer corners of his eyes to his jaw. "I think the body is more dangerous than the mind." He sat back, his eyes darting from man to man. He brushed his hands together as if cleaning them of ash.

"Mmm," Riley said, the way a fancy interviewer would on one of those big news programs. Sometimes Douglas thought it'd go better for her if she just asked one question and then refused to talk for the rest of the hour. He'd been in that place long enough to know the inmates hated silence, feared it. They'd sing, yell, or say anything to fill it. But she couldn't help herself. She had designs on something big, the way a teenager gets excited about all the things they'll do once they're an adult.

Douglas could remember wanting to be a garbage man, then a hockey player, and for a brief period let himself imagine becoming a teacher. Where had all that gone? When did it end?

"I used to spy on my neighbor," he said. "Was that the body or the mind?" He looked at Tim, at the flaky patch on the man's jaw. Every inmate seemed to have psoriasis or some kind of allergic reaction to the poison they washed the clothes with. For Douglas it was his knees and elbows, so dry he could write on a chalkboard with them, his ass crack twinging all day long.

"Talk about that," Riley said. "Don't give up on yourself."

"I tried to see into her bedroom," Douglas said. There were seven minutes left in Group, and then it was his and forty other men's turn in the TV room, then he'd try to fall asleep, try to pretend the lights weren't on. "I tried to see what a girl did in her bedroom. How often she was naked. If she touched herself. If she, like, measured her boobs." He thought of his mother standing on her scale, her splayed toes, her shitty posture, the hunchback and the potbelly as she leaned over, squinting. "I just wanted to know."

"That's called being a pervert, homie," Pete said. "A Peeping Tom."

"Shh," Riley said, flapping her hand. The folders in her lap began to cascade. "Go on, Douglas," she said, catching them.

Six minutes left. "I had girlfriends, or"—he shifted again—"girls who liked me, wanted to do stuff with me." The men sat up, more interested now. "But this girl, she was my brother's . . . They liked each other, I guess. And I could tell she didn't like me, not like those other girls. She didn't like being around me. You know how you can just tell when someone feels like that. She liked my brother Jayson, and it was like their first love, and her mom was the one . . ." He looked at Riley. She knew without him having to say it, knew his whole life story.

"This was Cece, yes?" she asked, her voice steady and controlled.

He nodded.

"Do you think," Riley said, uncrossing her legs, leaning over her lap, "that some part of you had an inkling of what was going on, that you knew your mom and her father were up to something, and you were trying to figure it out by watching the house?"

"No," he said. "I just wanted to see her naked. She could have been any girl."

Riley wrote something, nodding to herself. She looked at him again. "I don't believe that's true."

"Me either, bro," Pawel said. "You had a crush on her."

"And you probably wanted to have something over your little brother," Javi said. "That's how brothers are. Like I'd take a bullet for any one of my brothers but I'd also fuck their wives if the opportunity came up."

"Language," Riley murmured. She was still watching Douglas. He hadn't told her, had never told anyone, about watching his mother have sex with Cece's father. Riley knew he was holding back.

"Maybe," he said. "It doesn't really matter now. It's just something I did back then. I just wanted to see her without her knowing she was being watched, you know?" He sat back, hoping someone else would take the floor.

"Like I said," Pete said. "You were just a Peeping Tom."

"Did you . . . get excited by watching?" Riley asked. The men snickered, shifted in their seats.

"She means did you spank it," Javi said.

"Yeah, of course," Douglas said. "I was a teenage boy."

Riley nodded, took a deep breath. He knew she was gearing up for something. "Did you," she asked, maintaining eye contact, blinking rapidly, "ever watch your mom like that?"

Of course he did. He'd had enough time over the years to think about his relationship with Jackie, with the ways he watched her to figure out how he was supposed to be, what she wanted from him, the ways he felt in thrall to her moods. He'd watched her too closely. But she'd let him.

"My mom was lonely," he said. "I felt like that was our fault. Us—her kids and my dad. I felt like if I just watched her, maybe I could figure out what it was she wanted. Maybe I could give it to her." He was parroting a theory of Riley's, that as a child his concern for his mother had turned into an obsession, that boys often have a fierce love for their mothers, a rivalry with their fathers.

"You were in love with her," Riley said. She was pleased. "You wanted to be the one that made her happy."

"You wanted to fuck her," Pawel said. He was often in a combative mood, saying shitty things while examining a cuticle so he could pretend he wasn't being aggressive.

Riley waved her hand impatiently. "That's beside the point," she said. "Every boy wants to lay with his mother. Those feelings are the most natural thing in the world." She looked at Douglas. "Did you feel loved?"

He thought of what he wasn't saying, of his mother on the swing that day as he watched, her bony spine when she dropped the coat. "I know what you want me to say," he said. Four minutes left. "She made me feel a sort of torture that I know you want me to explain to you but that I am unable to explain."

"Don't let yourself off so easy," Riley said. "Deep within what you just said is something very real."

He laughed. "You're so full of shit, Riley."

"Hey," Javi said. "Respect."

Douglas's stomach churned. He shifted in his seat again, his foot knocking over the dregs of his coffee. He watched it trickle out onto the floor.

"All I'm saying," Riley said, "is after all the work we've done, you still don't know why you did what you did, right?" She waited, but he didn't answer. He knew if he stood, if he approached her, began yelling at her to stop, it would mean solitary, a tiny dark room with shit caked on the floor.

"Keep talking," she said. "Tell me about the torture you felt."

"Okay, fine," he said. He willed control into his voice. "I will fucking try. She made me feel like I should duck or put my hands up or back away, and then she made me feel guilty for feeling like that, because as my mother she could see it, she could see I just wanted out, but now I know all kids feel like that, all kids want to get away, it's the natural order of things to grow up and leave, but she . . . needed me. And at the same time, she could be so funny, and she didn't care all that much about our grades, and back before she lost the weight and started going around with Cece's dad she was just a mom, a normal mom, I see that now. Why couldn't I see it then? I watched Cece because I wanted to know what it was like at other people's homes. I just wanted to see something else. But then it became this thing I couldn't stop doing, and Cece was never even naked and she never touched or measured herself but I imagined myself there, walking into her room, the look on her face, the fear, how I could reassure her and show her she didn't need to be afraid. I just kept watching her reading or sleeping or putting stuff away and she seemed the kind of normal that made my whole world feel like it was going to crash down on my head. It was something I wanted, my whole body wanted it, and that's what I thought of that morning, how that quiet time in her room was gone for her, gone forever, and that was because of me."

He'd stitched the whole thing together from what the other men had said in Group, all of them obsessed with their own loneliness, how they were misunderstood or unique because of it, how they did their desperate things because they had no other choice. Some of it was true.

"Okay," Riley said. "Now tell me why you went to Cece's house, why you brought a crowbar."

"Damn, I didn't know it was a crowbar," Pawel said.

"Shh," Tim said. They all waited, leaning toward him.

He thought he was saying the things his mother wanted to hear. *I love you, you're pretty.* But he was just a kid. *I love you so much, Mom.* "I was just a kid," he said. He wanted Jackie to walk away from him and for the floor to open up and swallow her, as if she was never there to begin with. He wanted to orphan himself, erase himself, forget himself. "I do not want to remember these things," he said. They wouldn't change a thing, being remembered. "They won't change a thing." His father never wrote, never visited. He had other kids now. "Some people get do-overs." He was standing over Riley now and she was doing her best to hold her folders in place and keep his eye, to show him that she wasn't scared of him, didn't believe deep down that he was a misogynistic (a word she'd taught them) killer who she'd pushed too far. "Some don't." The other men started to shift and grumble.

Javi stood, putting his hand on Douglas's chest. "Back up, man."

He sat. That morning. Everyone wanted to know if Jackie told him what to do, and when, and with what. He kept rubbing his eyes. They felt wrong, like there was a bright light shining just beyond a fog, and he was trying to see through all of that. Or maybe that's just how he remembered it, now. There were buckets with garden shears and gardening gloves caked in mud. Tools hanging on the wall. A rusted rake propped in the corner. His legs ached from crouching so long. He smelled bread toasting, and then the smell got so strong he got a headache. He'd given up in the middle of plenty of chores. Said *fuck this* and wandered off. The lawn half-mown. The dishes still hot and soapy. His room cluttered and smelling of socks. But he stayed in that garage. He saw it through.

"My mom, she had remade herself into this new person. This thin stranger. But she was proud of it, we all could tell, the way she walked around and the clothes she started wearing and how our dad seemed a little afraid of her. She had surprised herself, and she loved when she'd run into people and they'd say, you look so different! She stopped eating. She chewed ice cubes all day long. She went too far, we all could see that, but she was also happy." He put his face in his hands. He had rough calluses from working in the prison yard; his palms were like sandpaper on his cheeks. "And I felt," he said, speaking into the darkness of his hands, "like I could relax a little. She didn't need me so bad anymore."

"This is important," Riley said softly. He could feel the men holding their breath.

"She was crying. She'd done all these chores, which wasn't like her." He forced himself to drop his hands. He looked at Riley. "I was angry."

Riley nodded. She looked around at the men. "A mother's emotions are difficult for children to process. In a child's mind, things are often black and white. Children look for solutions, for good guys to come in and stop the bad guys."

Did she tell him what to do? He tried to remember. He saw her and he saw her mouth moving, saw her weepy face. It had started when he was a boy, so little he didn't even have the words to ask her if she was sad, and why. He just knew he'd

put a stop to it. He'd make her feel better. "My little protec-
tor," she'd say, holding him close. Her softness, her warmth,
all for him. "She was happy, then all of a sudden she wasn't.
It felt . . ." He couldn't think of the word.

"Unbearable," Riley said.

"As soon as it started," he said, "I knew I had it all wrong."

"Mm," Riley said. "Your conscience kicked in." She
reached toward him, as though she could touch him if he
were closer. "That's a good thing. Know that that's a very good
thing."

He shook his head. That wasn't quite what he meant. "I
mean, I wished I was hitting Jackie instead."

The men nodded to themselves. He heard someone mut-
ter, "Jesus."

When he left the garage, there was blood in his mouth.
It had a tang, and he swallowed it down.

Later, in his cell, he waited. Sleep didn't come easy and his
mind raced, going over what he'd said in Group and how much
of it was true. He draped his arm across his eyes, trying to
block out the harsh lights that blazed all day and night. He
waited. Eventually, if he was as still as he could be, his body
would overcome him, and he'd drift into a dark sleep, a sickly
orange light creeping in at the edges. He'd dream. In his favorite dream, he was digging a hole with his brothers.

Adam

A pleasant crumpling sound, the sound effect he'd chosen from a list of dozens to signify that there was a notification on his dating app. It was Cece's idea to try online dating. She'd set up his profile the previous Christmas, visiting him in his new apartment. She bought him a skinny Christmas tree, dressed it up with twinkle lights and colored balls, made him pose next to it in a cardigan, holding an empty mug in the shape of a reindeer. "Look less bored," she said. He tried. In his picture he is just about to smile, the mug crooked in his hand. Almost immediately, the notifications came in at a steady pace. He still had his hair, though it was mostly gray, and daily runs kept him trim and lightly muscled. He was regional manager at his company, a comfortable position that allowed him to travel and afford his luxury American-made SUV, and his bedding was from a high-end home furnishing store (also Cece's doing)—nearly every woman he'd brought back to his apartment had commented on it. He was courteous and attentive. He held doors, he asked questions, he paid for dinner and drinks. He favored brunettes, no younger than forty, who emphasized travel and fitness in their profiles, and who seemed like they laughed easily in their pictures. Women who wanted companionship, an evening out, a nice man with clean sheets and good bourbon who didn't demand a blow job but accepted one with real gratitude should it be offered.

He pushed himself up from his chair, where he'd been about to drift off to sleep, watching a television show from his youth where a boy with divorced parents became a teenager. The TV was muted; the actor who played the boy seemed to use his mouth to convey any emotion. He smirked, sucked in his lips, pawed at his mouth with the back of his hand. His phone was on the small table where he ate his meals. There was a lighter ring in the wood where he set his drinks. Cece brought him a set of coasters from a brewery she frequented in the city where she lived, but Adam couldn't remember where he'd put them, and didn't care all that much anyway.

His phone showed a notification from a woman with wavy blonde hair. Even in the small thumbnail image he could tell she wasn't what he was looking for. Blondes, strawberry blondes, women with naturally flushed and cheerful faces, they reminded him of her. Of Theresa.

"It's okay to live a little," Cece had said as she finished setting up his profile. "No one likes to see a lonely old man." She was right—he did worry about becoming just that, a wrinkled fart who tried to engage the mail carrier in conversation about the weather, who no longer clipped his toenails because who would see them?

He knew Jackie lived with someone, and it galled him.

He lived a little. He had probably slept with twenty women that year alone. Rarely did they want a second date with him. He really didn't mind. He couldn't fathom keeping a conversation going beyond get-to-know-you drinks and postcoital murmuring. Already there were danger spots. Some of the women asked if he had children, and if he said yes, the inevitable next, if unspoken, question was *Where is the mother?* Finally he settled on *She passed away, many years ago. Very sad,* and moved quickly on to asking his date more about her life. Sometimes he said he didn't have children. It was just easier that way.

The crumpling sound again. A woman with thick, dark eyebrows and full lips had messaged him: *Hi ;)* He messaged her back and they made plans to meet at one of the three places he took dates. How had he never run into one of them, out on a date with a new woman?

"Not that it would matter," Theresa said from her corner. "Your mask changes. How can they keep up?" She was in the dress they'd cremated her in, the long shapeless thing that was in style when she died, patterned with small flowers, the black-eyed Susans Cece had placed in her hands at the funeral drooping now, petals drifting to the floor and disappearing. A shadow fell over her eye where the dent in her head was. Adam walked to his stereo and turned it on, the radio blaring. One of those new hip-hop songs where the guy sounds like he's so bored, he can barely move his mouth to make the words. He closed his eyes and counted to thirty. When he opened them, Theresa was gone. He kept the radio on as he wept, his mouth open in a silent scream.

The restaurant had an aquarium wall and blue lights around the enormous square bar. Adam preferred sitting there, closer to the bartenders, ordering appetizers and drinks and facing his date so his knee could brush hers. Amanda's eyebrows were even more striking in person; they moved on her face as though they had their own set of reactions. She gestured wildly as she spoke, her hands whipping inches from his face, her eyebrows rocketing up and down. Theresa never followed him anywhere, but he could feel her back at his apartment, watching the door, waiting for him to return. Just behind

Amanda, a man in a fisherman's sweater sat sipping his drink
slowly, and something about the way he angled his head made
Adam feel like he was listening in, amused.

"May I say something?" Adam asked, interrupting her.
The man in the sweater signaled for another drink, took out
his phone and began scrolling.

There was a way these things went, Adam had learned.
Either he spent the evening talking, and he and his date parted
with a hug, or one of them had to take it up a notch. He did not
want to go home to his apartment, or at least he did not want
to go home alone. The TV, the stereo, those barely drowned
her out anymore. She lurked and she stared.

He'd been running what he wanted to say over and over
in his mind. Amanda took a dainty sip of her drink, her eyebrows in anticipatory formation.

He brought a hand up to her face, letting his thumb gently rub her bottom lip. "You have the juiciest mouth I think
I've ever seen," he said.

She brought her hand up, laid it lightly over his. "I've
always been told I have a big mouth," she said, laughing. He
knew better. She was proud of those lips, maybe even had
them synthetically plumped from time to time. They were
two drinks in. If it were four or five, she'd probably take his
thumb in, suck it a little.

She pulled his hand away, held it in her lap. "You know,"
she said, biting her bottom lip, looking up at him from under
her eyebrows. "I know a little something about you."

"Oh yeah?" he asked. He wondered if he could free a
finger, press it in the V of her crossed legs.

She nodded. "I look up every guy before I meet them. I
looked you up." She was still holding his hand, still waiting
for him to react. He pulled free.

It felt like the lights had dimmed, the music surging, steel drums and some kind of horn blaring from the corner speakers. A bartender shook a cocktail too close, a violent clawing sound. "That was a long time ago," he said.

She cocked her head, took another sip of her drink. Adam wondered if he should signal for the check, if he should excuse himself to the bathroom but leave out the back door. She put a hand on his knee. "It's okay, Adam," she said. "I don't bite."

He felt an alertness behind his zipper that revolted him. Always, his whole life, he was helpless in the face of touch. His body betrayed him. He was desperate, starved, for someone to touch him. To keep touching him. For hands to cover every inch of his body. The man in the sweater was looking plainly at him now, his eyes darting from the back of Amanda's head to Adam's face.

"Do you know this guy?" Adam asked, pointing behind her. Amanda didn't turn around.

"I told you," she said. "I'm careful with who I meet." She made a careless gesture, her hand waving over her shoulder, but her eyebrows remained arched, tensed. "That's just my producer."

The man reached over her, his hand outstretched. "Jesse," he said. "We'd love to ask you some questions."

Amanda squeezed his knee, leaned closer. "We're interested in getting the real story from you. You could let the world know who you really are."

"We're true crime buffs," Jesse added, coming to stand beside her.

Adam stood, letting Amanda's hand drop away. "The only people who say that," he said, reaching for his wallet, pulling out some bills, "are people who've never experienced a tragedy."

"Oh, come on," she said. Her eyebrows were straight, her eyes dull. "You're a big boy. You can choose to be a good sport about all of this." She patted the stool he'd just vacated. "Let us buy you another drink." She raised a finger, turned to find the bartender, and he left, pushing his way out the door and into a warm night.

He'd seen the TV special about the murder. He'd watched Jackie try to paint herself as a victim, as a people-pleaser who didn't feel allowed to say no. "I lost my best friend," she said. He'd forced himself to watch, the TV on low because sound traveled so easily through the thin walls in their shitty apartment and he didn't want Cece to hear. They'd been there a year already, a ground-level unit in a complex by the newly expanded highway. Cece was finally sleeping again.

He wasn't.

Back then he took whatever came his way because he believed he deserved it. A man in the bread aisle at the grocery store spat at his feet. *Scum of the earth*, the man said, while his wife pulled at his sleeve. Cars slowed as they passed the house while he tried to pack it up. Tentative knocks on the door, growing louder, angrier. *We know you're in there*, the voices said. They yelled at him in the street, they called his work, they showed up in the parking lot and followed him to his car. *Coward. Scum. Pussy.* Mr. Delmonico told him in a flat voice how he watched a group of teenagers stab the tires of Adam's car. "Did you call the police?" Adam asked. Mr. Delmonico crossed his arms. "No." All of it, Adam received, accepted, didn't fight. It was what he deserved, a skewed bit of justice that his life was miserable because Theresa was dead. But Cece didn't deserve any of it. Didn't deserve to watch that man spit at him, didn't deserve to come outside ready for school only to see the tires slashed. He put in for a transfer at work, a great relief for all involved, then packed his clothes and the urn, told Cece to take whatever she wanted, and drove them a thousand miles away from that garage.

Still, the story never faded. The episode re-aired nearly every year after, first to add that Douglas wouldn't be facing a trial, then to add that Adam and Cece had moved and to please respect their privacy, and then it aired in the summer when everything was a rerun. Now, in the age of podcasts, it seemed one popped up every six months or so, retelling the lurid tale of a mother murdered by her husband's lover's teenage son. He had aged and didn't look so much like the old family photos they showed in the special, so there were fewer and fewer people who recognized him that way, but still. "True crime," a redundant oversimplification of what actually happened, was a genre that was only growing in power.

"Did you do it?" Cece asked him once. She was eighteen or nineteen, and he knew she was quietly researching what had happened, trying to see it from her own eyes rather than his. He owed her that, he deserved it. "Some people think you did it, that you framed Douglas." She looked so much like Theresa, the flush across her cheeks when she felt nervous or excited, her strong arms and long fingers, those eyes that deepened in color when they really focused on you.

"What happened was my fault," he said, his voice hollow and far away, "but I didn't kill her." She looked at him and he allowed it and he didn't move.

"I believe you," she said, and her face crumpled. He wanted to hold her, wanted to say he was sorry, but he wasn't owed that. Instead, he let her walk away, shut herself in her bedroom.

That theory was everywhere now. Douglas had a fan club of women who believed a teenage boy could never have committed such a crime, that statistics show it's usually the male partner who harms or kills a woman. Once, a reporter was crouched outside his door. She stood quickly and held up a small mic, her hand shaking. "Adam Linden, we're making a podcast called"—the name escaped him—"and we want your side of the story. Did you kill your wife?" He wasn't that hard to find. He hadn't changed his name or anything. Still, it rattled him, that a stranger would take the trouble to find his address, show up at his door, ask him about Theresa. "She was a real person, you know," he said. "She was a mother." He slammed the door in the woman's face, sank against it as she rained tepid knocks. Finally, she left. It probably made great listening. A month later, he moved to the new apartment, paid a service to remove as much information about him and his whereabouts as possible from the Internet.

He knew where Jackie lived, had even found images of the place online. Modest apartment complex that looked like it was made out of toothpicks and tongue depressors. He could even see cracks in the pavement of the parking lot. He knew she lived with a man, knew the man drove a years-old Toyota truck.

He knew Douglas had been transferred to a newer prison, knew it was something about black mold and an inmate dying that led to the old prison being closed. He knew Douglas had multiple online supporters, lonely people who created groups where they plotted ways to get him released early and talked about their own childhoods, how hard it was to have a slutty mother or too many siblings, how they'd heard Douglas had been caught masturbating and had been beaten by his father.

He knew Nick had a new family now, that he lived on the other side of the country. He knew all about Jayson's company, his beautiful girlfriend, his large, expensive dog. He knew Nathan had a nothing job at a whatever company. All he knew about Samuel was that he liked bands with singers who wore black nail polish and fishnet shirts.

He knew these things because he made sure he knew them. He checked in as often as he could, reading any new bit of information with zeal.

The last time he saw Theresa alive, he'd begged her not to tell Cece. They were standing in the kitchen whispering, though Cece was out, studying at a friend's or staying late at school—he couldn't remember what. The sky was dark out the kitchen window at Theresa's back. He watched his reflection, his slumped shoulders, the way he kept baring his teeth in anguish. "I'll do anything," he said, "to keep this family together." He meant it. He had no lingering feelings for Jackie, only a deep wish that he could simply pivot, face a different direction, and everything they'd done would be gone. It should have been that easy. "I'm sorry," he said. "I'm so sorry. I'll never stop being sorry." She was cold, unmoved. The phone rang and she picked it up. She twisted around so she could talk without looking at him. When she hung up she said, "Carissa said we can stay with her for a while. She's coming this weekend to help us pack." She walked past him, collected the kitchen trash bag, then disappeared into the garage to dump it in the can. He slept on the couch, left early so he could be out of the house when she woke. A few hours later, she was dead.

"Where were you?" he was asked by the cops, angry people that confronted him, and Cece. "Why weren't you there?"

"At the time," he said, or didn't say, or only realized now, "it seemed like the right thing to do. I was just trying to do the right thing."

His apartment was cozy; why did he ever leave? A tiny screened-in porch had views of the golf course and a man-made pond and, beyond that, a row of trees that seemed older than the town itself. He watched their tops sway gently, like tentative men on a dance floor. Theresa was agitated today, pacing from corner to corner, casting glances Adam's way like she was going to say something if she could just find the words. He dialed Cece.

"Do you ever see Mom?" he asked her when she picked up. He could hear some noise in the background, some laughter, something whooshing by, a distant siren.

"Sorry, Adam, it sounded like you asked me if I ever see Mom." She'd called him Adam for a decade now, setting an appropriate distance, he guessed, another thing he deserved.

"I just mean—does she visit you?" He watched Theresa crouch, her back to the wall, her elbows on her knees. He knew from past experience that she could hear both sides of the conversation, that she was listening intently for Cece's answer, for her voice. Tears crowded his eyes.

"Hang on," she said. He heard her cover the phone, heard her say something to someone, then he listened to her little panting breaths as she quickly walked somewhere. He had not been up to the task of being a father, a husband, but here she was, alive, breathing, out somewhere with someone, living her life. Now the tears spilled down his cheeks. "Okay, sorry, I just had to get somewhere quieter. No, Mom never visits me," she said. "But sometimes, you know how the sun will sometimes burst through a cloud, and all those rays shine down, and it looks like something you'd imagine a god making, or maybe the entrance to Heaven, or . . ." He waited, watching Theresa taking in Cece's words. "Or sometimes I'll see something moving out of the corner of my eye, and I'll look, and it's this amazing butterfly, or a hawk, or just something ordinary, like the other day I saw this mom give her kid a balloon, and tie it around the kid's wrist, and the look on the kid's face as he looked up at his yellow balloon . . . Anyway, those are the times when it feels like Mom is, I don't know, nudging me. Saying, *Look, Cece! Look!* Like she always used to, you know?"

They were quiet, Adam trying to swallow down the grief, so grateful to Cece for not hanging up, Theresa shimmering in and out of focus, her hand over her face.

"Why?" Cece asked. "Does she visit you?"

Adam watched as Theresa shook her head.

"No, no," Adam said. He wiped his face on his sleeve. "I guess she doesn't. But I'll be sure to be on the lookout for yellow balloons from now on."

"She'd like that," Cece said.

"Thank you for taking my calls, kid," Adam said.

"Of course." She said it quickly, so quickly that Adam knew she hid herself from him, hid her rage and disgust and maybe, now that enough time had passed, her true apathy for him. "I have to say," she said, and he heard that she was back outside now, was nearly ready to end the call, "I thought you were going to tell me that you were seeing Mom, that you were actually seeing her. Like you were losing your mind or something."

He forced himself to chuckle. "I'm sure that day isn't far off."

When they hung up, Theresa walked toward him. She got so close he could see the delicate layer of dust on her skin, could see the wrinkles at her knuckles. She bent so they were face-to-face. He stared into the shadow where her head was dented. The eye under the dent was deadened, milky white and staring at nothing, but the other one gleamed and searched deep inside him.

"Why don't you want her to know you visit me?" he asked. "Why don't you visit her? Let her see you, hear you?"

Her dress moved, caressed by air only she could feel. He could sense the shape of her legs, her knees. She had been so real, once.

"It's better for her that I'm a memory," Theresa said, her voice layering over itself, echoing. She raised her lip, bared her teeth. Her gums looked swollen, deep red at the edges. "You know what I want," she said.

"You're just my guilty conscience," he said, but he did what she asked. Raising his fist as high as it would go, he brought it swiftly down and punched himself in the throat. He did it again. Theresa's hair looked soft, almost touchable, but the dust was there, too. Not dust. Ashes. Their marriage, their home, the years they lived next to the Stinsons, his affair with Jackie, that was a lifetime ago. Several lifetimes. "You're not really here," he said, his voice choked. Again he raised his fist. He closed his eyes and thought of the evenings when Theresa lit tall candles and they ate pizza off their wedding china and she let Cece have glass after glass of soda as the sky turned from blue to soft pink to purple to a deep blanketing navy. What more could he want?

Samuel

Everyone had a story that was their defining thing. Unfortunately for Samuel, his story preceded him. He was the boy whose mother was a murderous slut. No honor in that, nothing to turn into sympathy. Everyone just looking at him like he'd be forever the progeny of a beast. And her children were probably the reason she went so crazy! Everyone knew women went a little crackers when they became mothers. What, was he unable to shut up? To get his own milk? To entertain himself for five minutes so his mother could think? No, no he was not. And so, she'd lost it.

Over the years, Samuel grew. He got fat, truth be told. He was heavy in every sense from sixth grade through tenth. He ate whole sticks of butter on numerous occasions. He buttered his pizza. He ate sticks of butter like corn on the cob. No one cared. No one saw. His father left, moved to a different state and eventually married a woman, Jenn, who had three children of her own. Meanwhile Jackie moved him and his brothers to an apartment with carpet the color of his earlobe, then a slightly larger apartment with cold tile in every single room. Jayson left, then Nathan. His mother worked at Walmart and then 7-Eleven and then a series of family restaurants where the portions were absurd, enough for three people to share. She had a boyfriend named Henry, a man with glasses and out-dated facial hair, a goatee that was nearly a perfect rectangle. Samuel sometimes picked up the phone to call someone and couldn't remember the number. His father was always in the other room, maybe try back later. His brothers, there were actually three of them. His life was solitude. His life was out of his hands. Every window just showed his own face looking back at him. There was nothing out there, there was only in here. He turned up the television. The louder it got the harder it was to hear. His mother came home and said she'd thrown Henry out, looked at Samuel as if it was significant to him especially. Samuel had some sort of realization that no one needed to eat all the time. In fact he could go for days without eating. He chewed gum instead. He could make an almond last an entire class period. What was an appetite, really? It seemed absurd, this urge to put something into his mouth, chew it up, swallow it, crap it out. Much more efficient, more powerful, to just move on. And on and on and on and on.

It would have been better if she'd gone to jail. He fur-nished her cell in his mind: metal bunk bed, dripping cinder block wall, a greasy-haired matronly psychopath as her room-mate. She'd hate the mirror above the sink. Too small, not clear enough. Or maybe she'd like it. Maybe it'd be a relief. He knew that feeling well. If he didn't know what he looked like, then maybe he wouldn't have to wonder if how he looked was acceptable to everyone he met. It is what it is, a favorite saying of hers in the Before. But she didn't go. She wasn't in jail, had never gone to jail. She'd left that to Douglas.

Did Samuel hate her? He'd watched plenty of television shows where the teenage kids yelled at their parents or glow-ered at them or just wanted to escape. It was a cliché, a given, that he as a teenager would be an ungrateful shithead. But yes, he hated her. He hated when she tried to act like a normal mom and he hated when she got that look on her face that begged of him something he didn't want to give. He hated how she walked like she was afraid she would make too much noise and he hated how she asked his opinion on where to hang this, if she should wear that. He hated that he was the one left there and he hated the thought of her being all alone. He wanted her to suffer but it made him sick to think of it. Eat? You want me to eat? He truly couldn't fathom how anyone could.

He had sores on his hip bones from where his pants chafed. His hands hung huge and paw-like from their bony wrists. He swallowed and swallowed and swallowed. He was at his job at the bookstore, typing a search term into the computer at the info desk. Starting at his ankles, up to his knees and pelvis and spine and neck, his body gave way inch by inch until he found he was lying on his coworker Rafael's shoes. He'd noticed them before, how they looked soft and childlike, not the generic black dress shoes the other employees wore, how this told him something about Rafael. Now, as he lay on them, he was grateful for the cushion. Rafael's face was at the very top of a narrow tunnel, peering down at Samuel with a look of anguish. *Rafael*, he tried to say, *I am tired*. He could smell the coffee in the cafe, he could smell that Sal was heating up one of those Asiago pretzels, he could smell chocolate and orange and something deeper, something like woodsmoke, and it felt wonderful to just let go and be folded into the memory of standing around the fire pit in the backyard with his brothers, how they held their arms out to keep him from getting too close, how even Douglas did that, how they were just kids in a backyard. It felt very possible to do a small thing, like snap his fingers or recite something, in order to arrive back inside himself in that backyard, but he couldn't figure out what that small thing was. He wanted to type it into the computer at the info desk or ask Rafael. *Please*, he wanted to say, *I've got to get back*. He smelled the dust in the carpet, the fabric softener in the cuff of Rafael's khakis. He closed his eyes and tried praying, but all he could come up with was *Please*.

Samuel had never, in his entire life, allowed himself to be led anywhere. He could remember distinctly fighting back, especially After, with all his might. No, he would not put on clean socks. No, he would not stop slamming the door. No, he would not walk next to his mother in the grocery store. No, he wouldn't like anything to eat. No. No. No. His hands, at rest, curled into fists. His body tight, ready for anything.

But there was nothing left to do but let Rafael lead him around by the elbow, into the break room for his things and through the store, everyone back at work tidying or shelving or ringing up the customers, everyone avoiding Samuel's eyes out of pity, and it felt like a gift. Rafael held Samuel's backpack on his own shoulder, pushed through the heavy wooden doors and led Samuel out onto the sidewalk, where the night air smelled of the fajitas from the place next door and the sky was the color of the denim lonely mothers wore.

"Well," Samuel said. "Thank you." He reached for his pack, but Rafael held tight. A small yellow circle wavered on the man's forehead and Samuel was confused, unsure what was happening. Was Rafael stealing his things? And then he realized: the old-timey lamp above them was reflecting off Rafael's forehead, and he was intent on bringing Samuel home.

"I live in a bad place," Samuel said. He was renting a room in a small, drafty home that had been divided into bedrooms and "kitchenettes," which were in reality foldout tables with a hot plate and a sink directly next to the bathroom. He was thinking specifically of Leslie, the neighbor woman he drank with, the large vein she had on the back of her left hand, the way she had begun to wait for him by her window. The way the blinds in that window had become permanently warped, so often did she pull them apart to look for him. The way he'd allowed her to leave her hand on his knee, both of them watching the lurid colors of cable news, the shouting somehow muted and the colors loud, the way he'd fallen asleep and had a dream that his mother was smoothing the hair from his face. Leslie's hair was stringy, the color of tree bark; she wore hiking sandals but didn't trim her toenails. They rarely spoke but they weren't alone and that was all that mattered. Samuel hated it, but those nights with Leslie had become his routine. He did not want Rafael helping him home. He did not want Rafael to see the missing third step leading up to the porch, the broken pane in an upstairs window, the hatchback parked at the curb with the blue trash bag for a back window. He did not want Rafael to see Leslie and he did not want Leslie to see Rafael. He did not want to answer questions, or anticipate any, or apologize, or feel defiant in the face of pity. "I mean, I can make it home on my own," he said, and more directly reached out for his pack.

"I'm not taking you home," Rafael said. He had a trace of an accent, something that felt familiar, like a voice in a sitcom. "I'm taking you to mine." He stepped closer and put his hand on Samuel's shoulder. "You should not be alone, my friend."

It felt like a kindness, a blessing that Samuel's knees didn't buckle for the second time that evening, that he didn't melt into Rafael's shoulder and weep. He had not expected it, not any of it, and he weakly followed Rafael to his car and folded compliantly into the cramped front seat. It smelled of strawberry chewing gum and the windows went up and down on hand cranks, and Samuel turned his head to watch as they drove by his own car, dusty and neglected, its floor mats and cupholders lined with trash, its tape deck that only worked half the time, its smell of breath and scalp and sweat. He realized, as his eyes snapped closed against it, that he was ashamed.

"Marcy wanted to call an ambulance," Rafael said, the *tick-tock* of his turn signal filling the silence. "I told her you would not want that. I hope I did not misspeak." Marcy was the manager that day, a sturdy woman with a thick sponge of hair and visible whiskers on her chin. She had a wicked sense of humor and an allergy to drama that Samuel respected. Nothing fazed her; he'd once watched as she'd walked a raving homeless woman out the door, her arm linked in the woman's as if they were old pals, nodding her head and saying, *Is that so?* until the woman was outside, quieted, blinking in the sun. If Marcy wanted to call an ambulance, how bad had he looked?

"Thank you," he said.

He'd chosen to live in Orlando because it was so far away from his childhood home, because it never got cold, because he could easily transfer to the bookstore (and to a new one in a different city should the feeling strike him), and because it seemed just anonymous enough to allow him to fade permanently into its mediocrity. The room he rented now was his third home since he'd moved to Florida, each dingier than the last, and sometimes he told himself he was in the "real" part of the city. Not the Disney-fied, palm-tree-laden, generic bland-o-rama, but where the actual human beings who worked the jobs to keep those areas cleaned and fed lived. In his heart of hearts he knew he was heading down. The bookstore was his only saving grace. It was intellectual, even considering the dumbass gift books and new age du jour and customers who planted their asses in a chair and stayed all day and only left when the store closed, leaving stacks of books and papers and cups and tissues in their wake. Even despite all of that, Samuel felt special. Elevated just a tiny bit. Like the rest of the world stood in the gutter, and he was on the curb. Rarely, a customer came in and asked about something worthy. Even more rarely, Samuel was at the info desk. But when those two things collided, and he found himself searching out an obscure tome by a writer who'd disappeared into obscurity after publishing it, Samuel felt like he was allowed proximity to the divine. At home he had a stack of thirty-seven pages of a novel he'd been writing for years. No one knew. Sometimes, he typed his own name into the search bar, imagining what it would be like to help a customer who wanted to read his book, his words.

They were driving through the "historic" part of the city, with its brick pavers and random fountains and trees dripping with moss. The sky had deepened into navy, purple at the horizon. Leslie would be expecting him home in the next hour or so, would have no idea why he wouldn't show. Something loosened inside him. He cracked his window, then rolled it all the way down. He wanted to stick his head out like a dog. The air was light, its scents skipping around playfully, orange blossoms and fried food and cut grass and exhaust. He wanted to ask Rafael where they were but he didn't want to speak. He let his hand drift along on the currents of air. Rafael turned and a trio of boys scattered from the road into the grass. He turned again and Samuel looked back to watch them, how they began kicking a ball between them, how the tops of their heads and newly broadening shoulders were bathed in light from the streetlamp, how they disappeared behind a tree and Samuel felt sad to see them go, but then Rafael parked in the driveway of a bungalow with red trim. "My sister lives there," he said. "I stay in the garage." He pointed at a small building just behind the house, also red-trimmed, with old-timey folding garage doors and pretty flowers clustered in pots around the sides. Samuel followed Rafael, feeling weakened yet romanced by the evening, despite himself. Rafael unlocked a narrow door and gestured for Samuel to go in.

"I've got leftovers," Rafael said, snapping the light on. "I like to make a big pot of something and feast all week."

Indeed, it smelled of cooking, something with onions and garlic, and Samuel found himself hoping for some sort of home-made pasta sauce. The garage was one large room, sectioned cleverly into distinct areas. The kitchen had a high wooden table; the seating area was also the sleeping area, with a couple of club chairs and a daybed, and there was even a desk against the far wall with a genuine typewriter on it. Not a vintage, just-for-show thing, but something that had been state of the art in the eighties, a beige workhorse that looked spiffed up and in use, judging by the papers stacked alongside it. It was bright and tidy in Rafael's home. Samuel had never suspected. In truth, he'd never considered Rafael's home life. His soft black shoes and earnest way with customers made him someone easy to ignore. Not like Drew, one of the stock workers, who had a face tattoo and wore T-shirts with different pictures of his pit bull printed on them. Or Shiva, who hennaed her hair and had been known to cry openly as she busied herself at the registers. What did it say about Samuel that he found it admirable that she didn't seek out comfort from others, but bore her tears in silence and never let it affect her ability to beckon the next customer in line? Rafael always seemed, to Samuel, part of the scenery. As recognizable as the face of a clock. He had a framed concert poster in the entryway, a band that was infamous but had always frightened Samuel a little, or at the very least required he gird himself before listening, and that said something about Rafael, too. He contained legions. Or he was legion?

I am legion. Jackie used to say that, smirking as if the world were taking her too seriously.

"You can take your shoes off," Rafael was saying. All at once Samuel realized he'd be seeing Rafael out of his wimpy shoes, and he felt a flutter of something he couldn't identify. Nervousness? Not quite.

"I won't stay long," Samuel said. "You can take me home whenever." Already he was planning it, how he could be dropped off at home or call himself a cab, could walk the mile or so to the store for his shift the next day and drive home and rejoin the battered loop of his daily life.

"You are fine, my friend," Rafael said. He padded over in black socks with lime-green seams at the toes and handed Samuel a short glass of something the color of topaz. "This will taste like shit at first, but stay with it." He tapped his own glass to Samuel's.

It was true, it burned immediately and smelled of gasoline, but as it crept down his throat it felt as if the sun were rising to meet it. He felt a gentle warmth spreading and he nearly sat down. "Oh," he said, and Rafael laughed.

They ate bowls of gummy pasta in a tangy sauce with crusty bread they tore with their hands. They balanced their dishes on their knees and watched *Jeopardy!* It wasn't unlike Samuel's evenings with Leslie, only he didn't feel that anxious, harangued feeling that he should be going, that he should be anywhere else. That if he stayed he'd be sinking another inch deeper into some sort of metaphysical bog, and was losing the will to do anything about it. In truth he'd been sure he'd have to sleep with her, sooner rather than later.

Sometimes he'd startle, shaving or driving along or changing the toilet roll, and he'd wonder just who felt sorry for whom.

"I have never seen you eat," Rafael said. He was clattering the dishes into his small dishwasher. He winked at Samuel and kicked the dishwasher door closed behind him. "It's good to see you can."

Samuel's face grew hot. He was used to being called skinny—his brothers called him Noodle—but no one talked about his eating. "I don't like to eat at work," Samuel said. This was the truth; the break room table was sticky and barnacled with dried bits of food from his coworkers' sandwiches and wraps and leftovers. The entire room smelled like the inside of a microwave and even as he couldn't look away from how others ate, it horrified him to think of what he would look like, how he wouldn't know there was a glob of mustard on his cheek or a jagged bit of lettuce in his teeth.

Suddenly, a memory: his mother dipping the tip of a spoon into a little tub of yogurt and then squirting the tiniest jewel of honey onto it. Precise, methodical, even loving. There couldn't have been more than a fingernail's worth of food on the spoon. His mother closed her eyes in ecstasy.

But it couldn't have been like that. He often hyperbolized in retrospect. He could ask Jayson or Nathan, but they had the opposite problem. All their memories had been honed down to the basics: place, time, characters present. Did they remember the Thanksgiving Jackie served pizza and scraped all her cheese into a pile that looked like innards? Was it the same one where their father said he was going out to find a turkey sandwich but didn't come back until the next morning, sheepish and reeking of cigarette smoke? *I don't know, man, all I remember is the pizza.* Or *Yeah, that sounds familiar but my memory isn't all that great, and anyway I gotta run, so-and-so's waiting in the car.* Samuel couldn't sleep until a memory became real, three-dimensional, until he felt as though he were walking through it. It was a comfort, like the way it felt good to probe soreness in his gums with his tongue. A sweet ache.

Rafael was bringing dishes of ice cream. He'd shaken rainbow jimmies over them. Who kept rainbow jimmies in their home? What sort of person was Rafael? His soft shoes, his soft belly and hands, his infuriating patience with elderly customers who left their crumpled tissues on the info desk as they dug through their pockets for the name of something they'd written down. And why had he brought Samuel here, to his home? Why not a cafe, or a coffee shop, or simply to the curb outside an urgent care?

"Thank you," Samuel said, setting his dish on a side table. He felt painfully full, his stomach loudly gurgling. He'd eaten what Rafael had given him because he'd felt shaky, starved. He'd swallowed some bites whole. He was embarrassed, but only mildly. He looked at the man, the way he ate neat bites of his ice cream, licking the spoon clean before going back for more. Samuel leaned over and placed his hand on Rafael's wrist. He waited for Rafael to look at him, and then he leaned in and kissed him. Neither closed their eyes. Samuel remembered doing something similar with his brothers, forehead to forehead, pushing and pushing back, staring into Nathan's or Jayson's or Douglas's animal irises and refusing to be the first one to give. He was always the first one to give.

"It is okay, my friend," Rafael said. His hand moving in circles against Samuel's sweater. Could he feel the bones poking through, a source of shame and pride for Samuel? Samuel put his hand to his mouth. The tears came when they came, he'd learned that well enough by now.

"I'm not crying because I kissed you," Samuel said.

"It is okay."

"I don't like being around people," Samuel said. "I'm not very good at it." It was pitch dark outside, the light inside Rafael's place spoiled somehow. Samuel wanted to squint, or shade his eyes. He took the napkin Rafael offered him and pressed it to his face.

"You have no family nearby," Rafael said.

This was, of course, true, yet Samuel couldn't imagine how Rafael knew it. He looked at the man. His hand was hot on Samuel's back. Why had he kissed him?

"You have no visitors at the store," Rafael said. "You bring no one to the parties. You receive no phone calls. You put nothing on hold for a sister or an aunt to pick up. You never bring leftovers to eat. You never purchase presents or ask for Marta or Denise to wrap anything. You don't leave early and you don't come late. You never miss a day. You take no vacations." He took his hand away. "This is how I know you have no family nearby, my friend. And this is how it has come to be that you feel you aren't good at being around people."

"You don't understand," Samuel said. He nearly laughed. He'd forgotten himself. He had an almond in his pocket; he'd been trying to save it for his ten-minute break. He should have just eaten it as he searched for—what had it been? A book about raising toddlers? Historical romance? A police procedural? But that hadn't been the real reason, had it? Had he really fainted because he'd fucked up by not eating the almond?

"I'm sure there is a lot I don't understand," Rafael said. He stood. "Would you like to go to the bed?" He held his hand out and Samuel took it.

A woman with stringy hair wearing a Christmas sweat-shirt had asked if he knew of any good murder books. Leaned her elbows on the counter and pulled her hair over one shoulder, the way Jackie used to. It came back to him just as he pulled Rafael's shirt over his head. He'd closed his eyes. That had been his big mistake.

Cece

Where Cece lived, the seasons were not subtle. There was no softening of the light. When snow fell it did so all at once, as if the sky could no longer hold it. The summers arrived one morning each June, roaring heat, days that never ended, until one morning in September when there was a chill followed swiftly by a freeze.

How had she ended up so far north? How had she come to look forward to short, gray days, snow up to her knees, the cold so brutal it had a sound, a snapping in the silence, a creaking underfoot? When she tried to answer that, she inevitably thought of him. Of Jayson. The snow was white at first but within a day or two it was grit and dirt and ash. At work she sat with her back to the window and typed in little boxes and larger boxes and medium-sized boxes, and her computer screen reflected the window just over her shoulder, the sky the color of her computer screen plus a little blue or a little gray. She typed and sent. Copied and pasted. Deleted and undeleted. She skimmed replies; she made edits. She missed him. But also, she'd been without her mother for long enough that she knew missing someone meant nothing. It changed nothing.

And it had been years. She wasn't a girl anymore. She went through a phase of wearing pantyhose, the way her mother had when they went to church on Christmas Eve, or when they'd gone somewhere special for dinner. It felt like a line she had to cross in order to fully embody her womanhood. Her mother, in the pantyhose, sidestepping—what? It was a moment Cece thought of often, a nothing moment, run through so many times in her mind that it had started to fray and tatter, but if she searched very closely the feeling was still there. Her mother, a woman in nude pantyhose, doing a little hop over something on the sidewalk. Maybe it had been an early moment of consciousness. Like, that's my mother and I am me. We are not the same. That's my mother and mothers laugh a little at themselves as they narrowly avoid stepping in/on/over . . . what? It had become absurd. She could never have put it into words, could never have even typed it into a medium-sized box. *That's my mother.* Delete. *Was my mother.*

But it didn't matter. And yet. If she added up all the seconds, minutes, hours, days in which she wondered what Jayson was doing, where he was, whether he was wondering about her, then Cece had spent half her life imagining him. There were times she wondered whether she'd even be disappointed should she discover herself there in front of the real him. Would his hairline have receded? Would he have awful breath? Would he be disappointed when he looked at her? Would they still know each other, their truest selves? She thought of him while driving (playing catch with him in the side yard, before they'd kissed, before their parents had kissed probably). She thought of him while washing dishes or doing homework or skimming emails (his profile, how his jaw was manly yet boyish and made her heart ache). She thought of him while masturbating (how tentatively he'd touched her breast under her shirt, how once he had, he let out a little scoff, as if it had been too much to ask of him), though she'd never been very good at getting herself off. She spent a long time deciding whether she deserved to, whether it would even happen, whether she was pathetic to live alone, never go out, her phone collecting dust and her television chattering away, and now here she was having sex alone, thinking about Jayson, hoping he was thinking about her.

She went on dates, set up by coworkers with their equally lonely or strange friends or cousins or neighbors. They watched each other from under their eyebrows, they fidgeted with silverware or itchy collars or napkin rings as though they were children banished to the children's table. "I googled you," a man with an old-fashioned name (Roger? Brandt? Something like that) said, plucking something off of the checkered tablecloth stretched before them and flicking it. Cece knew what that meant, though she herself avoided doing the same, knowing all too well how someone might want to keep parts of themselves hidden.

"Oh yeah?" she said, craning her neck for the waiter. She had cash in a variety of denominations, to make splitting the check easier. They always wanted to split the check, or they sat back and watched her pay the whole thing. One man nodded approvingly at the tip she'd left, then as they left pushed his way out the door and let it swing shut in her face.

"That's right," he said. He wanted her to start talking, but it wasn't clear what version he wanted. Her grief? Her rage? Her acceptance, her stoicism?

"Good for you," she said. She began counting ones onto the tabletop. She left a wad of money next to her plate. "Keep the change," she said to the man. "You've got something on your face, by the way," she added. It was true, he did, and she'd been holding back a rushing river of disgust the entire dinner. The air outside was hot and faintly wet and smelled of chicken, and Cece nearly shouted his name. She was done waiting for him to find her. She was on her way to find him. She could google Jayson. She could give in and finally do it. *I'm coming for you*, she wanted to yell. Just wait for me.

They'd had sex one time, after everything happened, huddled together at the base of a tree. They'd walked there in a daze, looking for a place to be together, alone. It hurt and they had no idea what they were doing, but it felt like the last time. Cece hid her face in Jayson's shoulder, pushed him deeper in. Douglas pled out soon after that; everyone scattered to the wind. "It's not that long until we're in college," Jayson said, panting. Cece knew what he meant though she hadn't bothered to imagine a future for herself. What was the point? She'd seen the end of things already. She'd thrown a clump of dirt onto her mother's coffin; she'd allowed words forgiving her father to tumble out of her mouth like wet dice. She was supposed to, what, keep going? It felt silly. Still, she had pushed her face into the space between his chin and shoulder, and she'd matched her breaths to his, and she'd ignored how a tree root was digging into her back, and she'd nodded so he'd know she'd heard him, so he'd believe she'd be right there with him, somewhere in the near future, free and together.

Douglas said the words "I hit Miss Theresa with a crowbar. I hit her until she was dead," with a small smile on his face that he seemed embarrassed about, a boy playing at manhood, unsure if any of it was real. "I feel remorse for my actions and I ask the judge for mercy." He'd stumbled over the word *remorse*, pronounced it "ree-morse." His hair was shaved off, his ears sticking out at extreme angles, his elbows and collarbones and jaw all painfully sharp. He was just a fuckup, a weirdo. A dime a dozen. And yet he'd murdered her mother. He'd killed his mother's best friend. He'd butchered a woman who'd made him pizza rolls and popcorn and once, in a brief crafty phase, a Christmas stocking with his name in green glitter glue. Cece hooked her leg over Jayson. She would not let go. She would never, ever let go. But within half an hour they were walking back, holding hands, and parting at a bus stop. She could not walk all the way back, to his house. She could not be near the place where her mother had choked on her own blood.

Cece had had sex dozens, maybe a hundred times since. She'd slept with Nathan one drunken night when he was in town on business, a fact that made her wince every time she thought of it. She pretended he was Jayson. He was close enough to Jayson. And with all of them, Jayson was who she saw when she closed her eyes in supposed ecstasy, when she played the part and made the noises and begged for more.

In the end, he was easy to find. There he was on Facebook, on LinkedIn, on Instagram, even Twitter. He'd been right there the whole time. His hair was longer, almost past his chin, and lighter. He was the founder of something called Life Awaits. He smiled in every picture. Cece felt a strange pressure behind her eyes. She wanted to cry. She opened her mouth, took a deep breath. In some of the pictures he was in sunglasses and she could see a woman with long, dark hair in the reflection of his lenses. It was hard to tell for sure, but the woman seemed pretty. She seemed happy, possibly even laughing. She was normal, unbroken, whole. Cece sent him a friend request, feeling brave and alone. Then she went out for a drink and brought home a gap-toothed man who fingered her and fell asleep against her stomach. She kept her eyes closed when he gathered his things and left, daylight peeking through the gap in her curtains.

She opened her laptop. Her Facebook picture was of a sunset and she did not allow herself to be tagged in photos. If he was looking for her, he wouldn't find anything of her there. True crime was huge, on TV and podcasts and in a million documentaries with the same ominous title cards. Her mother's murder was told over and over again. People contacted her, messaging her on Facebook and a few times at her work email. She'd been asked to be on podcasts about the case. *We just want to hear your perspective, give you a chance to talk.* She deleted each message and blocked the senders. Putting up a single picture of herself, updating her status to announce that she'd just had great drinks and a great time at some brewery, that was an invitation to the world to assume things about her. To assume she was okay, that it was okay to rehash what her mother's body looked like when it was found, to send another message asking Cece if she forgave Douglas.

For a long time, forever, Jayson was the only one who seemed like he understood. It had happened to him, too. But he'd been out there all this time, waiting to be found. It was she who was hiding.

Nathan

Hi.

Nathan pushed the stupid blue up arrow to send the text. He scrolled up like he always did, admiring the string of *Hi*'s that he added to, methodically, every single day. Cece never responded.

Hi

Hi

Hi

Hi

Hi

Hi

Hi

Hi

It began to look like a ladder, with a small person beside it, staring eye level at the ladder in confusion or wariness or rage or fear or bemusement, depending on Nathan's mood at the time. Today his mood was: tired. The little *i* with his strange ladder should just pack it in, lean the thing against the nearest house, walk or drive or bike away, never to return. He was still scrolling up, slowly. There had to be over a hundred *Hi*'s. He'd watched plenty of movies where, against all odds, a character hung in. Kept showing up. In fact, one of the movies may very well have been called *Against All Odds*. He wanted an outcome, an ending, permission to roll the credits.

And then what? was always the argument to be had. He'd deal with that when he got there. When there was a response, something for him to work with. He pressed the button to turn his screen black and tossed the thing onto his bed like it hadn't cost over a thousand dollars. Like he wasn't still paying it off.

In the shower he masturbated quickly, hunched over at the end and staring at his own feet as he came. Then he turned the water cold and washed up, his body seizing and then tingling. It had become a thing, this routine. The text, the shower. The coming under the hot water, the washing under the cold. Always, he toweled off with a lump in his throat. Was it normal? How would he know?

He checked his phone. A text from Nora, a picture of her smiling, a gold scarf around her neck. *On my way in*, she'd written. *Want a coffee?* It was baffling to him, this ability of hers to send him pictures of herself smiling, or looking off into the distance, holding something up close to her face with an excited or squealing expression. It was sweet, childlike. Sometimes it touched him, that near-innocence, brought him back to a time when all he wanted out of life was to shoot hoops, ride his bike, stay out of the house. Did she see that in him? Was she attracted to that sort of clean, easy boyishness he knew he could project? It was the haircut, so short on the sides that his ears shone, or it was the company softball team he coached, or it was the way he brought his lunch in a brown paper sack every day, or it was all of that. He looked at himself in the mirror. He was okay-looking. Mainly he just kept it all together. Combed, pressed, clean. He was choosy about his deodorant scent. He had muscles in his thighs and abdomen. He could objectively see why Nora, technically his boss—a woman so forthright and collaborative (words he'd used in the annual review passed around to all her direct reports) that you couldn't help but like her—had set her sights on him. They'd kissed, chastely, in the supply closet after hours. Did she know he'd had to tuck his erection under his belt? Neither of them knew how to proceed. And he was still texting Cece, still swallowing when he thought of her.

Surprise me, he texted back.

He went back to the Cece texts, hoping to see that she was typing a response. Nothing. It had been months, almost a year, since they'd run into each other at a bar in the icy city where she now lived.

He was there on a work trip, a phrase that sounded fancier than it was, which was a collection of meetings held in hot, dry conference rooms, bagels heaped on a platter and cream cheese sweating in its tub. The inevitable post-meeting drinks with the client, everybody loosening up and laughing too hard. He didn't know if he was supposed to offer to pay or if they were. They were all drinking Manhattans, which tasted medicinal, unpleasant, but round after round appeared. Eventually he roused himself, stood, said he was hitting the bathroom, but veered toward the bar. He wanted a simple beer, a glass of water. And there she was. Cece. A thick mustard-colored scarf piled around her neck, a double glass of something brown clutched in her hand, which was freezing cold and dry when she grabbed his arm and said, "Nathan?"

He felt sick, all of it rushing over him at once. The ambulance driving slowly away from Cece's house, silent, its lights flashing. His mother saying, *I don't know. I don't know what happened.* Cece drifting through the hallways at school, and him not knowing whether he should say hi. The cops saying they followed the trail of blood to his house, waiting until Douglas came home, blood dried in his hair, on his face.

She wrapped an arm around him. He could feel her laughing, could smell the whiskey on her breath.

"I can't believe it's you," she said, releasing him. He turned to acknowledge the woman she'd been talking with, to introduce himself, but Cece pulled him away, pulled him toward the back of the bar where there were high, small tables. "You know," she said, unwrapping her scarf, her hair crackling with static electricity, "for just a tiny moment I thought you were Jayson."

No one had ever said they looked alike, but maybe there was some familial similarity, something overtly Stinson about him. He didn't know if he'd have looked twice at her, couldn't sense anything overtly Linden about her. She sat, the stool tipping under her. Her scarf pooled on the ground. She didn't notice, was looking at him, something in her face he'd never noticed before, a relaxed, dreamy quality in her mouth. She was drunk.

He remembered a night as a child when he was supposed to be asleep, but he couldn't settle, the sheets sweaty and twisted but the air too cold when he threw them off. He lay still, willing darkness to crowd in from the corners of his and Sammy's room and quiet his mind. Then he heard voices. His mother, laughing wildly, something she rarely did. He crept to the door and listened. Theresa was there, too; he could hear muffled laughter. He'd noticed she often held a hand over her mouth and he'd begun to do the same, did it now as an adult, a modesty in the gesture that felt noble. He followed the sound, edged right up to the doorway into the TV room but just outside of the light. They were on the floor. He took in that they were barefoot, that their hair fanned around their heads, that the TV was showing a late-night talk show, that they were now laughing so hard that they were silent. Bottles on the coffee table. They turned toward each other and clutched shoulders. For a moment, he wanted to be part of it. To ask his mother what was so funny, to understand, to be included. Just as quickly, he wanted Theresa to get up, to sit on the couch, or better yet, to go home.

"Shh," he hissed from the dark hallway. And then, louder. "Shh!" He ran for his bedroom, pulled his bedding over his head. He waited, but nothing happened. In the morning his mother poured their cereal and drank black coffee, like always, ruffled his hair as he walked out the door to catch the bus.

He never liked being around drunk people, the way alcohol either muted or heightened their personality. But this was Cece. He tried to see her through it, tried to remember the girl he once knew. He'd forgotten how green her eyes were. He wiped his clammy hands on his pants, bent to retrieve her scarf.

"Oh, yuck," she said. She bunched the scarf and left it on the edge of the table. "So, do you live here now, or . . . ?" She leaned sideways to see beyond him. "Are you with your friends?" He looked back at his clients, at the skinny-necked man, Vernon, who'd insisted on the Manhattans, his colleague who preferred to talk while his thumbs moved furiously over his phone.

He explained about the work trip, about the forced Manhattans. She smiled a lot, and nodded, gave him her full focus, but her hand trembled as she raised it to signal for another drink. Her scarf began to drift toward the floor again, and he lunged to catch it, knocking her glass into her lap. For a moment, they were nearly forehead to forehead. This close, her skin shimmered. Strands of her hair clung to the stubble on his cheek. He pulled away.

"I'm sorry," he said.

"Why," she said, setting the glass on the table. "Did you kill my mother?"

Cold poured from his throat into his stomach.

She laughed, throwing her head back and slapping the table. "Your face!" she said. He could see that she was mostly faking it. He turned from her and went back to his clients, apologized for coming back without refreshed drinks. The music had gotten louder, and he was glad, because he felt sure his voice was shaking.

"We were just calling it a night," Vernon said. They shook hands and left. Nathan paid for the drinks with his company card, left the bartender a large tip. He shrugged on his coat, too thin for the freezing blast that he walked into as he left the bar. All along he felt something creeping, pulling at him, urging him to look behind him, see if she was still at her table, was watching him settle up, was following him out the door, her scarf forgotten on the floor. He called a car and waited, his back to the bar. By the time the car came she was there, and he held the door for her as she folded herself into the back seat. When he sat next to her, she took his hand. He felt sure she was crying, and emotion crowded in his throat, stung his eyes and nose. In the wash of streetlights that ran over her face as the car gathered speed, he saw that she wasn't.

In his hotel room, she lay her coat over the desk chair, took her time pulling off her shirt and pants and socks and bra. In her underwear, she climbed into his bed and pulled the covers up. He took off and folded his own clothes, left them in a neat pile on the dresser, and lay on the other side of the bed, on top of the covers, afraid he was misunderstanding something.

"You can have some blanket," she said. She made an opening, her arm arched, and he slid in next to her. Their thighs touched. He kept his arms by his sides. "You can touch me," she whispered. She pulled his arm over her, his hand resting on her back. He felt her nipples graze his chest. She moved closer. It would be so easy to join, just a swift pushing down of underwear.

"You're drunk," he said. He shifted away from her. He did not want her to feel how much he wanted to move closer.

"Not anymore," she said. She pulled him back to her. "Not so much anymore." She moved gently against him, rocking her pelvis, like she was trying to burrow deeper into the mattress. It lulled him. He wanted to fall asleep inside her and wake up inside her.

"We shouldn't," he said. That she wanted to be near him, that she didn't throw a drink in his face or run away or stand on the bar and shout that his brother had murdered her mother, it was wrong. She was looking for something, asking him for something that he couldn't provide. He felt sorry for her. He felt her warm breath on his neck. "You don't want this from me," he said. He forced himself to throw back the covers, to sit in the chair, her coat at his back. He folded his hands over his erection.

"You can stay," he said. He wondered where she lived, what it looked like, if she lived alone, if she was lonely. He thought of Jayson, his comfortable life, his fancy company, his pretty girlfriend. How he always gave the impression he was listening too closely. How he started, in the months after everything happened, to get up and run miles and miles in the darkness, how he still did it, his face angular and drawn, as though he was staying fit but it exhausted him.

"You should stay," Nathan said. "You can have the bed." He turned off the lamp that hung over the chair. Soft light from the parking lot flooded the room and he wondered if he should pull the shades. He would sleep in the chair, or wait until she was asleep and take a pillow from the bed and lay on the floor.

"I really thought you were him," she said. He heard her breathing, a sigh. "I thought you were Jayson. I never think about him." She sat up, reached over and switched on the light. In the warm yellow lamplight she looked like herself again, the girl who yelled over their fence and ate from their fridge and looked out the bus window at the same stretches of road, the same ball fields and strip malls they passed every day, turning every once in a while to say something to Jayson, to point at something so he could lean in and see what she saw.

"I think he tries not to think about you, too," Nathan said. She nodded. In the hallway, he heard the elevator doors slide open, then closed. She had goose bumps on her legs.

"You're cold," he said. He stood and waited until she lay back and he could pull the blanket over her. She held his hand and he let her, listening to the heat kick on and off, a car driving slowly into the parking lot. She tugged gently on his hand, and he slid in next to her, thigh to thigh, nestling his cock between her legs again, the blanket warm over his shoulders.

"I miss—" she said, and he kissed her. She pushed her underwear down, and then his, and guided him in. Quietly, they moved together.

In the morning, Nathan woke to the winter sun blaring in through the window. Cece was gone.

He checked his phone. Still no reply from Cece. They were playing at something, that night in his hotel room. He knew it, even then, that they were attempting to reclaim parts of themselves from Before. In the days after their night together he convinced himself that there could be something beautiful, something worthy, that rose from the devastation Douglas had left behind. This was getting harder and harder to believe.

She'd cried, her face against his shoulder, and he'd pretended not to notice. He buried his face in her hair, which smelled like weed and woodsmoke and plums.

Cece

There was a message from Jayson. He'd accepted her friend request. *Cece, wow*, he wrote. *How are you?*

It was a stupid question, a nothing question, but coming from Jayson it also felt sincere. She fetched a beer and drank half before she replied.

I'm okay, she wrote. *I had too much wine the other night and started going down memory lane. You know how it is.* She stopped herself from adding *lol*, which all too often felt like an escape hatch: Don't worry, I don't have a drinking problem! I didn't message you in a moment of pure loneliness. Lol!

They went back and forth, she filling him in on where she lived, what she did for work, and he describing the business he'd started in maddening jargon that was all the worse because he never mentioned his personal life. Never said *we* the way all couples did. He had that same boyishness, that earnestness, or maybe Cece was seeing what she wanted to see, or maybe he was doing to her what she was doing to him, editing himself into the character she was expecting. For example, he was up front about how pleased he was to hear from her. *I miss you all the time*, he said, right in the middle of telling her how he'd spent Christmas with his father. She didn't know if he meant it or if it was a platitude, if he pined for her the way she pined for him, the specific way his neck smelled and the feel of his forearms as she gripped them that day in the car, the way he kissed her like it was a question. The way he knew her as she was then, Before. How his hand was slightly larger than hers, and warm and dry, and how he wasn't embarrassed or shy to hold her hand. Did he mean he missed her because she was home to him, the way he felt to her? Outside her window, snow was falling sideways, crazed by the wind.

She turned out the lights and read what Jayson wrote, over and over. *My dad has these little kids now*, he said. *His wife is nice.* Never any mention of Jackie, or Douglas. His dad's house was big enough for the family, but visitors slept on the couch, and it was hard to sleep there and he found himself wondering why he was there, a grown adult, no longer a child, visiting this strange new iteration of his father's life. And then: *I miss you all the time.* And then: *Gotta go, big plans tonight!*

I miss you, too, she typed, then deleted. Instead, she wrote: *Big plans, huh? You proposing to someone?* He read it immediately, but he never replied.

Days went by. She made out with a young female coworker at the office happy hour, a monthly event at which everyone made poor choices, egged on by the endless open bar and the roaring fireplace and the fact that many of them were single, because theirs was the kind of job that held them in thrall by promising a collaborative work environment that actually meant "cultlike slavishness to the deadline, and the deadlines within the deadline." But there were fun snacks, and a tread-mill in one of the offices, and a shower, and there were the monthly happy hours. Cece had fallen victim to the coziness that started the evening too many times to count, the fire and the nifty drinks poured by very serious bartenders and the way it felt good to laugh in her coworkers' faces, how it felt good for them, too, how if you were outside it might look like they were all just screaming, teeth blushed with mulled wine, arms around necks and shattered glass everywhere, but truly it was a necessary catharsis, because it shamed everyone back into complacency, back into gratitude. They were employed and someone wanted to pay for their drinks. Look outside, look how freezing cold! We could be out there! Serena, her coworker's name was. Newish and eager, the way Cece used to be. *She'll learn*, they all said to each other, jaded laughs covering up the rage. Cece had gotten stuck in the corner somehow, a rookie mistake, because she'd have to ask six people to shove over if she needed to pee or to escape, and Serena was one of them, so close that Cece was sitting on half her purse and Serena's elbow kept digging into her ribs. It didn't take long for Serena to be drunk, too drunk, her V-neck splotched with the Midori sours she kept ordering, the V so stretched out, so painfully overworn, that Cece could see that she wasn't wearing a bra and didn't even need to. Poor Serena, she had no idea. Cece crossed and then double-crossed her legs, squeezing the urine back into her body, or so she told herself.

"I've been messaging my high school boyfriend," she said. If she turned the attention onto herself, maybe Serena would quit it with the drinks, and maybe Cece could get some water into her so she'd have to pee as well, and they could both ask everyone to shove over and then Cece could walk the mile back to her apartment, sobering up in the freezing cold.

"What?" Serena said. She looked at Cece and, just for a second, Cece saw that she wasn't actually drunk, or she wasn't as drunk as she was pretending. There was a shrewdness, a fear Cece recognized as a young woman's determination to hang in, to prove herself in these rituals that seemed male-dominated or just male in general. Drink. Drink more. Now drink even more. Now be a fool but don't embarrass yourself. And do it without seeming ugly. The waitress who brought more drinks looked like Jackie, the low ponytail and the eye-rolling and the pretty, tired face. Cece wondered if she truly remembered what Jackie looked like. Didn't she have curly hair, bigger boobs? Were her fingers short and stubby like the waitress's?

"What did you say?" Serena said, and it was clear she was making an effort to slur. Cece felt impatient that Serena didn't know anything about her, that there wasn't a shorthand between them, because she wanted so desperately to say, *That looks like Jackie*, and for Serena to have a certain look on her face when she said it. That was why she messaged Jayson in the first place, wasn't it? Because he knew everything. She looked down at her phone and there was nothing. She could get up and climb onto the table and stomp over everyone's drinks and be out of there in a heartbeat, *in two shakes*, as her mom used to say, and she could at the very least call her father. She could say what happened and she could say, *I miss her so fucking much*, and she could let it land like a brick to his head because she had never allowed herself to hurt him like that, not ever, because if she did he'd know there was no turning back, and even though that was true, Cece needed to know there was someone out there who hadn't given up on her.

"What?" Serena said again, her face shaped into something conspiratorial, something in on it, and Cece felt for her, felt for Roslyn stuck humoring Will and his endless chatter about politics, felt for Kari and the way she had to baby everyone because she was in HR and she couldn't seem too threatening, felt for Micki and Sarah and Britt and Fabiola and Amika, because all of them said sorry before they began speaking, and Cece said it too, all of them falling over themselves to have a say without saying it too loudly, too bluntly, too readily.

Or maybe Cece was just thinking of her conversations with Jayson. All of them, the polite and sassy and funny messages, all of them poor masks for what she actually meant: *I need you.* She opened her Facebook app and wrote it and sent it, and then she drank Serena's drink and asked for another and another and another, and by last call it was just the drunkest of them left, and Cece played one round of spin the bottle in which the bottle landed on Serena and their teeth clashed together and their tongues slipped around and Micah and Zack cheered them on and high-fived. She did walk home, the cold burning her cheeks. She'd never thought too long about how Jackie was somewhere out there. What was the point? Where did it leave her? The ice and snow were loud under her footsteps, so loud it sounded like violence. Her lips felt chapped and bruised. Idly, she thought about killing Jackie. Driving to where she was, murdering her. Jackie pleading with her to stop, but letting herself be eased to the ground, her hands weakly batting at Cece's arms.

At home she plugged in her dead phone and drank hot water from the tap, trying to get warm and sober up. Her socks were wet at the toes and she pulled them off and left them where they lay. If anything, she felt even colder.

There were messages from Jayson, stacked atop each other on her home screen.

I'm worried about you, he said. *I can tell you're not okay.*

He said he had a girlfriend and her name was Kyla and she knew about Cece and what happened when they were kids, knew Jayson loved her and always would.

What the fuck, she wrote to him, *does this mean?*

She considered holding her head under the faucet, considered a cold shower, considered walking outside barefoot into the ice and bathing herself in the ever-pinkening sunrise. What was the saying? Pink sky in morning, some sort of warning? She sat in her bed, listened to her roommate begin shuffling around in his room, remembered she'd promised to buy coffee on the way home and hadn't. Her throat felt raw and she realized she'd been laughing and screaming into her coworkers' faces, that she'd have to chime in on mockups and memos and deliverables as if she hadn't told her boss to shove a tampon up his ass, and he hadn't laughed with shocked, pleased delight.

Jayson hadn't read her message yet.

I'm not okay, she wrote him, *but I'm also fine.*

Kyla. What kind of name was that?

Cece fell asleep and when she woke up she'd realize she'd slept too hard on her shoulder, and it would ache halfway into the next week, when the invite for the next happy hour would ding into her inbox and she'd have stopped checking to see if Jayson had replied yet, stopped asking around if anyone else wasn't receiving messages, dialed her dad's number and hung up, dialed the number to the house on Hot Springs Drive and listened as a confused-sounding older woman asked if this was Diana calling, said that it was okay, Diana didn't have to be afraid.

Cece knocked softly on her roommate's door, but he was at work. His room was neat as a pin, everything just so, his bed made and the pillows fluffed, vacuum lines in the carpet. He'd told Cece he used to get depressed, but his meds made everything seem more possible. Cece often wondered if they only helped him get even more tight-assed, if they pulled taut any slack and made him believe it was all under control, finally. They were in his spotless medicine cabinet, set primly in their orange bottle on a paper doily so tiny Cece wondered if it was from a dollhouse. The pills were enormous. Cece held them in the palm of her hand, weighing them. One by one she put them back, deciding each time. Was she trying to feel better, or was she trying to stop feeling?

Her roommate came home and she had three left in her hand. "Honey," he said. He held her wrist lightly as he took the pills from her. He hadn't even taken off his coat. Jewels glittered in his hair. "Is it raining?" she asked. "No," he said. "You're just crying." They ordered pizza and they ate it on his bed, and Cece knew this meant she'd scared him, and she felt vaguely bad about it, but also like something had shifted, righted itself inside her. She didn't have it in her, in the end. To do what they had done.

Jayson

He was due to travel to a country he'd never seen before, and he'd been studying up, attacking the language and culture barrier the way he'd learned, by buying all the travel guides he could and watching random tourist videos on YouTube and subscribing and following anyone who seemed popular there, at least a million followers and no overt problem areas (racism, checkered past, support of dictators, etc.) and he was going to fly commercial and sit in economy even though he could afford much better, even though Dawn in PR said it was better to show financial solvency by flaunting it a little, even though he got motion sickness and a teeny bit claustro-phobic, because sitting in economy he could better observe people, those visiting and those returning, those worried and those excited. He could feel that he belonged, that he could listen well and speak even better, that he could help solve the problems he had become an expert at solving. He had a special neck pillow and special headphones and breath mints and travel socks and a download of Kyla's favorite meditation and morning stretch, he had granola bars made from ancient grains and cacao, he had dried dates in a little pouch and he had mint tea bags to settle his stomach and he had, in case of extreme boredom, his tablet with a whole season of Kyla's favorite show. He knew how to pack for weeks inside a single bag. He had learned the politest way of letting a seatmate know that he wasn't up for chitchat. He had music and his favorite pen clipped onto a brand-new journal. He had the promise of Kyla herself, arriving a few days after he would. He had the notion of asking her to marry him on a sunset boat tour that, he had been told, would cost him three times the going rate simply because he was American.

But he wouldn't be going, and the reason he wouldn't be going was because of his mother.

"Do you really want to get married?" Nathan had asked him at least three times. "Dude, are you sure?"

He felt as sure as one could be. Kyla was tall and strong and smart and beautiful. Her brows were straight and dark and her eyes were always searching his; her fingers were long and slender and her elbows and knees were bony and he could see the child in her, still, the serious, unflinching child who'd once fallen off her horse and limped the mile back home, where just before she fell unconscious she asked if someone would please make sure Freckles got the apple he expected after a ride. She grew up with money and she'd attended the sorts of schools Jayson read about in books, but she'd made her own way in the world, had bought her own small condo with money she made all on her own, and she cooked pies when she felt sad and she loved to read in bed and she was utterly whole in a way that felt precious to Jayson, something to be awed by, something to protect, though she needed no protection he could offer. And she loved him. She said it often and without reservation. She knew everything; he'd let it all out one evening when he felt prickly and annoyed and he thought he wanted her to leave but it turned out he wanted her to know him, to really know him. She'd been to visit Douglas, bought him whatever he wanted out of the vending machine. She'd sent

Jackie Christmas cards. She'd stuck around. He was lucky, so lucky. How could he not marry her?

It was just that it felt like he'd left something behind, something he'd been entrusted to carry, something he wasn't supposed to forget. It tugged at him, this feeling that he was pushing forward despite part of him being held fast to where he was. He'd been able to ignore it, to let it fade, but Cece reaching out had shown him he wasn't as clever as he'd thought. He hadn't escaped; he'd never escape. Cece wasn't okay, and when he thought about it for longer than a moment he knew he wasn't totally okay, either. Was anyone okay, he asked himself, but then he looked at Kyla and knew yes, there were people who were mostly okay. There were people who didn't worry so much about being seen as inherently good, trustworthy, upstanding, helpful, useful, moral, nice, smart, worthy. Who didn't divide their days up by the minute with tasks that would be proof of those qualities, who didn't ask and re-ask if something was okay, who didn't deprive them-selves of most pleasures because that was a slippery slope, or so he'd come to believe. Some people just lived their lives as best they could, safe in the knowledge that they didn't have a dark side to shun, they never had to confront emotions or situations in which they came dangerously close to a side of themselves they'd locked in a dungeon and oh what in the hell was he talking about? He was talking about Jackie. He was talking about evil. He was talking about the thoughts he hid from himself, the ideas of revenge or wounds or erasure. He was thinking about how good it had felt, that first time with Cece, how they'd fit together so easily, it was almost like lying down only suddenly he was inside her, how they'd both known exactly how to move, how she'd kissed like there was a sob trapped in her throat. Why was he thinking of these things? Sex with Kyla was great. Her breasts were just a tad too large to fit nicely in his hand, and it was more than he could bear some nights. Her abundance. But Cece. He saw her as the Cece he'd known then, a whisper of her as a child still in her face, in the cheeks and at the jawline, her eyes still trusting and open . . . He was broken, that was the point of all of it. He was strange and sad and no matter how hard he tried, how well his company was doing, how good he was to his employees and neighbors and Douglas and Jackie and his father and Kyla, he was still Jayson at soccer the day the cops drove slowly onto the field and pointed right at him. He was terrified and dumb and disgusted and relieved he had done nothing wrong. *It wasn't me. I didn't do it. I didn't know.*

It was Jackie's fault he wouldn't be going. His therapist asked him to repeat it.

"I am not going on the trip I'd scheduled. I won't be asking Kyla to marry me in four days. I am not going on this trip and I am not asking Kyla to marry me because I have deep issues related to my mother"—here his therapist, Dr. Kyriakos, which was his first name, interrupted him, so Jayson amended—"related to what my mother did, and if I don't resolve them, and the tangential but no less real issues I have with Cece"—his therapist hummed in disagreement, so Jayson again revised—"to the unresolved sexual and emotional yearnings I have for Cece, whose mother was killed by my brother as egged on by my mother, then I won't be the partner I know Kyla deserves and, down the line, I won't be the father I hope I can be."

He squinted at Dr. Kyriakos, who was scratching notes onto his yellow legal pad, his elbow jerking as though he was annoyed, put out, which never failed to put Jayson slightly on edge, even though intellectually he knew that with the angle of the pad and the pencil, his arm would of course have to move like that, that Dr. Kyriakos wasn't angry with him, didn't have the capacity or emotional connection to even attempt it, and he knew all of this because they'd worked it out over three hour-long sessions just when Jayson thought he'd been making progress. "My friend," Kyriakos had said, which was how he always referred to Jayson, "you are tense beyond your wildest imagining." He puzzled over that phrasing for days. Had he ever imagined his stress level? "You are consumed with being good, with being liked, with doing everything so right that the past becomes irrelevant." Irrelevant! If only.

Together, they told Kyla that Jayson would be taking a break. "From work," Kyla said, no question mark at the end, but Jayson could see uncertainty creeping in, her mouth curving up on one end and firmly pursed at the other. "Yes, from work," he said. "But also from everything else. Not," he rushed in to add, "because I want to. I don't want to take a break. But it's clear I need to. I want to be as whole a person as I can be for you."

"I see," Kyla said. She hated platitudes, vagueness. "No one on this earth is whole," she said, facing Dr. Kyriakos. "You, above everyone, know that." She turned back to Jayson, took his hands in her cool dry ones. "I'm worried you're setting unrealistic expectations. For yourself, and for me." She moved closer so their knees were touching. "I'm not a sweet little girl who can't handle pain or truth or"—she faltered, her eyes roving as she searched for the word—"whatever. You're putting me on this weird pedestal. You're making me feel like you don't actually know me."

Always, always he was comparing whatever she said to his memories of what Jackie used to say, how she'd behave. She'd gone through her silent phases, where she wordlessly handed them their lunches, their folded shirts, their backpacks, her robe open over her pajamas or clothes; she'd gone through phases of talking sharply to everyone she encountered: her family, the cashier for asking if she wanted plastic or paper, a neighbor in her way as she pulled into the driveway, the television when it wasn't tuned to whatever she wanted to watch. She had her sayings (*You win some, you win some, Crying only leads to more crying, You look good enough to eat!*) and she seemed, especially after she'd lost the weight, to want her boys to know she was a complicated, emotional person who'd stumbled into motherhood through no fault of her own. *How should I know? Well, what do you think?* She told them to *beat it* and *get lost* and to get out of her sight, but she'd touch their shoulders and ask what they were thinking; she'd loop the rest of them into conversations she was having with Douglas (*Douglas says no girls are that interesting to him. He's lying, right? He just wants his old mom to beat it, am I right? Jayson, tell me about Dougie's girlfriend. I know he's got one!*) She could be too real, because she was relentless and loud and she wouldn't let them leave until she was satisfied, but also, because of all that, she was somehow unreal as well. It was as though she was acting the story of herself out as she was writing it. Impossible to tell where the truth lay.

Kyla never reminded him of Jackie. He ran her every word through that sieve, was relieved each time to know that Kyla was just herself. Still, the anxious feeling never went away. Always, he waited for it to happen. For him to wake up and see that he was in love with a woman too much like his mother. He'd worked through this with Kyriakos. Going over and over his fears helped, but then he'd need to go over them again. And again.

He looked at Kyla. "I think I know you," he said. He pulled his hands from hers and put them to his face. He could smell the citrusy lotion she used, stamped faintly on his palms. The light from the room, from the sunlight in the window, made his palms seem orange. *Jaysie thinks if he can't see us, we can't see him, isn't that funny, Dougie?* Always, his mother was there. He pulled his hands away. "Or at least, I know what you aren't, and I don't think it's fair to love you for that."

Kyla looked at Dr. Kyriakos, back to Jayson, then out the window. He felt that he had gone about it all wrong, had turned the session into something fraught, his throat already hurting from a welling up of emotion and an inability to set it free. *No, no,* he wanted to say. *There's nothing wrong, here. Everything is actually just fine.* He wished he had the ring with him, wished he could show it to Kyla as proof of something.

He had forty employees. He had two separate assistants. He knew how they all saw him, because he'd worked tirelessly on his image with his PR folks. Young, open, serious but charming. Dedicated, handsome, going places. He thought of the burnt-coffee smell of his father. The old man never had an assistant, though there was a woman who always looked damp sitting at the reception desk in the front of the showroom, her knees together and her feet splayed under the desk, sucking on a butterscotch. He had condescending thoughts about her, about his father and his willingness to repeat the same joke over and over, about what the woman's crispy-looking hair and his father's poorly shaved jaw said about them, and he knew he should break these thoughts down with Kyriakos, to release them and understand that everyone, every single person, had their own humanity that was important and yet none of his business. Kyla cracked her knuckle and he had the wild thought she was trying to hurt herself. He felt like he was attempting to stir wooden blocks into something smooth.

"I see what's happened here," Jayson said, offering his hands up and out, as though they were holding a large bowl. "I'm not using the correct tools." This, Kyla could understand. Kyriakos ran his hand through his hair, down his thick beard.

He had piercing gray eyes; Jayson was convinced they never blinked. Jayson turned to Kyla and with revulsion saw that she was crying, her face dripping. "It's fine," he said. He forced two Kleenexes from the woven box Kyriakos kept into her hands. "Don't you see?" He pushed a trembling wave of hair behind her ears. His throat was dry; the ache had grown. The wooden blocks tumbled from his mouth, wrong, all wrong, everything all wrong. He found he couldn't stop telling Kyla it was fine, when what he meant was, *This? All of this? This whole hour and parts of the days leading up to it? Poof, gone.* He had the familiar feeling again, that his life was stalled, and it was stalled because he had stopped to ask a question. Fucking Kyriakos! Who was in charge here? *No one*, his mother mouthed. *No. One.*

That night, he bought a ticket. He studied Cece's latest picture. Snow, and lots of it. Her face framed in fur. He zoomed in, in, in, on her lips.

Mike Shasta

Mike Shasta ran into Jackie when she served him an Arnold Palmer at the Applebee's near his worksite. He hadn't seen her in decades, since back when they were both in high school 280 miles away from that Applebee's. He studied the small rectangular pin that bore her name, set at a slight angle just above her left breast, and because he knew her face before he remembered her name, he stared hard at it as he tried to place her.

"Sir," she said. She was laughing at him, and he was sheepish, and the whole thing became a story they embellished, each adding a tiny new detail, explaining to friends and acquaintances the amazing story of how they were brought (back) together.

She'd been a real teetotaler in high school, the kind of girl who pursed her lips at you if she saw you having any kind of fun, and Mike was always having fun. She got good grades and told everyone who'd listen how she was going to Europe as soon as she could. She wasn't all that memorable, really, though he heard she'd never gotten to Europe and instead had married Nick Stinson, also generic in his way (sweaty, big, nice enough) and had a whole litter of babies. Mike went to his fifth and tenth high school reunions and found himself groping and hot-mouthed with some old classmate or other, everyone high on fumes of nostalgia and treating it like their last chance to catch some tail. He didn't go to the fifteenth or twentieth, because he'd gotten married and had a kid of his own and life seemed to gray over for him, as though a years-long winter had descended, he trapped in the stockroom of his wife's father's grocery store and the kid asthmatic and ever fearful and, in his teen years, interested in eyeliner. It was his wife who suggested the divorce, maybe just to snap Mike out of whatever it was he couldn't shake, and it did the trick but not the way she wanted, because he agreed and walked out of the house into the sunshine and never looked back, and she treated him like a common criminal because of it. The kid began calling him Mike, not Dad. Picking black nail polish from his nails instead of meeting his eye. When the job came up a half day's drive away, Mike jumped at the chance.

Jackie was the kind of woman he could understand. Made it clear she had her own thing and he had his. Didn't want him to open doors for her or buy her flowers, but insisted he make dinner three times a week. She had one of those feminist vibes going, but not too man-hating, just enough where she didn't give a flip if he came home late or went out with the boys two nights in a row or forgot her birthday, so long as he apologized like a man and didn't care where she went all day every third Sunday.

She never said where in Europe she was going. That thought occurred to him from time to time. Not that she ever mentioned it now that they were together. She didn't.

Mike told the guys he was dating a grandmother and they all got a kick out of that. Not that the babies were ever around, but she had pictures, called herself a grandma on their first date. Kind of kinky. Imagine him, Mike Shasta, trying to get up a granny's shirt! But that all wore off in time. She was just

Jackie, her hair smelled like peaches, she had a trim waist and straight teeth and she stocked her fridge with his favorite beer.

Later, she confessed that the grandbabies in the pictures weren't hers. She'd seen the frames at Target, liked the look of the kids, liked imagining her boys had babies and families and gatherings at Christmas where they all wore the same red plaid sweaters. He had long understood that her boys didn't involve her all that much in their lives. He got it, understood why she would make something like that up.

Mike Shasta, if he was being honest, had experienced loneliness before he landed Jackie. He had a sparsely furnished apartment that felt like it was built from cardboard, a downstairs neighbor who clutched her purse close when she passed him in the hall, a tiny covered porch off his itty-bitty dining room, where he played guitar in the evenings and smoked a joint or two. Life had simply proceeded, day after day, Mike Shasta lost in the everyday worries of keeping a job, paying the bills, wondering about his kid (who had a new name now, a woman's name) with increasing plumes of anxiety in his gut. They were speeding by, faster and faster, the weeks and the months and the years, and now after the divorce time seemed to have slowed way down. A luxury he'd have killed for, back when they were all in the same house. *Just hold on here, just wait*, he always wanted to say. He couldn't get his bearings, couldn't get a full breath. Wanted to say to his child, *Hey, I'm no angel*. Wanted to let on that he knew how to party in a harmless way, but he never did say it, missed his chance, felt disgusted at the thought of connecting in that way. *Pick up this damn room*, he said instead. *Wipe that shit off your face. Get a hobby, get a job, quit being a drip.* The fear in his belly like fire. Would this kid ever be happy? What would it take? And now Mike Shasta had none of that. He had his small porch and the sun taking forever to set and his neighbor being carried out on a stretcher, a sheet over her face, her cats moving in and out of the open doorway crying like infants. He could text his kid now:

Hope you're doing good.

I am, thanks.

It wasn't nothing.

"Invite your boy over sometime," Jackie said often. "I'll feed him a steak dinner." It was touching, but Mike had the feeling if they had to deal with each other in person it'd ruin the tentative cease-fire they'd come to.

"I will if you will," Mike always said, because he knew that'd be the end of it.

"Accommodation is what you got," his buddy Troy said. Troy was the philosopher of the group, seemed to have kept a goatee just so he could stroke it as he thought aloud. "At a certain age, you don't have a relationship or a fuck buddy or a marriage. You have an accommodation. You get a warm body and she gets the same. Which is better than going it alone." He clapped Mike on the back. "Am I right?" The other men nodded and clinked beers. But it was more than that with Jackie. There remained the perfume of mystery, something she kept only for herself, something that made the seed of jealousy, of envy, appear inside Mike Shasta. Over time, it began to bear fruit.

It was easy enough to ignore. Jackie wasn't a touchy-feely sort but she was physical, brushing up against him when she had plenty of space to pass behind him in the bathroom, or leaning over him as he sat at the table going over his bills, her tits mashed pleasantly, her breath cool on his ear. She didn't like to hold hands in public or kiss hello but she'd be there in the passenger seat on the phone, her other hand rooting around in his lap, unzipping him. *Hey,* he'd have to say, sometimes. *Hey . . . hey.* She was unique, kept him interested.

Her birthday approached and Mike Shasta made an error in judgment. Didn't every woman want to be pampered, showered with presents and love and all of that? He'd been feeling especially grateful for her, for the way she'd sit with him during the game, comment on the players' hairstyles or whatever even as she knew what *pass interference* and *offsides* meant. How she shopped every Friday afternoon, how the pantry never felt bare, how she didn't get on him to pick up his wet towels or wash the car or whatever bee used to catch in his ex-wife's bonnet. Knowing he had her made him feel like he had some wind in his sails, like, yes, he wasn't all that great a father but at least someone liked him, at least he wasn't totally hopeless. He'd started calling his kid once a week, just brief chats, no pressure, using the kid's preferred name, and he owed it all to Jackie. She saw him and she accepted him, no catch. So he wanted to do something for her, wanted to make her feel appreciated, special. He wanted to throw her a surprise birthday party. He wanted to give her a ring in front of everyone, including her boys. Not that he meant marriage. Mike Shasta wasn't that clueless; he knew better than to think Jackie wanted to be trapped like that again. But still. A nice ring, something with sparkle, personality, nothing too gaudy.

What he did, his ultimate sin, was to go through her phone and find her boys' phone numbers, though he could only find three of the four. She talked about them often enough, Samuel, Nathan, Jayson, and Douglas, and he figured the other three could get word to Douglas for him. He sent a group text. He asked for Douglas to be included. He told these men he'd never met how much it would mean to their mother, how important it was for her to have her family there on her birthday. His heart swelled and his eyes filled. Mike Shasta imagined inviting his own kid. It'd be awkward—Jackie had mentioned how rowdy her boys had been back in the day, and his own quiet, weird kid might feel overwhelmed—but still, his kid could be a part of something important in Mike's life, see that Mike wanted it that way. He texted his kid, kept it simple, nonthreatening, no pressure or expectation, just a simple statement of when and where and the hope she could make it.

And that's where we leave Mike Shasta, the Mike Shasta that existed prior to Jackie coming home while he was making spaghetti in her kitchen and telling him he had to leave, that she never wanted him to darken her door again, that he owed her for a half shift at Applebee's because she had to leave early, tell her boss she was ill so she could come home and toss Mike Shasta out on his ear. Not that he didn't try. He apologized and begged and tried to hold her steady so she'd look in his eyes, see Mike Shasta, him, good old Mike Shasta who, exhausted by his divorce, was so easygoing that he couldn't even bring himself to yell back at her, shake her a little, ask her if she was crazy, all possibilities that felt like bridges too far for Mike Shasta. She broke free of him, threatened to throw a can of baby peas at his head, and he ran out and down the concrete stairs and into the parking lot. It was a gorgeous day. Warm but not hot. The smell of lilies and fried food. It was quiet and Mike Shasta listened to his every breath. There were no fewer than three bright-orange vehicles in the lot; something about that felt fortuitous. Where did she go on those Sundays? Didn't he have cause to storm around as well? To throw cans? Not that he would ever throw a can at a woman. She always came back tired and distracted, prickly. Some sort of obligation she dreaded and didn't want to discuss. He unlocked the driver's-side door and sat sideways, his feet planted in the parking lot. An attractive older woman in an apron and name tag nodded at him and got into her little orange car and drove slowly out.

There were plenty of fish in the sea for Mike Shasta. He was tall and trim and had a nice head of hair. He made decent money and he liked to go down on a woman. He kept his truck clean. He paid for dates; he couldn't stomach the idea of splitting the check. What sort of man split the check? Definitely not a man who used gel and liked the taste of pussy. Mike Shasta felt himself get indignant. His phone buzzed, a reply to the group text he'd sent. *My mom would hate that. No offense. This is Samuel by the way.* Mike Shasta had gotten it all wrong. He pulled his legs in. He didn't have very many things at Jackie's, nothing he couldn't just replace at any Walmart. He stopped for a submarine sandwich at the grocery store and he saw the woman from the parking lot at the next counter over, replenishing the donut case. Her hair was caught in a hairnet. "I like your orange car," he said. His heart was pounding; he didn't really know what he was doing other than some vague attempt at doing the opposite of what Mike Shasta would normally do. "I read once that lots of artists, their favorite color is orange." He held his sandwich like an axe. The woman nodded and thanked him and it didn't appear her English was all that good and then she asked Mike Shasta if he wanted a free donut from the day-olds and the whole thing made him feel silly, exposed, a hot embarrassment rushing up his neck and face followed quickly by the tug of exhaustion. What did he think was going to happen? What was his endgame?

He pondered these questions as he worked through his sandwich in his quiet apartment. He could smell the walls; he could smell the carpet. His whole world smelled like a white box, despite the sandwich. Mike Shasta had to ask himself: Did he want someone in his life? Someone to answer to? Someone to count on, to ask him to fix the drain or help pick out deck chairs? Or was it that he'd been conditioned to want it? He had a small, squat window above the sofa and it leaked white light down the wall, weakly, as though the sun could begrudge whomever she chose. Mike Shasta thought of his friends, of their wives and girlfriends, of the easy way his buddy Paul's wife, Sharon, gave him shit in the same moment she kissed him hello. "I hope you had your shirt tucked in at work." Of his friend Marco's girlfriend, Dana, a plump and easily blushing woman who nonetheless giggled helplessly at all their dirtiest jokes. Who offered a joke of her own on occasion, her voice going to a whisper at the punchline and her whole face the color of a strawberry. There were people out there, Mike Shasta assured himself, and that was the whole point. People were the point. A person needs people. Mike Shasta used some of the bread crust to blot the mustard from his chin, and then ate that, too. So, sure, it was society demanding he couple up. But it was also an ancient requirement, probably going way back to the time of the mastodon. A woman had her role and a man could not fulfill that role on his own. And vice versa, though, if Mike Shasta was being honest with himself, all the women he'd ever been with had seemed so much more alive than he ever was. So in tune with microscopic shifts in mood or weather or thought, so impatient with him that he hadn't caught on (his ex-wife) or so ready to clue him in on something he'd missed (his high school girlfriend, Mikaela, who he often tenderly remembered telling him what all the bases meant). He could see himself reflected in his television screen and with a start realized he had never even turned it on. Had sat hunched over his secondhand coffee table eating and staring at *himself*. His hair seemed wild, the way it did after sex, and he had to wonder if that was how he'd looked all day long. The window was reflected there, too, a bar of light hovering over his head as though Mike Shasta were perpetually having an idea. "This is just silly," he said, out loud, to the Mike Shasta shadow in the television. He took his trash to the kitchen, tidied up, and marched over to the card table where he had his PC and turned it on. Waited the long minutes it always took to get started. Double-clicked the Internet icon and waited some more. With two alternately curled and jabbing fingers, Mike Shasta put Jackie's name into the search engine. He figured out pretty quickly where she went every third Sunday.

Jackie hadn't killed anyone; even the prosecuting attorney admitted as much. Her son said the same. Mike Shasta looked at every photo of the boy available to him. He was handsome, in a squirrely way. As though he'd never understood the concept, couldn't sit still long enough for anyone to get a good look. This Mike Shasta surmised from the boy's first mugshot, the shadow from his Adam's apple, the way his eyes seemed to look directly at Mike Shasta and also what was behind Mike Shasta. There were two more pictures of Douglas, one from the hearing of him looking back over his shoulder as though the cameraperson had shouted his name, his hair too long and his jacket too big, and one from a more recent mugshot, where he'd widened and the muscles in his neck seemed to have subsumed that boyish Adam's apple. His mouth was open and his two front teeth were visible and he looked more terrified than he did in the other two photos. Mike Shasta thought of the time he found out another boy at school was pushing his kid around, of how Mike Shasta himself had been pushed around by a boy named Ken when he was in school, how Ken had made him feel terrified, hunted, angry, how he had wanted someone to do something about it and the only thing that had happened, at the end of the day, was that Ken's father had gotten a new job and they'd moved out of state. How the best-case scenario was to be ignored. How being invisible felt like the greatest possible outcome for all involved. And what sort of life is that? To want to disappear? Douglas looked like he wanted to disappear. Mike Shasta, for the first time, cried hard and ugly. Around the time of the bullying is when his kid had started to wear eyeliner. It only made the kid more visible, more of a target. All of a sudden, Mike Shasta could see the bravery in that. He put his fist to his mouth but he couldn't calm. Mike Shasta cried bitterly, looking at that picture of poor, stunned, numb Douglas. And then Mike Shasta drove to Jackie's and asked to come in.

Jayson

A man lived there. Shame crept up Jayson's neck as he sat in his rental and stared at the door he'd just seen the man go through, the door he knew was Cece's, because he'd walked up those steps and stood before it, staring hard at the rusty numbers nailed there, before hurrying back to his car and panting as the heat blasted out of the air vents. Eventually he switched the heat off. It was a warm day, considering it was winter, and this was the north, and there was snow on the ground. The sun was out. A car pulled in two spots over and the man got out and jogged up the steps and let himself in to the apartment. Guiltily Jayson checked his phone, prepared to respond to a text from Kyla. It felt like she knew, could see him, see how desperate he was for a glimpse of Cece. But there was no text. He'd asked for space and she'd granted it. It was a relief, and that made him feel even worse.

He shrugged out of his coat, a charcoal-gray peacoat that looked like any other peacoat but for the enormous patch on one arm and the fact that it cost eight hundred dollars. Kyla had convinced him to buy it, convinced him he could afford it. "You're the founder of the company," she always said. "It's okay to look the part." He thought of the blond wood all over the office, the warm tones and enormous windows, the cool wall color and furniture and the warm, quirky accents. A lime-green pot holding a fiddle-leaf fig; bright orange poufs found in what Kyla called "gathering areas." He thought of how many weeks they'd agonized over his business cards, whether or not to include his middle initial. He thought of how he had a dozen different denim button-downs in his closet, how they were all different but only a certain type of person could know that. He used to have a dozen different pairs of mesh basketball shorts flung around his room, handed down from Douglas. Nothing smelled awful in his life now, not the way it did in that room he shared with his brother, or inside the refrigerator once his mother stopped caring about food. Everything was neat and tidy and cleaned and available. Nothing ignored, neglected, forgotten. He cared deeply about that. Didn't he?

He turned on the radio, preset to a top 40–type deal. He was searching for a specific kind of song. Something he could blast loud, something they—Cece and the man—might hear as Jayson peeled out of the parking lot.

Kyla made ceviche and Kyla never painted her toenails and Kyla had a library card and Kyla drank tea. Kyla had thick hair and a mole on her cheek. Kyla loved him. But she let him go and he couldn't tell what he actually felt about that. He looked at his phone again. Nothing. He unlocked it and scanned through Cece's Facebook, zooming in on her face, her lips.

There was this day when he'd run into her at the mall after her mom died. Was killed. He still remembered the look on her face when she saw him, still remembered how it felt knowing that she didn't hate him, that she wanted to hug him, touch him, kiss him. He was—only now did he truly realize this—hoping for that again. Hoping for that look to come over her face when she saw him, adult him, standing outside her door.

He got out of the car. He walked up the steps. He knocked on Cece's door. It opened.

"I'm sorry," he said. She'd opened the door and it jumped from his mouth. His mother had been happier during her affair with Cece's father. "I'm sorry," he said again. He could have told somebody. His father, or Cece's mother. He hadn't told anybody. That was the thing he'd done for her, the thing he'd done to make her feel better. He'd protected her.

"Who is it?" The man from before appeared next to Cece. "Wait, is it—is that Jayson?" he asked. He pivoted so he was standing between them, his back to Jayson, facing Cece.

"It's fine," Cece said. "I'm fine." Jayson could see her face over the man's shoulder, how tired she looked. Was she ill? He fought the urge to apologize again.

The man turned, offered his hand. "Shawn." They shook. He looked concerned for Jayson, worried for him, and Jayson began to wonder if he'd met Shawn before, maybe at some event he'd spoken at, some airplane ride to somewhere. How did he know his name? Why did he have that look on his face? Shawn pulled him inside, closed the door behind them, and only then did he let go of Jayson's hand. The short foyer was narrow, and Jayson was half standing inside the laundry alcove. "I'll be in my room," Shawn said.

"I'll make tea," Cece said. Jayson followed her deeper into the apartment, sat on a barstool at the countertop that divided the kitchen from the living space.

What had he imagined, buying his ticket, flying here, driving into the parking lot, knocking on her door? He'd just felt a pull, a gnawing. He had to see her. He had the resources where such a thing was comically easy. He could afford the last-minute ticket, the rental car, the luxury hotel.

Seeing her, he believed, would make other possibilities become clear. He'd see her face and know she was now a stranger. He'd rush back to Kyla, apologize, never look back. Or. The sheer force of the pull he and Cece had on each other would drive them together, mouth to mouth, stumbling through the short foyer and past the kitchen and into that room with the rumpled bed and the shoes all over the floor, where he would be inside her within seconds, and they would be breathing into each other's *How?* and *I missed you.*

Or there was another possibility, one in which she slammed the door in his face, or screamed at him, asked him why he was doing this to her, and he slouched home to Kyla, burning with shame but cleansed from the urge to ever stray from her again.

Instead, he watched as she heated mugs of water in a small microwave, her shoulders looking impossibly small inside her cardigan.

"How's work?" he asked. He tried to remember the name of the company, or any of her coworkers. *I need you,* she'd written. The jolt that had given him, as though he'd been sleep-walking and suddenly realized he was meant to be somewhere else, meant to be standing with his arms outstretched, meant to be catching something. He was needed; how could he ignore that? He'd worked on his response with Kyla. It seemed the only ethical thing to do. Kyla was worried for her, worried for this woman she'd never met who happened to be his childhood love, the girl he'd lost his virginity to, and why was that such a major thing in everyone's life? Sex was such a normal activity, especially when you considered every human being was also an animal. But it was. Major. They'd tried once, twice, and there had been some barrier, something preventing him from pushing in. He hadn't wanted to hurt her and they'd looked at each other with relief, gone back to just kissing and touching. That day at the mall, though. They'd walked out, through the parking lot, along the roadside, holding hands, Cece sniffling and wiping tears. They had nowhere to go and still they walked. He spotted the park he'd gone to as a child for summer camp and he took her there, through the dusty playground and past the picnic tables and further in to what felt like a forest but was only a brief clump of trees surrounded on three sides by busy four-lane roads, so that the traffic sounded like a constant rush of water, and she pulled him close to where she was standing against a tree and kissed him, and he began to cry, and even then he was grateful Douglas wasn't there to see it, even then Douglas made him feel like shit, and he pushed that all away and suddenly it was easy, so easy, they were finally united and if it hurt her it was hard to say because she was already crying. He pulled out and came against her leg and apologized.

"It's okay," she said.

He had the same feeling then that he did now, watching her study a box of cinnamon tea. Like he was supposed to say something, but the thing he was supposed to say was so terrible as to summon an ending, a crash, an explosion, a mess. *I'm sorry my mother did what she did to your mother.* Even now, it was hard to say his mother killed her. Because, technically, she didn't. That was part of it, but also, he did not want to say it. He did not want it to be true. *I'm sorry my mother was a monster. I'm sorry my mother is a monster. I'm sorry she is my mother.*

"I'm sorry for just showing up like this," he said.

"Why are you here?" she said. "Where is Kyla?" She pronounced it wrong, and she looked at him, quickly, and he knew she was embarrassed to say the name out loud.

Her cardigan slipped from her shoulder and he could see she still had freckles there. Her green eyes had a gray shadow to them now, like a storm was brewing. She had chapped lips and she bit at them. They'd helped each other up, brushing dirt off their legs. They'd walked back to the mall. She'd called her father. Jayson had waited just inside the door, unseen, and watched her get into the front seat. The car pulled carefully away and was quickly out of sight. She switched schools, moved away. It felt like a punishment he deserved, the freedom she required.

"I'm here to see you," he said. "I wanted to see you."

"Oh," she said. She took out a tea bag. "Oh," she said again, looking at it like she wasn't sure what to do next. Jayson had the urge to hug her, bring her close, or do something else inappropriately familiar, like cuff her on the shoulder or poke fun at her bare walls, something that would get them back to where they once were. Easy around each other. Relieved, even. He wondered if this was something he should break down with his therapist, if it was yet another example of the ways in which he was not normal, not okay. His mother had never apologized. Over the years he'd wanted to scream at her, to hit her, push her out the door and lock it behind her. But he could never say what he'd truly lost, because what he'd lost was Cece, and what Cece had lost was so much more, so much greater, that he felt like a fool. He hated his mother, and he loved her. He remembered how it felt, waiting for her on the soccer field. Her, his mother. Anciently familiar, as deeply a part of him as his own breath, as the grass under his feet. And then she was gone, studiously erased and written over. Kyriakos said all men had a hard time with maturity, with seeing their mothers as women. He wanted to tell Cece about his therapist, wanted to show her that he was also Not Okay, that she shouldn't feel alone. But then Cece was sinking to the floor, and the microwave was beeping, and then she was crying into her hands, so Jayson didn't say a word, just came around and sat down next to her. He stared at his shoes. They were that modern type of dress shoe, the kind with an athletic sole, and Kyla had helped him choose them from a catalog. She'd called them up and ordered them in his size, asked about inserts. It had felt old-fashioned in a charming way, Kyla once again so capable that it made him want to laugh, though later Kyriakos had asked if Jayson enjoyed how Kyla mothered him, if she was a solace in that way.

The floor was tiled, and cold, and the grout was crumbling in places, and under the lip of the cabinets there were crumbs and a nickel and a twist tie. "I'm sorry," Cece said, and for an absurd moment Jayson thought she meant to apologize for her poor housekeeping. She had calmed some, was pushing her hair out of her face and delicately touching the corners of her eyes, her cheekbones, the tip of her nose. Down here, with her lips and face slightly swollen and her eyes on his, searching, he could finally feel her. Cece. Right here, nearly knee to knee with him. He saw the birthmark on her calf, slightly faded, saw her green, green eyes. "I missed you," he said. He reached over and brushed a tear from her jawline. Often, quite often, he found himself confronting the idea that being a man only required pretending to be a man. He had no idea how to accomplish it otherwise. Walk across hot coals? Survive in the jungle for thirty days? Sleep with a different person every night? He thought of his father, who tucked in his shirts for work and wrenched them free the minute he was home. How manhood was half pressed, clean shirt and half wrinkled, sweaty shirt. Jayson realized (nudged by Kyriakos) that he'd decided he just needed the right gear, the correct abbreviations, the walking style. He could just pick these things up from other men he ran into, quite possibly doing their own version of pretend. He could edit, add, expand, contract. He could not identify when it was that he'd crossed over from the Jayson from Then into the one he was Now. From boy to adult. He left his hand on her face; she turned to more fully rest her head there. His hand caught the new tears. After a bit she took his hand, rose, led him into the room with the messy bed. At first they lay facing each other, hands on each other's faces and shoulders, forehead to forehead. "I feel like crying," he said, though he couldn't stop smiling. "I know," she said. It was just that he'd found somewhere to put it down, all of it. Finally, they pressed their lips together, and then their bodies.

"Is this okay?" he asked her, something he'd said years and years before. "Can I?" He just wanted to look at her, but then he wanted to touch, and they were skin to skin and she shivered but blazed, and he wondered if she had a fever. It felt so good to kiss her, each of them gentle with the other. He kissed her freckles, her sternum, her hip. They kept their pants on; he couldn't figure how to get them off and it seemed like a faraway problem, when what they were doing felt so good. Bright joy, like the breath just before a plunge into cold water. He had the wild thought that they should just sleep, that there was a deep weariness in both of them as they touched and kissed and breathed into each other. He sat up to pull the blanket over his shoulders, then lay back on top of her. He rocked against her, felt her ankles crossed over his back. She pressed a hand against his pants, held him. "Cece," he said. He kissed her with his eyes open. This close, she looked like a child, younger than when they'd started everything, her eyes huge and clear.

"Jayson," she said, and they laughed, and then it was too much to bear; she unzipped him and pushed down her pants and guided him in, her other hand on the back of his neck, and when it was over, after he tried to pull out and she held him fast, watching his face as he came, they slept, something like a yawn trapped in his throat, or a sob.

He dreamed of Theresa, a thin scrim of her holding something out to him, wanting him to take it. It looped. She was saying something; her mouth was moving and sound came out but he couldn't understand what she was saying. He woke in the dark, unsure if it was night or if it was just dark in the cave of her room, with its square window and the blinds pulled tight. He remembered Kyla, remembered his office and apartment and car and life, as though he'd watched it on TV at some point. He crept into the small bathroom and tried to make his face appear, tried to see himself and not the shadow in the mirror. "Come back," she said, and he turned from the trick mirror and found his way back to where she was waiting. He felt heartbroken with exhaustion.

Cece looked like her mother. Had anyone said that to her? He wanted to tell her. It felt important to tell her. The same lopsided lips. The broad, delicate shoulders. Something else. But he was inside her again, his chest to her back, the sex not the point, it seemed, more the closeness. She turned to kiss him and he closed his eyes.

Jackie

I have a shoebox of photos on the shelf in the closet, behind some sweaters. Not very many, but enough. Over the years, I've lost track of so many things. No one told me my lot in life was to never understand how good things were in the moments when they felt so bad. I have a picture of the boys in front of the hole they dug in our backyard. Douglas—he must be only seven or eight—is holding tight to Jayson's hand, and Nathan has his little chubby arm around Samuel's neck, and Samuel is making a face like it hurts, like he's just about to burst into tears. I remember taking the picture, and I remember tossing the shitty disposable camera aside so I could tend to Samuel before he lost it, before there was yet another problem for me to deal with.

Now when I look at the picture, I see that Douglas isn't looking into the camera. He's looking at me. Picture after picture, my boys as babies and kids and teenagers, Douglas is looking at me. I didn't see that then.

I couldn't see them all, not all at once. I didn't even try.

He was getting weird, spending all this time in the bathroom or locking himself in his and Jayson's room. I could feel him slipping into this other version of himself, slipping into a darkness I had come to know. Everywhere I went, he followed. I didn't want him to follow me anymore.

I did worry about him, looking back.

Everybody wants to know why he did it. Why would a teenage boy do that to his mother's lover's wife? His mother's friend? They all think he only could have done it if he'd been told to. They all think I told him to do it. I've thought about that a lot. It used to get me so angry. The first thing they do is say you were a bad mother. As if that explains everything.

Maybe that's true. I did love my boys.

If I'm guilty of anything, it's showing Douglas that it's better to stop something before it gets any worse. He was just a kid. I never told him to do a thing.

The most terrible part of being a mother is knowing your children will love you no matter what.

In a way, she would always be beautiful. In life she was a normal amount of pretty, a rushed, squinting human woman who got food stuck in her teeth and wore outdated sneakers and danced clumsily and never did anything with her hair, though that hair was thick and shiny and she had lovely, delicate hands and a pleasing, sometimes gorgeous face. But now she was frozen in memory, in photographs, and I know for a fact that those are always much more attractive once time has passed. She looks impossibly young in the one picture I've kept of her, of both of us. We're standing in the driveway (if what Samuel tells me is correct, some version of me out there in the multiverse is standing in that driveway forever, or maybe over and over, something like that, some kind of purgatory), flipping the bird at whoever took the picture. My guess is Nick, though the angle makes it seem as though someone shorter took it. Maybe it was one of the boys, or Cece. We dared each other into irreverence like that. Or maybe I did that to her.

She'll always be beautiful. They said it on television about her; they said it in her obituary. As if a woman's one shining accomplishment is to hold tight to her looks, as judged by— whom? I'd love to say men, because it's true, and it's easier, but it's also true that we women look just as hard. If her thighs were thicker than mine, or she had more cellulite, or her boobs weren't as good, then I won. And I needed a win.

The house stood empty for a long time. I started going over there. It was easy to get in before Adam put the house on the market, before the realtor began making sure every door was locked. Adam never came by to check on it, to run the taps or cut the grass. He left his toothbrush. Two pairs of dress shoes. A ratty old briefcase. All of their furniture. Food rotting in the fridge, the bananas in the bowl on the counter turning black and petrifying. There were clouds of fruit flies, and then there were dead fruit flies dotting the floor, and then even those disappeared. We'd spent a lot of time at her house, Theresa and I. Mine was too loud, too sticky. I could hear myself think, sitting right there and watching her in the kitchen, wiping things down, arranging and rearranging. We distracted each other from eating. She kept her fruit bowl stocked. I looked at my stretch marks. I bit my tongue. I chewed ice.

The other day Mike caught me doing that. Chewing ice. Said it sounded awful, like my teeth were breaking. It would take me a lifetime to explain. How can I explain? I had absolute control over myself at one time. Never before and never since.

I forgot what it was I was so sure of. That's it, right there, the truth of my life. I forgot what it was I was so sure of. I smelled Adam's shirts. I lay in their bed. I took a shower, the water cold and weak. I stared at myself in that mirror Theresa had by the door. I forgot what it was I was so sure of. It had felt like mine, like something that had been mine from the start, something I'd had to fight for. Adam, that quiet, organized house. This version of myself that was cold to the touch, impervious, sure of something. Douglas used to look at me, first openly and then, as he got older and we both had more secrets, out of the corner of his eye. He was so good at picking up on clues, at sensing changes before even I knew they were imminent. I always thought I'd be the kind of mother who could hold it together, at least until her kids were in bed and she could drop the mask, maybe dunk her head in a spiked punch bowl or smoke something in the dark corner of the backyard, some small reclaiming of herself, of the parts she couldn't let her children see, because it would frighten them, it would confuse them. Sometimes I'd wake and think, if no one talks to me for the first hour of this day, I can be the best mother ever. If I am allowed to pass through this house, pee in silence, drink a hot cup of coffee, think a private thought, without someone asking me something or telling me something or hollering, I will be okay. I will be perfect. But it never happened. I don't recall silence. Never a moment of it. It got to be that I preferred that kind of chaos, that din. If I sat, I'd only have to get right up again, so I never sat. I never paused. I barely breathed.

Pepper said stay-at-home mothers lived in their workplaces, only they never got to punch out. She had such a creamy face, such brushed hair, unwrinkled clothing. I stared and stared at her trying to figure out if she had kids. She sent me an email, after everything, asking me not to come back. Said

I'd endanger the progress of the rest of the group. I thought
of Kevin, his thin wrists and small hands, his enormous ass
and belly. I thought of Dreama and Carrie and LaTosha. I
watched them all so closely, how LaTosha knitted during meetings and shook her head in sympathy and Carrie and Dreama
held hands the whole time and Kevin had a high, infectious
laugh. I thought of Theresa, how she pumped her fist in exactly
the same way each time the weigh-in went well for her. It'd
be easy to never return there. That place, those people, they
were in another multiverse. I'd stepped through the veil into
a different one, where the sounds were louder and the colors
were sharper and where I missed the days that drove me crazy
in the first place, the days when my boys wouldn't leave me
alone for one goddamn second and I was their whole world.
I was only pretending, you see. I was only pretending that
there was anything more to me than what I was. Just a mom.
Tale as ancient as the ancient gods. Step into your boredom.
That's what I'd say to me if I could travel through the veils.
Sometimes the sun will be the perfect yellow, not too hot,
and there'll be a breeze, and you'll look up at just the right
moment. That's all you'll remember, that's all that matters,
and thank goodness.

Was I beautiful, though? The thought plagues me. Maybe
that's my problem, has always been my problem. The beauty
I see when I notice an attractive woman, that feels very different from the beauty I felt when I was most likely beautiful,
or pretty enough. A beautiful woman—right?—she has long
legs, easy hair, nice teeth, something that is unique to her, like
freckles or a long neck or interesting lips. She laughs but she's
not trying to get you to look at her. She's laughing because
something is funny; she's delighted.

Theresa will always be beautiful, even in the pictures
where she clearly has cankles. Is there anything we see that

isn't through the lens of someone else's viewpoint? By that I mean men's. Did I think she was beautiful, do I think she was beautiful, or am I assuming she was because I know what men like? I know it as well as I know the backs of my hands, or the lines on my face. I learned it by osmosis. I learned it in the seventh grade when I didn't develop as quickly as other girls and they pretended to write on my front like it was a chalkboard. I knew it when my father asked me why boys never called. I knew it when my father offered to buy me lipstick, dresses, prettier shoes. I knew it when my mom wrung her hands and listened as he offered and offered. I knew it when, finally, there was Nick, and I gave it over to him so fast my head spun. I thought of my father, how, perversely, he'd be relieved. I thought of how I knew something about myself, now, and I knew it because a man had shown it to me. I was the outline of something, and Nick had filled me halfway. That's what I thought. Now I know he just made my lines thicker, that I was still see-through. I knew it when Nick showed me videos of what he'd like to try, women being mounted like dogs and men spitting into their hands. I knew it after all my babies, when I was asked again and again if I was trying to lose the baby weight. I knew it when I'd show up wearing color on my lips, mascara, and I was told I looked great. I knew it at Get Skinny when we all confessed how we wanted to be seen the way we'd been when our husbands first married us, before. We wanted to be invisible again. We were too visible, and ashamed.

When I think back to the time when I was beautiful, the moment Nick first saw me or after I'd lost all the weight, I see who I was, a girl with scraped knees well into teenager-hood, a girl whose father asked, again and again, if she was *funny*, meaning *lesbian*. She was just a sketch, just some quick brushstrokes, not even fully conscious. I'm talking about the time when Nick decided he wanted me. I'm talking about how I'd barely understood how to hook my bra and there I was, engaged to be married. And I was relieved! I wasn't funny but I saw my father's point: no one seemed to want me. There was barely any me to want, and maybe that's what Nick liked about me.

I began eating. You can't help it during the pregnancies. Believe me, I tried. You can't help your urges, even when you know you'll throw it all up in an hour. I ate and I felt powerful. It was a thing I could do that would pass some time. Those early days with one, two, three, four little boys, sometimes eating was all I could do for myself. The one thing I could do to remind myself I was a separate person with my own mind and body. I was trying to fill myself out, be visible. Solid, recognizable. I expanded and I had a good time doing it. Did I? Now when I think about how I ate, I feel horror and shame and sometimes I laugh. But at the time I just felt free.

Was I beautiful then? My unique body with all its folds and strain, the physical map I'd made of all the ways I'd tried to create myself? Beautiful enough to hook Theresa. There was something in me just for her. I still believe it. Ours is a love story.

There was this one evening when we drove home from a meeting and stopped for French fries. No one had had a good weigh-in that evening and we all watched each other with pale, weary faces, pretending to listen, but really going back over our counts for the week, every meal and snack and little cheat. The following week Pepper confessed that the scale needed to be recalibrated, and everyone had an extra-good weigh-in, but still. We never trusted that thing after that. Theresa and I stopped for French fries and ate them smeared in ketchup and washed our hands of the stench in the restaurant bathroom and drove home with the windows down. "I needed that," she said. That's what I mean. That's what I was, just for her.

The French fries on the way home from a weigh-in. When I hugged her goodnight, her hair smelled like hot oil and salt. That's what I was for her. The wedge of darkness under the door. The fang. The edge.

I'm trying to get somewhere, to say what I have to say.

Was I beautiful that first time with Adam? What was it about me? But men are so easy. There's beauty and then there's a hot, wet mouth. I felt beautiful and I guess what I mean is I felt powerful, like the world was actually a very easy place if you just took what you wanted.

If I was the darkness, does that make Theresa my light? I don't buy that. I refuse. I had plenty of light. Me holding my babies in the wee hours. The lists I used to make. The way I'd wash each apple and dry it and place it in a mixing bowl for easy grabbing. The way the sun caught in my freshly wiped tabletop. The care I took, folding little T-shirts. I signed Jayson up for soccer; I told Douglas he was just a normal boy feeling normal feelings. Years and years and years of care, all me. Somewhere along the way, I made a friend. I stopped washing my curtains. The garden went to seed. I watched the dust twirling in the sunlight. I let the coffee go cold. I wondered why no one in the house knew how to make a bed, replace the toilet roll. I wondered why everything had an unpleasant smell, and why it was my fault. Theresa woke early to tend to her home. She said it was her job. Was she my friend, or were we two proximate women, one sure of her reasons and one less and less so? *Look at those two*, I heard one of the husbands say, once. About us. Were we friends, or were we just the same species, mired in expectation?

These days they tell moms to let it all go. To ignore societal expectations. To live without a vacuum, to forget washing their hair. Everyone's accused of being too hard on themselves. Here's my secret: No one noticed the house was crumbling around us. Not really. Not until it was crumbled, I mean. Then they noticed. Before that? We all enjoyed dropping our tooth-brushes on the floor, never flushing, wiping sticky hands across the sofa. We giggled like we were getting away with something. Didn't we? Then it was too late; I no longer remembered how to care. How to even fake caring. That's the thing no one wants to admit: a home is held together by care, and quite often the one who cares is . . . well, you know. I remember how that man from the television show was careful about where he rested his elbows. How he squinted through the dusty window. How, still, I wondered if he found me pretty. Hoped he did.

Mike is next to me. Everything out of his mouth is rounded, the way a child speaks to himself. I watch him say that life is complicated, kids make mistakes, even big, irrevers-ible mistakes, that it was just a terrible accident. He loves me unconditionally, the way I love my boys. I used to want that kind of devotion, or I used to think I wanted it. I let him hold my hand. Far off, I hear thunder rolling toward us.

I will turn to him, right now, and I will tell him the truth.

PART III

Douglas

"Everything okay?" he asked his mother, and she collapsed to the floor, like someone had swept her legs out from under her. He grabbed her arm, tried to haul her up. It felt like a broomstick, too thin. Disgust welled up in his throat. She wailed, her face in her hands.

Behind him, he heard Nathan go up the stairs, go into his bedroom and close the door. He longed to do the same. Why couldn't he? He stood, looking down at her, and he nearly did it. Nearly walked away and shut the door against her.

"Get up," he said, and he willed his voice to be gentle. He went into the kitchen. Jayson was just standing there, his hands at his side, listening to their mother cry. Douglas ignored him and filled a glass from the tap, brought it to her. "Here," he said, "water."

She sat up and leaned against the wall and sipped at the water, her hand shaking. He held the glass for her, brought it gently to her lips. As a little boy, he used to ask her where her mother was. "You know where," she'd say. "She lives in Colorado!" But how, he wondered, could she go through life without one at her side? It seemed to him that she was motherless. That no one looked out for her, dressed her wounds, cradled her, cared. It was easy to do those things for her, to run up and hug her when she seemed sad—a safe bet—to ask her simple questions about her day. He knew because of it that he was closest to her, that he was her favorite.

"Tell me," he said. He listened as she told him about Mr. Linden, how they were in love and only wanted to be together. Mrs. Linden found out and wanted to destroy them. Douglas sat beside her, numbness flooding his body, his heart hammering dumbly.

"She said she's going to make sure I never see my boys again," she said. He saw, he knew, that she was making up parts of it as she went along.

"Dad won't let that happen," Douglas said. He thought of his father, of the way he walked slightly pigeon-toed, belched loudly, sucked in his belly when he wanted to impress people. Old man things, pathetic things that made Douglas feel a deep sorrow. "She won't actually tell," he said.

"If she does," his mother said, "I'll kill myself." She dropped her head again, brought her hands to her face. Douglas heard Jayson leave the kitchen and go upstairs. He'd surely heard it all. Douglas held his mother the way she used to hold him when he cried, his arm tight around her bony body. She was smaller than any girl he'd ever touched, smaller than he'd ever been as a child. "I will," she whispered. "I really will."

Cece

Jayson got on her laptop and bought himself a ticket home. It was over two thousand dollars and he paid with his debit card. Cece felt the gulf between them, as though she'd blinked and was suddenly on the other end of a bridge, her hand over her brow, looking for him. "I'll be back," he said. He kissed her and she wanted to pull his coat around her, shut herself inside his warmth. "Or you come," he said. "I want you to come." She imagined herself walking around his apartment, touching items his girlfriend had chosen, fitting herself into his life where she could. First, she'd stop drinking so much. She'd clean her room. Get a haircut. Buy one or two nice tops from a boutique.

"See you soon," she said. She walked him to his car, waved as he pulled slowly out of the parking lot. She waited until his taillights turned at the corner. She waited until it began to sleet, the freezing droplets working their way into her collar, down her back. Carefully, she picked her way around patches of ice and up the stairs. It was the afternoon, a nothing part of the day. Shawn was out; she'd be all alone in there, waiting for Jayson to turn around and come back to her, knowing he wouldn't.

* * *

There was paper in a box under Shawn's desk, and she found a pen in the junk drawer in the kitchen. The words came easily and her pen could hardly keep up. *My mother saw you*, she wrote. *She tried to help you.* She was inelegant and unpolished and free. *I've thought of you and your family every day of my life. I know it's the same for you.*

Evening came on quickly, as it always did in winter in the Midwest. Out her window she watched the lights of a plane track across the sky. She could go to him. She could use her credit card. She could. *That is over for me but it never will be for you*, she wrote. Then she put on her coat and scarf and tucked her hair into her hat and walked the three blocks to the mailbox, tears and snot freezing to her cheeks—cheeks so much like her mother's—and dropped the letter in. *Dear Jackie*, it began.

She turned on all the lights in the apartment. She turned on the TV, then muted it. She saw her mug in the sink from the tea she'd made the day Jayson came. She rinsed it out, filled it with the brandy Shawn kept on top of the fridge. She could not lay in her bed, though she was dying to, because it smelled like Jayson.

The brandy made her feel like she was slowly melting. She told her phone to play a song that her mother loved, a song about dreams. She swayed to the song, remembering how her mother had sung it to her sometimes. A night when she'd had trouble falling asleep, her mother's cool hand on her cheek, her face shaded. It had probably happened just like that on many nights, but they'd all consolidated into one memory for Cece. Her mother's soft voice, the hallway light at her back.

And now Cece could feel her there, as though something had unlocked and her mother had stepped through. Honeysuckle and lemons and cheap apple shampoo. She was dancing, her arms waving in the air. Cece didn't so much see her as know she was there. They danced together, the radio cycling through a song from Cece's high school days about something terrible but unnamed happening to some teenagers. Eventually, Cece realized she was dancing alone, all the lights blazing.

Acknowledgments

Thank you to Roxane Gay, who has given me so many opportunities over the years. Roxane's generosity and sharp, terrifying, brilliant editing have made me a better writer again and again. She published me in *PANK*; she published me in *The Rumpus*; she's publishing me now. It is the honor of my lifetime to be seen and read the way she sees and reads me. Thank you, Roxane.

Thank you to my agent, Jim Rutman, who always seems to know exactly what I need to hear. Thank you, Jim, for always leveling with me, and for believing in me.

Thank you to the team at Roxane Gay Books and Grove Atlantic. Noah Grey Rosenzweig, thank you for your excitement about this book and for shepherding it and me! Alicia Burns, thank you for your keen copyedits. Thanks is also owed to Sinclair Blue.

Thank you to Chip Kidd for such a gorgeous, perfect cover.

Thank you to Alex Higley, a dear friend and collaborator.

Thank you to the independent bookstores all over the country, but most especially those in Chicago. I feel very loved and supported by my community here. I must especially call out Javier Ramirez and Kristin Enola Gilbert at the excellent

Exile in Bookville, who have become friends and, occasionally, my partners in mayhem.

Thank you to everyone who's asked me when the next book is coming out. I hope you're as excited as I am. Thank you for sticking with me.

Thank you to my husband and children. Family is our sacred mission.

I wrote this novel during the first eighteen months of the pandemic. I wrote pieces of it sitting in my car, or while one of my children was in virtual school and the others napped, or in the dark hours of the early morning when my sick pit bull, my sweet Coco, had to go out. This is the first book I'm publishing as a woman in her forties, as a mother of three. It feels like a fucking *miracle*. Just, thank you.